Larry, t,
buying my book,
I appreciate it,
Enjoy the book
Thanks

# GATEWAY

## by Jim Keane

2022, TWB Press
www.twbpress.com

# Dedication

To my dad, Thomas Keane, a great father and friend who loved life and passed away too early. Whenever I see an MTA bus go by, Dad, I think of you. See you in the afterlife. Up Kerry.

Love, Jim.

# GATEWAY

Edited by Terry Wright

Cover Art by Terry Wright

ISBN: 978-1-944045-92-0

**More works by Jim Keane**

## The Midnight Train Murders

A disgraced journalist, hoping to regain his prestige, investigates the murder of passengers on the midnight train to Crotonville, a reporter's dream story that turns into a nightmare.

**www.twbpress.com/themidnighttrainmurders.html**

## Astra's Revenge

When a syndicate assassin kills the mother of a circus fortune teller, he can run but he can't hide from Astra's black magic and her crystal ball.

**www.twbpress.com/astrasrevenge.html**

# Chapter One

I turned up my collar against the February cold as I hurried to Clancy's Deli in the Bronx. My nostrils bristled in the frosty air, and I squinted against the evening sunlight reflecting off the icy pavement. I could have been home, warm and cozy, drinking beer and watching hockey on TV, but I had to get dinner for my mom.

As I entered the deli, a bell rang above the door. Inrushing cold air made the sawdust on the floor scatter like snowflakes. The place smelled of Chicken Noodle Soup, and spicy sausage hung in rows above the counter. An old Irish tune, *Danny Boy,* added a bit of heritage to the deli's atmosphere. Déjà vu hit me like a board, as this must've been the millionth time I'd come to Clancy's, but only one of a handful of visits without my dad.

Nearing the cash register, I noticed Clancy wrapping an order for a waiting customer, an elderly, stooped woman in a dark wool coat that dusted the floor as she moved aside.

Clancy taped the package closed. "Well if it ain't Sean Calhoun. Be right with you, laddy." He was a big man with white hair, wore a stained apron over a t-shirt that revealed his burly arms tattooed with anchors, ships, and sails. He handed the neat brown package to the old lady. "Thank you, missus."

She nodded to both of us then shuffled out the door.

Clancy pulled off his thin food-prep gloves. "What can I get you, Sean?"

"Dinner. Mom's not up to cooking."

"Ah, yes. Sheila. Not seen her around since..."

"The murder. It's all right to call it for what it was." I leaned on the counter. "She won't leave the house. It's not safe in the city, she says."

"Your dad was a great man."

I reflected on that. "For a bus driver, Dermot was a hero to many people around here. We miss him very much."

"A shame what happened to him."

"Mom's not been the same since."

"Next time, bring her with you."

"Fresh air would do her good...but she's not ready yet...maybe no time soon, either."

"Grief takes time to run its course."

"It's been a year, Clancy. I sold my flat in Yonkers, moved in with her here, tried everything I could to get her to move on, see her friends, get back to living again."

"You're a good son, Sean. Don't give up on her."

I pressed my lips together and shook my head. My life had been turned upside down, a temporary upset, I'd hoped, but there now seemed no relief in sight. When Dad died, so did Mom.

"So, what's for dinner? Got fresh shepherd's pie."

I sighed. "Okay. Pie for two, and I'll take a pint of that chicken soup."

Outside, I carried the warm brown bag in the crook of my right arm and savored the aroma. A BX-34 bus lumbered down the avenue. Standing at the curb, I imagined my father behind the wheel, maneuvering the behemoth bus along the narrow streets like a ship's captain navigating rough waters. "See you tonight, Dad," I muttered to the passing bus as if the past had been but a bad dream.

I trudged across the street where McGee's Irish Pub spilled music and laughter across the sidewalk. If not for the meal I carried, I might have been tempted to step inside and join the frivolities. I envisioned foaming pints of Guinness and amber shots of Jameson lined up on the bar for dossers and slags getting schnockered, arm-in-arm, singing and dancing like there was no tomorrow. What a reprieve I would find from caring for my grief-stricken mother, keeping the household afloat, and not thinking about my murdered father for a few hours into the night.

However, my mother needed my help until she recovered from Dermot's murder and moved on with her life.

I reached my parents' house, a two-story with a cracked concrete driveway, the same driveway where Dad had taught me to ride a bike.

*That's it, buddy, you can do it. Keep your balance.*

At seven years old, I'd gotten so good I'd ridden up and down the street, pretending I too was a bus driver making stops to pick up imaginary passengers.

My vision of father and son in the driveway morphed into a present reality, a white Ford Taurus parked there now, engine pushing vapor out the tailpipe. The sight of the man behind the wheel sent adrenaline boiling through my veins: not from fear, but from excitement. Hope. Maybe today the news would be good.

As I reached the car, the driver's door swung open, and Detective Mullen from NYPD's homicide division stepped out. He was tall and slim, wore a trench coat, collar up-turned, and a red yarn cap his grandma might have knitted. "Mister Calhoun."

"Detective. What are you doing here?"

"Just checking on you...your mom." He held out a gloved hand.

"Look..." I shifted the brown bag to my left arm and accepted a quick handshake. "Mom's not doing well. If you don't have my dad's killer in jail, your being here will only upset her. She's walking a thin line, you know."

"We're not giving up." Mullen glanced toward the house, the lighted front window, the silhouette of a woman standing behind the shade, peeking out. "But still no leads."

I could only imagine the horror Dad had faced, the hooded and masked punk demanding money from the coin drop-box, his demand bolstered with a gun, a 40 caliber, as evidenced by the slug the coroner had removed from his chest. Dermot Calhoun must've explained he had no key, no way to give the thug what he wanted. However, to press his demand further, he turned the gun on the passengers. The bus's security cameras caught the last moment of Dermot's life, the split-second decision that he'd made to leap from his seat and shove the robber backward out the open door, even as the gun discharged, and in the following second, Dermot had the whereabouts to close the door, locking the punk outside and saving the lives of his shocked passengers.

I shuddered. "He died a hero, you know."

"Yeah. We'll get the bastard sooner or later." Mullen got back in the driver's seat. "Tell your mom that, will ya?"

As disappointed as I felt, I knew finding one killer in a city of eight million folks was not an easy task. "Thanks for stopping by." I indicated the brown bag. "Dinner's getting cold."

Mullen closed the door and reversed out of the driveway.

I watched the taillights and vapor recede down the block then walked to the front porch where I stomped snow from my shoes. The silhouette in the window backed away. I wished she hadn't seen Mullen, as he had a way of sending Mom into a tailspin. She could never get Dermot back, but bringing the killer to justice would go a long way toward mending her broken heart.

I entered the house, expecting to see Mom standing there, but she wasn't in the living room, not on the couch, and not in the Lazy Boy. The television was dark.

"Hey, Mom," I called out. She wasn't in the kitchen. I set the brown bag on the table then walked to the staircase. "Are you up there? I brought dinner."

"Why was that awful man here?"

"Come on down."

"I'm not hungry."

"Got Clancy's shepherd's pie. Get it while it's hot."

"Did he catch Dermot's killer?"

"Mom, don't make me come up there and get you."

She grunted. "Give me a minute to freshen up."

I set the table: plates, bowls, utensils, poured water for two. Opening the brown bag released an explosion of aromas only found in the Bronx. The diversity of ethnicities, those from the old country who'd brought with them their family's culinary skills, tempted and tantalized the palates of many New Yorkers.

*Maybe tonight, Mom and I can have a decent dinner together.*

While I waited for Mom to join me, I dished up the shepherd's pie and poured soup into the bowls. I was hungry enough to dig right in, but I'd wait for her. Talking with Clancy about my dad, and after Mullen showed up, my memories wouldn't leave me alone. I pulled out my cell phone and flipped through photos I'd saved. My favorite was when we sat behind home plate at the Yankees game. It was Saturday afternoon, the Red Sox, when Aaron Judge blasted a home run to seal the Yankees' win.

*Dad had worked a lot of overtime for those tickets.*

I missed him, his counsel, his laugh...I couldn't help myself, but I had to hear his voice, so I clicked on my saved voicemails.

*"Hey, bud, looking forward to a beer with you at McGee's after work."*

I wish I'd answered that phone call, but I was buried in a problem at Vericom, troubleshooting a router glitch that had knocked out cell service to a lower east side borough. How was I to know he'd be murdered that night?

*I never got to say goodbye.*

Fighting back tears, I played the message again.

*"Hey, bud, looking forward—"*

"What are you doing?" Mom shouted from the doorway behind me.

I closed the voicemail. "Ah...sorry, Mom."

"You torture me with that? And that detective...he's

worthless. Couldn't find a killer if he tripped over one."

"He's trying, Mom." I turned to see her standing just outside the kitchen, a specter, a shadow of her former self, dressed in a nightgown and slippers. Her thinning hair was streaked with gray, her body gaunt, and her face hadn't seen makeup in a year. Dad's murder had sucked the vibrant life from her as if the killer had shot her through the heart, as well. "Come and eat, Mom."

She shuffled into the kitchen, slippers scuffing tile, sat across from me, and looked into her bowl of soup as if it were deeper than the deepest ocean.

"Chicken Noodle, Mom. Clancy made it special for you," I lied.

She was just going through the motions of life, dead inside yet unable to fall, though I knew she would if she could, even pull her own plug and be done with it all. Yeah, like Clancy said, I was a good son. I didn't want her to quit on life, give up...she had so many good years left in her, if only she'd let go of the past, let herself laugh again, tell funny stories to her friends...*I'm too stubborn to quit trying.*

"It's...not...fair," she muttered and looked up from her bowl, her eyes all soupy with tears. "He was a good man."

"I know, Mom."

"Taken by some scumbag Mullen can't even find."

"The cops 'll catch him." What else could I say? As long as they were looking, as long as it wasn't a cold case, there was hope for justice. Maybe then she'd get on with her life.

She lifted her spoon as if she fully intended on eating her soup. "Dermot...my God...he come from Ballybunion in Ireland, a proud and determined man."

"I know, Mom. Eat your soup."

"Just a suitcase in his hand...no money...no family...just a dream," she managed between heavy sobs.

"The American Dream. He found it, all right, driving a bus. Many don't." I dug into my shepherd's pie. Clancy had a gift with ground beef and mashed potatoes.

"I met him on that bus, you know."

"Mom, you get like this every time you see Mullen."

"He's no damn detective—"

"Mom. Please. You've got to snap out of it."

She started to hyperventilate, she was sobbing that hard. The spoon fell from her hand, and she shrank back in her chair, hands over her face, her entire body trembling in despair. Every time she talked about Dermot, she would lose it all over again, relive the night Mullen and his partner came to the house, told her they were sorry...but her husband had passed.

I wasn't there. I was at McGee's waiting for my dad, his pint of Guinness at the ready. When he didn't show, I called Mom to see if he'd forgotten and showed up at home. A man answered, Mullen I'd find out later, but mostly I remember the wails in the background, a woman's loss vocalized in a way that left no doubt our lives would never be the same again.

I ran all the way home, could hear her cries halfway down the block, cries that continued throughout the night and into the next day, and the next, and the next. I was powerless to stop her crying, to help her breathe, as I was now, at dinner with my mom.

# Chapter Two

After a depressing dinner, I decided to walk to McGee's for a Guinness, or three, and let off some steam with the boys. Decked out in a heavy coat and snow-boots, I announced from the door, "Mom, I'll be back later."

"You be careful out there," she shouted down from upstairs. "I don't want to lose you too."

"You can come with me if you want."

She responded by slamming the bedroom door.

I retraced my steps the three blocks back to McGee's Pub. The Saturday night crowd was a rowdy, noisy bunch, a conglomeration of Irish die-hards, blue-collar workers with dirty hands and soiled garb, Polish construction workers wearing white and yellow hard hats, and lassies from who-cares-where in short skirts and deep-diving necklines, some more professional than others. Yeah, someday I'd like to get married, settle down, have some kids of my own, but not today and definitely not tomorrow, either.

Guinness in hand, I flung a few darts, slapped a few backs, but mostly bellied up to the bar. The walls rattled to the quick tempo of fiddles, flutes, bagpipes, and bodhrans; I could hardly hear myself think. It was paradise.

A familiar body nuzzled up to my back. Her perfume had that come-hither fragrance that begged for attention.

"Sean," she breathed in my ear. "You wanna dance?"

I wasn't in the mood for kicking and stomping, but a good hug was in order. After I set my pint on the bar-top, slowly, as not to appear too eager, I turned to the visage of Miss Bridget O'Hare, and what a fine lady she was. Deep green eyes greeted me with delight, and her dainty nose, lightly splashed with freckles, touched my nose, softly, as a butterfly wing would caress the air.

She slipped a bare arm around my neck and set a pout on her lovely pink lips. "What's the matter, baby? Your mum again?" Her wavy red hair would envy Rapunzel.

"She's having a rough night."

"Then loosen up. I can help you forget."

I drew her in and hugged her, and as she melted into my arms, my mind drifted to a time before Dad's murder, before Mom's fall into grief, when Bridget and I didn't have a care in the world. Were we in love? Maybe. Did we talk of marriage? A little. Mostly we enjoyed each other's company and let the future be what it would be. I could only hope a time would come when we might reignite those passions.

"Sean, please," she whispered. "I've missed you so."

"I know. But not tonight."

She pushed away from me, and that pretty face put on a mask of hurt. "I won't wait forever, Sean."

I wanted to grab her, pull her back, kiss with the passion she deserved, let the fire in my heart show her how much I missed her, too, how much I wanted us to be together, like the old times...but instead, I let her go, let her walk away, again.

My heart sank. I was trapped in a life not of my own

making, all on account of one punk with a gun. Even with all the hoopla around me, I couldn't escape the fact that my mood had plunged to a depth greater than where it was when I'd first entered McGee's. I slammed the rest of my pint, worked my way through the throng of happy people who didn't carry the weight of murder on their shoulders, and stepped outside. The cold air quickly sobered me. I set out for home, well, my mom's house; it never really felt like home, just a return to my boyhood bedroom until life got better for Mom. Then I could—

Spinning tires behind me interrupted my pity-party, and I turned to see a black SUV, boxy like an FBI Yukon, pull a U-e down the block, its four tires throwing ice and rock salt and engine roaring. Looked like trouble brewing, a possible drive-by, lots of that going on these days, so I ducked into the alley, turtled my neck into my coat collar and stuffed my hands in my pockets. The alley wasn't terribly dark, as back doors were lit, and the streetlamp sent a shard of light my way, though I did pick up my gait until an odd sight presented itself.

A homeless man, I first thought, lay on the ground, his back braced against an old wooden fence that surrounded a trash bin, and I could see that he was in some distress the way he was panting hoarsely. I assumed he'd been mugged, as no one would choose to lay among all the broken glass strewn about. As I neared him, I saw his jacket splayed open and he was clutching his stomach with bloodied hands...like he'd been stabbed or shot. I had to blink to be sure my eyes were working correctly. Then a hot-flash of fear jolted me to action. I glanced around to be sure the mugger wasn't still nearby, saw nobody and realized it was up to me to get this poor man some help.

With my heart pounding as if it would escape my ribcage, I ran to the downed man. "Hey, mister. What happened?" I knelt, careful of the glass shards, and looked him over. He was wheezing, and spurting blood leaked from a wound in his chest; his blue button-down was awash in red. "I'll call 9-1-1."

He moaned. His bloody hand dug into this jacket and pulled out a cell phone. "Take it." He wheezed. His eyes darted back and forth frightfully as he held out the phone to me.

I baulked at taking a blood-smeared phone, HIV and all. "No thanks. I have my own." I fished my phone from my coat pocket and fumbled as I attempted to dial 9-1-1.

"No cops." He jabbed his phone at me. "Take it. Be quick...and run."

"But you're going to die."

"Nothing...can stop...that now." Calmness passed over the man's face as he gazed up at the starlit sky. "I'm coming, Miriam."

I followed his gaze. The moon scowled down on the alley like the skull of a demon with crater eyes and glinting teeth. Irish music pumped from McGee's, and newspapers swirled around nearby garbage cans. Tires skidded as the black SUV appeared at the end of the alley.

The injured man's face drained of color. Life was running out of him with each throb and spurt from his chest. He gasped, coughed up blood, "Guard it...with your life," and pressed his phone into my left hand.

"What's so special about it?"

"You can speak...to the dead." His voice was but a

whisper.

An icy hand gripped my throat. What a crazy thing to say.

He wheezed. His face went slack and his head lolled to the side.

"Oh, God." I couldn't believe I'd just watched a man die. That icy hand on my throat tightened. Looking at the bloody phone, I decided to grant his last wish, that I guard it with my life. "It's in good hands, sir." After pocketing the man's phone, I punched 9-1-1 into my phone, but before I could press 'send', car doors slammed and fast-approaching footfalls stopped me.

"There he is." Two guys dressed in black suits were running toward me, coattails flapping, mere silhouettes against the streetlight glow behind them. One thug brandished a gun.

My stomach clenched. I thought I'd lose my Guinness, sprang to my feet, and backed away from the dead man. Whatever happened to him, it was a good bet these two brutes were responsible.

"Hold it," the smaller of the two shouted at me, his demand bolstered by the wave of his gun.

I thumbed 'send' on my phone and stashed it in my pocket, hoping the cops would hear what was going on, hopefully without recording my own death.

The thugs ran up to the body and bent over it. "Give us that phone, O'Malley." When he didn't move, the smaller goon checked the man's neck with two fingers then turned to his partner and frowned. "He's dead, Frank."

"Don't get stupid on me now, Bart. Has he got the phone?"

While the sawed-off thug rummaged through the man's bloody clothes, I took a quiet step backwards, my heart racing and my brain screaming, *"Run."*

"It's not here."

Both men turned and glared at me. "Where's the phone?"

I raised my hands.

*Guard it with your life.*

"What phone?"

The big lug stepped toward me. "How'd you get blood all over your hands?"

"Shaving."

"Give me that phone, you fool."

*Guard it with your life.*

"Shit." I took off running down the alley.

"Get him," the big gunman shouted.

A flurry of footsteps thundered behind me. I expected to hear a gunshot, feel the burn of a bullet, see the ground rush up to meet me, but for some reason they didn't shoot. Maybe they wanted me alive to interrogate me at length to find out what I knew about this phone worth dying for. These guys had evidently shot O'Malley while I was inside the pub, didn't hear a thing, just stepped out into the middle of their mess.

I broke out of the alley and onto the side street, my boots begging for traction on the icy pavement, and sprinted past three houses, all with their lights off. No refuge there, and running in snow-boots was no easy matter. I cut across a front lawn. Gnarled tree branches hung low and scratched my face as I charged through them with reckless abandon. If I didn't lose these guys fast, I would surely run out of steam.

My mom's house was coming into view, but I realized I couldn't duck in there. These goons would know where I lived, so I kept running, passed the house like all the others, and hoped the cops would figure out what was going on and triangulate on my phone to locate my position.

Suddenly, the supersonic crack of a bullet whizzed by my ear, missing me by inches, followed by the gunshot. I ducked but stumbled on the curb. If I fell, I was dead. So much for my lengthy interrogation theory.

I caught my balance and raced the goons to Martine Avenue and then cut through an apartment complex where I lost them in a maze of parked cars. Nearly spent, I took refuge behind a landscaping truck to catch my breath. My heart was slamming around in my chest like a wild animal in a cage. Behind the cover of lawn mowers and ladders, I watched the goons stalk past me and go the other way.

"Where did he go?"

"He couldn't have gone far," the man named Frank said. "I'll bet that prick is watching us."

"Yeah. He's a dead man walking." The smaller goon seemed to be the meaner of the two.

"Let's split up. We've gotta get that damn phone."

Icy fear bristled my neck hairs. Split up? They'd be harder to keep an eye on. What was so damn important about that cell phone? How did O'Malley get it...and from where? And how could it be used to talk to the dead? I knew cell phones, how they worked...and their limitations. That was my job at Vericom. I could guarantee anyone there were no fiber optic cables to Heaven or Hell. To make such a call would take an otherworldly medium unknown to man. Any such notion one existed would be a scam, at best, though O'Malley seemed pretty confident of his cell phone's ability...sincere to his last breath. And those two goons seemed like true believers. *Crap.* By now, I'd lost sight of them both.

I wished I'd stayed in the pub for a second pint.

A window opened on a third-floor apartment above me. A woman wearing curlers in her hair stuck her head out. "Get out of here." She stabbed a finger at me.

"Shut up, lady," Frank shouted from somewhere close and off to my right.

I ducked low and scooted to the front of the truck.

"I'm calling the cops," the woman cried. "This is a safe neighborhood."

"Come on, Bart," Frank said. "Let's go. We lost him."

"Mr. Massey isn't going to be happy with us."

As they strolled back the direction they came, I duckwalked to a dumpster and peered down 233rd Street where an NYPD cruiser drove slowly by, its overheads flashing. A block away, another cruiser seemed on the prowl. I figured they were looking for me, so I broke into a sprint toward the street. The back window of a parked car in front of me exploded. Its burglar alarm chirped and bugled. I hit the deck as shards of glass rained down on me.

Frank was hootin' and hollerin'. "I told ya the rat would skedaddle if he thought we'd left."

Footfalls were coming at me fast. "Shit." I scrambled to my feet and hauled ass past a shuttered gas station and an old motel sign flashing: *Vacancy*, then scrabbled up a grassy knoll where I ducked behind a wooden fence that I was sure a BB gun could penetrate. When I looked back, sure enough, the goons were on my trail up the hill thanks to my boot prints in the snow. From this vantage point, I could see the patrolling cop cars were farther away than ever. Triangulation wasn't an exact locator, and its limitations plagued me big-time.

I took off for the crest of the hill, keeping the fence at my back to block their view of my escape, though every boot print I left in the snow would lead them closer to the place of my death.

As I crested the hill, bright headlights flashed on and stopped me cold. A siren bleeped and overheads came to life. I must've looked a sight, breathing hard and bloody hands up in surrender. My first thought was *I'm going to jail.* My second: *Who's going to take care of Mom?*

I turned to look back down the hill, where Frank and Bart were hightailing it down 233$^{rd}$ Street. Whoever their Mr. Massey was, I had a feeling he was going to throw their shit in the fan. No love lost here.

I turned back to the cop cars in time to see a white Ford Taurus pull up. The driver's door opened and out stepped Detective Mullen. At first, relief nearly swept me to my knees, but on second thought, he might think I had something to do with O'Malley's death in the alley. "Crap."

"Mister Calhoun. Where is your cell phone?"

"Cell phone? My cell phone?" Or did he mean O'Malley's—

"No. Mother Teresa's cell phone."

"Oh, that one. It's in my pocket."

"Answer it please...and tell the dispatcher you're safe and sound."

"The lady?" *Oh.* I got out the phone and put it to my ear. "Hello?"

"The police are there now," a woman's voice said.

"I see that."

"You can hang up."

"Okay. I'll hang up. Thanks." I felt like a ditz, hung up, and by the time I put the phone back in my pocket, Mullen was standing in front of me.

"You want a ride home?"

"A ride? Sure...but don't you want to know why those guys were chasing me?"

"We already know. I'm a good detective, believe it or not. Tell your mom that, okay?"

"Of course. I'll tell her." I got in the passenger seat. The heater was blasting. I held my hands in front of a dash vent, betting he didn't know about O'Malley's cell phone.

The squad cars shut off their overheads and drove away.

"So..." I grabbed a breath. "Who were those bad guys?"

"We're working to ID them now. Got their SUV, for starters. That's more than your dad's killer left at the scene."

"Yeah. Good for you." I strapped myself in and slumped in the seat. As Mullen drove, I thought about telling him some names: Frank, Bart, Mr. Massey, their boss, then kept that information to myself, to see how good a detective he really was.

Mom would certainly approve.

# Chapter Three

**N**ew York City, the City that Never Sleeps, the Big Apple, this was the city Ronald Massey called his playground. Real estate, that is. *Build upward, young man,* his father would say. Along a stretch of West Side Highway, with magnificent views of the Hudson River and New Jersey beyond, he'd built a row of skyscrapers, some 20 stories, some double that, which housed expensive condominiums and office suites, one of which was his own, Massey, Inc., a penthouse perched high above the hustle and bustle of the little people below.

This was where he sat, sixty floors up, his broad oak desk stretched out before him, monitoring his array of computer screens, ever vigilant over Wall Street, local and national news, and the weather. He'd made his fortune in the high-rent district, but his passion was cell phone technology and its ever-evolving challenges. The center-most monitor on his desk showed an eight-camera view of the activity in his sub-basement laboratory where his scientists and programmers toiled, at the moment, frantically in search of one goddammed cell phone.

A quad security monitor set to the right of an elaborate phone panel replayed the betrayal of his lead technician, Arthur O'Malley, stealing the one-of-its-kind phone. Cameras recorded him hunched over a terminal keyboard as he circumnavigated intricate security protocols and downloaded the data files to a flash drive then erased all the backups with a format command. His vast knowledge of the inner workings at Massey, Inc. enabled the backstabbing thief to quell any alarms and notify the mainframe that all systems were operating normally. In a last twist of the knife, he glared into the exit camera and left a message. "Mister Massey, you may be rich and powerful, but you cannot play God."

"...*you cannot play God.*"

"...*you cannot play God.*"

Massey slammed his fist on the desktop. "I can do anything I want, you traitor." Every time he heard O'Malley's voice, his blood pressure shot up, and his heart became a sledgehammer battering his ribs. Bad news for a cardiac patient and two-time flatliner.

Yeah, Ronald Massey might have been six-foot-five and 250 pounds, but as big and tough as he was, at sixty-five years old, he wasn't long for this world. If a man didn't have his health, all the riches he'd amassed in life were worthless. Such was the fate of New York City's Number One real estate tycoon. Where he once traveled the world hobnobbing with other moguls of similar stature, sailing the French Riviera, big game hunting in Africa, whale watching in Antarctica, and multiple trips to Las Vegas on gambling junkets, he now pretty much stuck around Manhattan, nursing a bad ticker.

So here he sat, chucking Nitro under his tongue and fighting for breath, thanks to Arthur O'Malley's thievery. Well, his time was coming. When Frank and Bart get their hands on him, he'll cough up that phone, all right, then be on his way to meet his maker. Nobody steals from Ronald

Massey and lives to tell about it.

If someone were to walk into Massey's office and see the Bible on his desk, so out of place among all the technology, it would be easy to assume he was a religious man. To the contrary, he hadn't wasted an hour in church, praying to some benevolent god for forgiveness. All that preaching about Heaven and Hell would only piss him off. Nobody knew the truth about life after death, yet the Bible touted the goodness of Heaven-goers and the evilness of those bound for Hell. If the scriptures were right, he would surely burn for eternity, as he didn't get rich by being Mr. Goody-Two-Shoes. Now the question remained: What awaited him in the afterlife?

Nobody knew.

However, Massey was on the verge of finding out. He hadn't been idle during his battle with heart disease. No, he'd been quite busy, as witnessed by the centermost monitor on his desk, eight views of his team at work on the biggest breakthrough in all of science and religion. Screenshot number three revealed the discovery of a lifetime, a constantly fixed camera image aimed at the object that would transcribe the future of mankind on this measly, insignificant planet called Earth. But first, he needed that damn cell phone.

The intercom buzzed. "Mr. Massey."

He pressed a button on his phone panel. "Yes, Janice."

"You have visitors."

"Who?"

"Mr. Coletti and Mr. Marconi."

"Send them in."

The massive double doors split at the center seam, and

the two dolts lumbered in. Their black suits looked in need of a good pressing, like they'd been slept in all night. While the doors closed behind them, they approached the desk.

Right away, Massey noticed their hands were empty. "Where's my cell phone?"

Frank took charge. "Some wise guy got away with it."

Massey stood. "And O'Malley?"

Bart spoke up. "He's dancing with the devil, sir."

"You don't know that for a fact."

"He ain't breathing," Frank said. "We chased him 'til the cops showed up."

Massey paced the office. "So O'Malley passed the phone to someone, and you idiots let him get away."

Bart shrugged. "That's pretty much what happened, sir."

Massey stopped pacing and faced his hired guns. Bart may have been the shorter of the two, but he had a rap sheet as long as his arm. He grew up on the mean streets: petty thefts, muggings, bank robbery. He'd rather shoot a man than look at him. He had no family to claim as his own. Frank hailed from Riker's Island, a survivor among the most feared criminals in the city. His size alone wasn't as intimidating as his quick temper. Hard to believe he was a married man, had a wife and a home in the burbs, but he threw it all away for fast money and a life of crime. Though they'd both found a home here at Massey, Inc., their value solely depended on their performance. Today, their report cards were bleeding 'F's.

"What do you know about this wise guy?"

Frank ventured a guess. "He must live in the Woodlawn section of the Bronx, probably within walking distance of McGee's Pub."

"That's where we seen O'Malley," Bart put in. "He spotted us and took off running. I put a couple of bullets in his back, but by the time we got the SUV turned around, we'd lost sight of him."

"He didn't get far," Frank added. "Halfway down the alley, but I got some bad news."

Massey's head felt like it would explode. He took a calming breath.

*Watch that blood pressure. Don't let these guys set off a heart attack.*

"What could be worse than losing the cell phone?"

"When we got back to McGee's, your SUV was on a tow truck."

That put a jolt in his chest. "Now the cops will come around asking questions." The thought of throwing these two fools off the roof was tempting. To watch them plummet, screaming their heads off as they fell to their deaths, that would be music to his ears. Of course, it would be messy, and he didn't need that kind of police attention.

He scoffed at them then retreated to the desk and sat in the high-back before his knees could give out completely. Options and contingencies raced through his mind. He had dozens of Cadillac SUVs, hard to keep track of them 24/7. He could say this one was stolen. However, explaining why it was found at McGee's was the least of his problems. He had to get that cell phone back.

He chucked another Nitro, stood, tested his wobbly legs, then: "Follow me, boys."

"Where are we going?" Bart asked.

"To Hell if you believe it's possible." Massey led his

two buffoons out through the double doors and into the corporate lobby, across the marbled span lined with gold-trimmed windows to his private elevator. Chrome doors slid open, and he ushered his boys into a plushly carpeted and heavily mirrored cabin. The doors closed. He punched the button labeled *SB*, and with a bump, the elevator began its sixty-plus-story descent, bypassing the residential floors, but with stops at the business floors, mostly insurance companies and stock brokers, the gyms, spas, sports center, the main lobby, and on down to the sub-basement where the elevator stopped with a subtle bump. The entire ride down had been tense with silence, Massey admiring himself in the mirrors while his boys stared at their shoes.

The doors opened to a vast white room, seemingly alive with the thrum of fans exhaling ionized air from rows of computer servers and banks of blinking lights. Scientists and programmers sat at terminals, much like NASA techs during a space mission, watching their monitors, typing and thinking. Other technicians milled about, checking hardware configurations, switching mainframes, and collecting data on laptops and tablets. None of them so much as looked up to acknowledge Massey's presence, their chores were that vital.

Massey led his wide-eyed idiots past the rows of blinking and beeping servers to the main terminal where he stopped next to Carl Carlson, a young electronics engineer he'd hired right out of MIT five years ago. He was perfectly capable of stepping into the lead Technician role, as O'Malley's departure had created a sudden vacancy. Carlson looked every bit a college student: scruffy brown hair, Yankees t-shirt, blue jeans, and Chuck Taylor sneakers, yet he had one of the brightest minds in the business. For that and his loyalty, Massey paid him well.

"Mr. Massey..." Carlson didn't even look up from his iPad.

"Any progress?"

"We've broken through the alpha wave barrier to get at the inner frequency, but fine-tuning the waveband across miles of concrete and steel has been problematic."

Massey frowned. "Whoa, whoa, there. The layman's version."

"Since the missing cell phone doesn't contain a SIM card, which would have made tracing it much simpler, I have to make the frequency of the obelisk feedback on its chip in the phone, hoping to get an echo readout for its present location."

Massey thought maybe he could be of some help. "Would knowing the general area where the phone may be located make the search any easier?"

"Definitely. What do you know?"

"Concentrate on the Woodlawn section of the Bronx...see what you come up with." Massey turned to his bruisers. "Maybe you guys aren't as worthless as I thought."

Bart moaned. "Gee thanks, boss."

Frank, a sharper tack in the pail, had to ask, "Did he say obelisk? What obelisk?"

Carlson jumped on that one. "Good question. It's not really an obelisk by definition, more like a magic stone, but it's not really magic and it's not just a stone. It's more of a boulder, but for lack of a better term, we call it an obelisk. Right over here." He led the dumbfounded goons around the back of the servers and presented them with a magnificent sight.

Massey got a kick out of seeing their drop-jawed expressions.

There before them, on a fenced raised platform, rested an odd-shaped rock, egg-like, perhaps ten feet high, its shell the color of granite with crystalline nodules protruding from its surface, as if greater beauty and treasure lay deeper within. The spotlights shining down on it created the illusion of something otherworldly. It vibrated ever so slightly with a soft hum, as would an element of nature that defied known physics, Massey believed.

"It's some kind of trick with the lights," Frank said.

Carlson held his iPad like a schoolbook. "All matter vibrates in some way, to some degree, which resonates a frequency, or pattern of frequencies, unique to its atomic structure. That frequency can change depending upon forces acting on it, say a touch, a tap, a strum, or even by moving the object. This rock emits a frequency unlike any other element on Earth. It's a stable frequency that doesn't change when any external force is applied." He swept his free hand to the high-tech assemblies around them. "It takes all this equipment and computing power to harness the frequency, and the more we studied it, the more we came to understand how special it is."

"It's a rock," Frank said.

Massey scoffed. "To a bonehead like you, maybe, but to an inquisitor like me, it's a possible communication link, a means to an answer to the age-old question... What lies beyond death?"

"Nothing." Bart grumped.

"Come on," Frank jumped in. "You're telling us that cell phone O'Malley stole is connected to this rock?"

"The frequency," Carlson said. "We matched that phone's frequency with the obelisk's frequency. With the frequency of the transmitter and receiver paired, communication is possible. We were testing the application when O'Malley contacted his dead wife, Miriam. Or so he'd claimed. Before we could repeat the test and verify the results, he stole the damn phone."

"And..." Massey added. "He stole the data and deleted our files. Now we're back to square one."

"Not entirely. We have the frequency." Carlson stepped away to instruct his team on the possible position of the lost phone in Woodlawn.

Frank asked, "What about all those cell phones?"

Around the base of the obelisk, cell phones lay scattered about like the bones of some electronic beast, busted and discarded iPhones and androids, Samsung, LG, and Sony with the latest generation technology. Also, at a distance of three feet, a fence had been erected, not a sturdy barrier, by any means, just a simple wooden rail fence that seemed completely out of place.

Massey stepped up to the fence. "Out of all those cell phones, none of them worked. It wasn't until Carlson tried an older model, a Motorola StarTAC flip phone he bought at an Army Surplus store in the Bronx for five bucks. With it he got a frequency match, but only after he'd inserted a tiny crystalline chip from the obelisk into the SIM slot. We don't dare take another chip from the stone, so it's imperative we retrieve that stolen cell phone."

"Why the fence?" Bart asked. "Is the obelisk

dangerous?"

He didn't want to talk about what warranted a fence but thought it best to elaborate. "Late one night, the cleaning lady was down here doing her job, and curiosity must've drawn her to look under the blue tarp we put over the obelisk. At first, I thought there'd been a glitch in the video camera that stands watch over the lab, 24/7. One second she was moving around under the tarp, and then there was a white flash, and she never came out. A closer inspection of the obelisk's surface showed no evidence that it had done anything to cause her disappearance. However, just in case some alien activity was at play, the fence went up, and I put everyone on notice to stay clear."

Bart laughed. "Alien?"

Frank waved him off. "Where did it come from?"

"Uganda. In the Rwenzori Mountains. On safari there a few years back, I heard the locals talk of a stone monolith the natives used to communicate with their ancestors in the afterlife. I set out to find it, and find it I did, and with much effort, I brought it out of the mountains to its resting place here."

He shuddered at the irony of such a stone, for him to have come into possession of it as his own life started slipping away. If it was somehow connected to the afterlife, as the locals believed, be it Heaven or Hell or oblivion, he was determined to learn the truth.

"Got it," Carlson announced, standing at a terminal in the first row, his hand on the shoulder of a woman working a keyboard, their attention on the glowing screen. "It's at a cemetery in Woodlawn."

Massey couldn't contain his excitement, though he

knew he should have tried, as his heart rate jumped to supersonic. The map on the screen showed the phone's location with a pulsing X. "Lock on it."

"Present coordinates are 40 degrees, 53 minutes, 3 seconds by 73 degrees, 52 minutes, 12 seconds," the woman reported.

Massey slapped Carlson on the back. "See? That wasn't so hard, was it?"

Carlson keyed his iPad. A similar map came up. He handed it to Frank. "Think you can bring back that phone this time?"

"No problem." Frank stared at the blinking X.

In all the excitement, no one was paying attention to Bart, and in all his stupidity, he leaned over the fence with an outstretched hand and grabbed one of the obelisk's crystal nubs. It had to be worth a fortune, but no matter how hard he pulled, it wouldn't break off. Instead, a fiery crimson hole opened in the middle of the crystalline rock, and as if the devil himself inhaled a deep breath, a swirling gravitational field sucked Bart into the obelisk. He didn't even have time to scream.

Frank closed the laptop and tucked it under his arm. "Come on, Bart. Let's go get that damn cell phone."

No reply.

Massey turned to the obelisk where Bart was last standing. *Oh, no. Not again.*

"Bart," Frank shouted.

"Mr. Massey," Carlson muttered. "We've got a problem."

Frank spun around. "Where the hell is Bart?"

Jim Keane

## Chapter Four

**B**art couldn't believe what had happened to him. His body felt as if a soundless clap of thunder had thumped him, then some otherworldly force had sucked the air from his lungs. He wasn't sure if he'd passed out, as his world went from the sub-basement lab to this strange landscape in seemingly a split-second. It might have been minutes or hours for all he knew. He had no sense of time and space as he trudged through a burnt forest of blackened trees, his shoes stirring up the ashes on a meandering trail to who-knew-where. A tailwind pushed him forward like a giant hand pressing on his back. Though he wanted to turn around and run back to the lab, that relentless wind pushed him onward with a purpose, it seemed. The putrid smell of death hung in the air, a mix of rotten eggs and spoiled milk; and the sky, if there was a sky, was obscured in acrid smoke. Shades of gray drifted around him, no color, no life, and his dusty black suit seemed the perfect attire for this...place.

*What is this place?*

Certainly, the landscape was far too vast to be inside the obelisk. He must've passed through a portal of some kind, to some other universe...or worse...to the land of the dead. The thought of being dead caused his heart rate to falter, which gave him instant solace.

*Dead people don't have beating hearts.*

He trudged along for an indeterminable amount of time, an impossible distance, until the smoke lifted and a blackened hillside came into view. At its summit, a large black shape loomed over the desolation, a familiar shape in its height and breadth. He squinted.

*The obelisk?*

How could it be set before him when he'd just passed through it somewhere behind him? Maybe it was the exit, a way to get back to the lab, to Frank, and their mission to find that damn cell phone. With boosted hope, he scrabbled up the hill, clawing at the ashen ground, his shoes losing traction again and again as he fought to make progress toward his salvation.

However, the gloomy sky unleashed a thunderous boom and a torrent of rain, not just any rain, but rain that burned on contact, acidic in the way it sizzled his skin and set his suit afire, melting his watch, his belt buckle, and even the gun tucked in his waistband. Within minutes, he was lying in the ashes, naked, his skin blistered, smoldering and stinky. If he had to describe the pain, he'd liken it to his flesh being consumed by a million voracious maggots.

Writhing in the ashpit of Hell, he screamed, "What's happening to me?"

*"You're on the other side now,"* a gravelly voice echoed above him.

"Am I dead?"

*"Not yet."*

"That's not entirely comforting," he shouted.

*"Crawl to the obelisk on the hill where you will know the meaning of your life before we cast final judgment upon you."*

"Final judgment?"

*"Crawl, you fool."*

And crawl he did, through the ashes and over the burnt tree roots and scalded rocks of Hell's half-hectare under the relentless bombardment of acid rain until he reached the base of the obelisk. Amazed he was still alive, he crawled through an opening where he found instant relief from the torrential onslaught. The cold air offered no relief from the burn in his lungs or the heat of his blistered flesh, but he found the strength to stand. Above him, and beyond the transparent dome of the obelisk, the light came in flickering waves, as if the sky were on fire, a sky he was certain didn't exist but in his own perception.

Stranger still was the perception of his physical being, now dressed in jeans, a wife-beater-t, and Jordan tennis shoes fit for fast getaways. He felt the lump under his belt where he'd always carried his gun, a .40 caliber Beretta PX4 Storm.

*"What the hell?"*

He took a curious step forward, and suddenly found himself back in the Bronx, standing in front of Tony's pizza under a violent gray sky. His only perception of time came from the traffic, the cars and trucks slogging by, models twenty years old or older.

"Are you just going to stand there gawking..."

Bart nearly jumped out of his sneakers. The voice belonged to Frank, and he was standing right beside him.

"Or are we going in for lunch?"

The MTA D train rattled by.

"We got a Brinks truck to rob, remember?"

"The truck, right." He and Frank had planned the

robbery weeks ago, at the Fleet Bank on Bainbridge Avenue. They'd staked it out, and every Friday at 1:30 pm, a Brinks truck dropped off bags of money for the paycheck-cashing rush on Friday evenings.

The next thing he knew, they were sitting at a small table inside Tony's, eating pizza: thin crust New York Style with pepperoni and dollops of cream cheese. He looked around, amazed at the authenticity of the place, the narrow aisles between dark wood tables, the aroma of mozzarella and basil, pizza dough slightly singed in a wood-fired oven. It was as if the obelisk had sent him back in time and given him a second chance at life, a chance to turn from his criminal ways...

"We should have a thirty-second window." Frank swigged Guinness. "As soon as they open the back door of that armored truck, we pounce on them."

Frank Coletti was the mastermind, Bart Marconi, the follower. Whatever Frank wanted, Bart went along with it.

"Sure, Frank. What about the alarm?"

"We'll be in and out of that truck before anyone notices."

"And we're still going to shoot the guards?"

Frank nodded. "No witnesses."

"Makes sense." Bart chewed pizza; it tasted real, as if he were truly at Tony's with Frank, finalizing the plan, and not in the hellish world of the obelisk.

"Even if a passerby sees us, our masks and hoodies would make it impossible for anyone to identify us, but we'll be up close and personal with the guards, so they have to die."

Bart wanted to say, *"Count me out. I'm going*

*straight. Been to Hell and it ain't no fun.*" But the words wouldn't come out. Obviously, history was going to repeat itself. There'd be no reprieve from his past.

"We gotta split up afterwards," Frank said.

"Split up?" Bart pressed his lips together. He didn't like the idea any more now than he did back then.

"I'll take the train. You take the car. We'll meet up at McGee's Pub."

"What about lying low?"

Bart smiled. "After we celebrate."

"You're a crazy son of a bitch."

"Just stick with the plan, Bart."

The next thing he knew, they were parked across the street from Fleet Bank, sitting in an old Ford sedan, the engine idling with an ominous lope that shuddered the steering wheel. The dash clock showed 1:30, and right on time, the Brinks truck pulled up and stopped in front of the entrance doors. Leaves and dust took flight in the wind. Bart was suddenly wearing a ski mask and hoodie. He glanced at Frank, now dressed the same. They pulled out their guns. It was showtime.

Two Brinks guards got out of the cab, one driver and one delivery boy. As soon as they opened the back door, Bart and Frank confronted them, brandishing guns. Both guards threw up their hands, turned their backs to the robbers, and dropped to their knees. Obviously, neither were prepared to risk their lives guarding money that didn't belong to them.

Frank climbed inside the truck while Bart held his gun on the guards. He already knew how this would play out and abandoned the plan. However, as he lowered the gun, his arm popped back up. His feet were glued to the ground. The obelisk had made him a passenger in his own past with no way to alter the outcome. Yeah. He was in for a wild ride.

The first thing that went wrong, a bus rolled up on the scene and stopped alongside the Brinks truck. Then a female bank customer strolled out, immediately spotting the guards on their knees and a gunman standing behind them. She screamed.

Frank tossed out sealed white packages of bills, which hit the ground behind Bart. When he turned to look at the loot, one of the guards got a backbone, wheeled around and grabbed Bart's gun arm. The gun went off and sent the bullet ripping into the top package of greenbacks. Frank jumped out of the truck and waylaid the guard with the butt of his gun.

"Pop 'em both." Frank picked up an armful of loot just as sirens screamed from down the block.

Bart knew he hadn't killed anyone that day, so he snatched up the ripped packet of money, just as he'd done before, and again he regretted it right away. As he took off running, money spilled out from the rip, and the wind sent riches flying down the street.

"Let's go," Frank said. "Stick to the plan."

As the bus had blocked a straight shot to the car, Bart took the long route around it, spilling cash as he ran. Passengers piled out of the bus and started chasing the loosed bills.

An old woman shouted at Bart, "You should be ashamed of yourself."

It was Mrs. Cradwick, his teacher in grammar school,

but he was sure she couldn't recognize him in this getup. He darted around the bus and through the throng of money-grabbers, jumped in the running getaway car, and tossed his half-empty bag of money on the seat. That's when he spotted Frank hightailing it down East 205$^{th}$ street, heading for the train, his hoodie jacket stuffed fat with packages from the heist.

*"Stick to the plan."*

Bart gunned the engine and tore away from the curb. The excitement and fear burning in his veins felt exactly as hot as it had felt on that fateful day on Bainbridge Avenue. The terror of the high-speed chase that followed, it felt the same, as well, and when it was over, the cold steel of handcuffs replayed the same agony of defeat.

The obelisk was a cruel storyteller.

Now, in an orange jumpsuit and shackles, he stood in front of a judge. Frank was there too, as his escape had not been any more successful.

"Ten years." The judge slammed the gavel down.

A swirling sensation landed Bart back in the obelisk under the dome of fire, again naked in his acid-burned skin. Lying on the cold floor that offered no relief from the heat, he recalled how he'd spent five years at Upstate Correctional Facility in Fishkill, New York, whereas Frank served all ten on Riker's Island, mostly because he'd pistol-whipped the guard. After his release, Bart returned to his life of petty crime and left bank robbery to the professionals. When Frank was eventually released, he chose a different path, swore off a life of crime, got a real job, married Clarissa Bow, bought a house in the burbs, and fathered a beautiful baby girl they named Chloe.

Bart's respite down memory lane came to a sudden and brutal end. The obelisk replayed his life of crime with a montage of stills and clips of the criminal acts he'd bestowed upon his fellow citizens of New York City: the muggings, purse snatchings, robberies, and shootings.

The obelisk suddenly threw him into a dark and warm August night where he stood on a street corner, watching patrons go in and out of the convenience store. Its register had to be brimming with cash. He pulled on the ski mask, shoved his hands in his hoodie pockets, and gripped the .40 caliber Beretta in his right hand.

He shivered with excitement brewing in his chest. When it appeared there were the fewest people inside, he made his move and opened the door while drawing his gun to show he meant business. "Give me your cash." He waved the gun at the clerk, an old guy; he might have been sixty, who certainly wouldn't put up a fight for the store's money, not while facing the gun, for sure, but he didn't immediately comply.

"You think I'm playin', old man?"

He held up his hands. "It's not worth it, son...maybe twenty bucks in here, but I might have a couple bucks in my wallet. You can have it. Just take it and go."

Bart knew the big bucks were in that register. He'd seen all the customers coming and going, so he held out for the bonanza. "You're lying." He swiveled the gun barrel toward customers huddled in the back aisle. "Open it, or I'll start shooting 'em, one at a time. You hear me?"

"No need to hurt anyone." The clerk opened the drawer.

Bart stretched over the counter and grabbed

greenbacks from their slots. When he pulled back and realized how few bills he'd grabbed, that really pissed him off. "That's all?"

"I told you—"

"Where's the safe?"

"I can't open it. No key. Only the owner has a key."

"You talk too much, old man." Bart shot him in the chest then turned his gun on the customers. "Nobody move."

Their faces were etched in horror.

The clerk lay on the floor in a growing pool of blood.

*Dumb bastard should a given me the money.*

He took off running down the street but ended up hanging out the passenger window of a black SUV, firing his gun at O'Malley's back. He was getting away with the cell phone.

Frank cranked the steering wheel hard, which sent the SUV into a tire-screaming skid, whipping it around to give chase in the opposite direction. O'Malley was nowhere to be seen.

It felt good to be working with Frank again, though their new boss, Ronald Massey, seemed a bit ruthless in his disrespect for law and order. If they didn't get that cell phone, their lives wouldn't be worth two nickels. So far, Massey had been paying them well, which made it possible for them to afford these black Armani suits and paten-leather shoes.

Frank slammed on the brakes, stopping at the mouth of the alley behind McGee's Pub. Bart jumped out and started running toward O'Malley but landed face-first on the cold hard floor of the obelisk, again naked and burning up.

"Are you kidding me?"

Haunting laughter surrounded him.

Instantly, he was sitting in the back of a stretched limo with Frank, who was pouring himself a drink from the carbar. Bart immediately recognized the scene of wealth, plush leather seating for a dozen passengers, the neon ceiling lights that gave the interior the feel of a disco. He'd just finished up a 90-day stint in jail for breaking into a parking meter, and Frank had offered to give him a ride and a place to hang out. He'd never said anything about picking him up in a chauffeured limousine.

Frank's brother-in-law, all spiffy in a three-piece suit, sat in a swivel chair with a drink of his own in hand, a tall glass, complete with an umbrella and a wedge of orange. Yeah, his wife was none other than Frank's sister, Sharon, who'd married the richest man in New York City, Ronald Massey. He leaned forward and offered a beefy handshake. "Good to meet you, Mr. Marconi." His voice had that oily slick tone of a politician. "Frank's told me a lot about you. I understand you might be looking for work."

Bart accepted a handshake with the devil, and then Frank handed him the drink he'd prepared. "Rum and Coke, right?"

The engine revved with an odd gurgling sound, and yet again, Bart landed on the floor in the obelisk, and again his blistered flesh radiated pain to the nth degree.

*What is this shit, Ground Hog Day?*

*"Welcome back, Bart Marconi,"* the malevolent voice echoed around him. *"As you have seen, your life, even your mere existence, has no redeeming qualities."*

"I played tuba in my high school band."

*"You grew up on the mean streets, dog eat dog, survival of the fittest, but that's no excuse. There is no defense for your criminality. You have been judged and sentenced accordingly."*

The floor dropped out from under him. Down, down, down he fell. Utter darkness surrounded his tumbling body. Terror, true terror, visceral in every way, borne of fear and pain and hopelessness, infected his brain as viciously as feeding piranhas, each fighting for the biggest bite, each bite a migraine as sharp as a steel blade, lethal as a lead bullet.

"You gotta be shittin' meeeeee."

# Chapter Five

**F**rank gripped the steering wheel of his black Ford Crown Vic. He liked the feel of the heavy car, the growl of the gas-guzzling V-8, and the fretful looks he'd get from motorists, as if they thought it was an unmarked police cruiser. Since he'd lost the company's Cadillac SUV in the alley behind McGee's, Massey had made him use his own car to chase down the stolen cell phone. According to the laptop Carlson had given him, the blinking X was still at the cemetery in Woodlawn, and this time he wouldn't fail to retrieve that phone.

A taxi raced past him, horn blowing as it cut in front of him and weaved through traffic on the West Side Highway. Frank wished Bart was riding shotgun; he would have popped the cabbie with his .40 caliber, but instead, his sidekick had disappeared, nowhere to be found in the sub-basement lab. It wasn't until Massey played the security video that they'd solved the mystery; the obelisk had opened up, and the soles of Bart's shoes were the last they saw of him. Screaming mad, Frank wanted to take a sledgehammer and bust that rock into a million pieces. He'd have done it to get Bart back, but no such hammer was to be found in the lab, and Massey convinced him to calm down and stick with the plan. "Get that damn cell phone."

Yeah. The stakes were high in this game of cellular

cat and mouse. All the best-laid plans in the world, all the best intentions, meant squat when his daughter's life was on the line.

After his release from Riker's Island ten years ago, he'd set out to go straight. No more bank robberies, no more contact with Bart, the bad seed, just the American Dream: a job, home, and family. Yeah. It all started with good intentions. He'd always been good at stripping cars, so he got a steady job at Big Al's Garage. He and Al went way back, and he had no problem hiring ex-cons. Frank's first paycheck for an honest week's work had given him a sense of pride.

One day at work, he met Clarissa Bow, a classy gal in a business suit, when she came in to pick up her car. Their attraction was immediate and intense, and as it turned out, over the next year, they were married and bought a house in the Bronx.

He thought he could never be happier until the day Chloe was born. He was ecstatic. The next nine years were paradise. He loved being a father, husband, and a productive citizen with no court dates or probation officer meetings.

And then everything fell apart.

Just thinking about what had happened created such a storm inside him, an adrenaline-fueled rage, that he gripped the steering wheel and gritted his teeth.

*How could life be so cruel to a little girl?*

A car horn blasted next to him. He'd wandered from his lane on the Henry Hudson Parkway and nearly caused a wreck. Startled, he shook it off and checked the laptop. The blinking X was still in the cemetery.

He remembered the night he'd come home from work, the night Chloe came running to him for his usual welcome-home hug, her scream as she tumbled to the floor, the shock that belted him in the chest. "Chloe." He ran to her and knelt. "What's wrong?"

"My back hurts."

He lifted her to her feet, but her legs were wobbly and she couldn't stand.

Clarissa rushed up. "What happened?"

"Call 9-1-1."

Frank's eyes teared up, and he had to blink a few times to clear his vision of the roadway ahead. The events that followed that fateful day had changed the course of his life, Clarissa's life, Chloe's, and their American Dream.

Their lives crumbled on the day Chloe's doctor diagnosed her condition. In the hospital room at MSK Kids, she was in good spirits, a bubbly and giggly nine-year-old lying in bed. Flowers and cards were set around the room, and a poster of Buzz Lightyear hung on the wall. Frank and Clarissa stood at her bedside.

"You want to go for a ride?" Frank asked her.

"Can we go to the gift shop?"

"Sure. Why not?"

Frank scooped her up in his arms and set her in a wheelchair parked by the door.

Clarissa positioned Chloe's feet on the footpads. "Don't be gone too long, now, you hear?"

"Ah, Mom. I'm not driving." She smiled up at her dad. "Onward, slave."

Just as Frank turned the chair for the doorway, the doctor walked in. "Where are you going, young lady?"

"For a ride to the gift shop."

The doctor turned to the hallway and summoned Nurse Debbie. "Take Miss Coletti to the gift shop. I need to speak with her parents."

Chloe giggled. "Can I get some gummy worms?"

Nurse Debbie laughed. "We'll see." And rolled her out.

Frank remembered the angst that roiled in his stomach. They'd been waiting on the MRI results, and it was time to face the truth about Chloe's condition.

The doc came right out with it. "She'll never walk again."

"Why? What...what's wrong?" Clarissa spluttered, fighting back tears and raw panic.

Frank didn't know what to think. What to say.

"She has an inoperable CNS tumor at L2," the doc went on. "It's crushing her spinal cord and cutting off nerve impulses to her lower extremities."

"Inoperable?" Frank managed.

"Sorry."

"So that's it?" Frank spat. "There's nothing you can do?"

"Not entirely," the doc said. "Stem cell therapy has shown to be helpful, but it's experimental and not covered by insurance."

"How much?" Clarissa asked.

"Each treatment is fifty thousand dollars, and she'll require multiple treatments. However, positive results are not guaranteed."

"We don't have that kind of money," Clarissa cried. "What are we going to do, Frank?"

"I need to make more money."

*Make more money. Make more money.*

He careened the Crown Vic down the exit ramp for Woodlawn Heights.

The solution threw him back into a life of crime, working for Ronald Massey as his hired gun. An enforcer. A cell phone hunter. Massey had made him a deal: "If you bring that cell phone back to me, I'll pay for Chloe's treatments." *Incentive*, he'd added. Massey never did anything for nothing in return.

Frank wished Bart was with him on this hunt. He'd have no problem shooting the fool who had taken the phone from O'Malley. However, if it came down to it, Frank was willing to do whatever it took to get that phone, including murder and going back to prison...for his daughter.

## Chapter Six

Ibrushed snow from the small plot of grass at my feet then dropped to my knees in front of my dad's grave. The gray marble headstone with a green inlaid shamrock had cost me plenty, but Dermot Calhoun deserved a marker to lay witness to his presence and passing on this earth.

*BELOVED HUSBAND AND FATHER – REST IN PEACE*

"Dad, I don't know if you can hear me, but coming here makes me feel closer to you. I miss you. Mom misses you. We wish we could have had the opportunity to say goodbye."

My eyes burned with fresh tears. Death's finality seemed so cruel, especially to Mom. Her headstone lay next to Dermot's, blank in its context and void of content, lying in wait for her time to pass into the afterlife. Would she cross paths with Dad under some ethereal rainbow in the clouds? Nobody knew, of course. I could only hope they would have such a sunny and happy reunion.

Being a scientist of sorts, an engineer and technician who manipulated atoms and coaxed electrons and photons into signals that carried voice, text, and video, religion never weighed much on my life. The tall statue of Jesus, arms outstretched, palms up, that stood at the entry to this cemetery was a nice touch, but to me, that was all, a man from history who'd tried to teach the masses to be kind to each other. It was only after Dad died that I hoped Jesus was right, that Heaven existed, and that Dad was looking down on me from some lofty height, guiding me, protecting me, but logic told me that couldn't be true. If it were true, why had he abandoned his wife? Why would he let her suffer so much pain? Still, I hung on to hope and looked up to a wintery sky. "Dad, if you can hear me. Please help Mom before grief kills her."

How I wished we could have a normal conversation again, exchange ideas back and forth over a beer at McGee's. My dad was a great man. Not because he had cured any diseases; nor won any great battles of war; nor would the world ever remember him in the archives of influential people, celebrities, or heroes. He never wrote a song or penned a novel, and his singing voice was gruff and bold when he belted out an old Irish ballad.

Dermot Calhoun was a great man because he was a dedicated provider for my mom and me. He was resolute in his commitment to his family and his thirty-year marriage, as well as my occasional scraped knee that required a Band-Aid. Whether it was a church fundraiser or a Boy Scout jamboree, he was always there to lend a helping hand.

Yes, Dermot Calhoun was a great man.

Every time I visited my dad's grave, I promised myself I'd be strong. I wouldn't cry, but I was human. This was my dad. He deserved every tear I shed for him.

There was so much more I wanted to do with him: Yankee games, movies, road trips...we'd even planned to go back to Ireland and see my uncles and cousins, hear the old stories, or just hang out at a pub to enjoy a few beers and dance the night away.

I was such a fool.

I'd taken him for granted, never thought he'd be killed. My dad would live forever, but he didn't, and now all that we had is gone, all on account of one punk with a gun. Mullen has had no luck finding the murderer, and I thought there was nothing I wouldn't do to get justice for Dad, justice for me, justice for Mom. An eye for an eye... I wouldn't care if the whole world went blind, but I was sure my dad wouldn't want me to go off half-cocked and seek justice on my own.

"Ain't that right, Dad," I said to the sky.

As if in response, a cell phone rang in my pocket, not my cell phone, but the dead man's cell phone. Its ringtone was that of an old landline, whereas mine chimed a tune. My cell phone was 4G and streamed movies. O'Malley's cell phone could talk to the dead. It was an old Motorola StarTAC flip phone with an extendable antenna, famous for crappy reception and dropped calls. I had to wonder who would call such a phone. A telemarketer, probably, to tell me my car warranty had expired. I reached into my coat and removed the murdered man's cell phone. The tiny display read: *out of area.*

The phone stopped ringing. I regained my feet and walked to a nearby bench where I sat and recalled last night after Mullen dropped me off at home. I needed to know more about this phone, who was the carrier, who'd last purchased it... I'd cleaned the blood off the black housing and phone pad then removed the back and the battery to get to the serial number, which could tell me a lot about this phone. However, to get that information, I'd need to access a secure database at Vericom...I'd also noticed an odd chip of crystal in the SIM card slot, which made me wonder how it was possible for the phone to even ring, much less complete a call. SIM cards assigned each phone to a Mobile Switching Center frequency...

The phone rang again.

I blinked.

*What the hell is going on? Do I dare answer it?*

A cold wind picked up, and the skeletal branch of a tree waved above me. Someone wanted to talk to the murdered man, O'Malley, I supposed.

*"Are you going to answer the phone or just stare at it?"*

Now I was talking to myself. That's how freaked out I was.

I poised my finger over the send button, took a breath and gave it a stab. "Hello?"

*Static.*

I pressed the phone closer to my ear. "Is anybody there?"

*Static.*

I extended the antenna. "Hello?"

*Static.*

"Who is this?" Then a chilling thought froze me. Maybe it was the bad guys from last night, trying to get a fix on the phone...triangulate its location. I never wanted to see those thugs again. Fear tempted me to close the phone, end the call, until I realized how impossible it would be for them to find the phone without a SIM card.

*Static...* "Son?" *Static...*

*Son? Did the familiar voice say son?* It sure as hell sounded like my dad. "Hello? Dad?" I jumped to my feet and turned a dizzying full circle, hoping to get a better signal. "Dad?" My heart was beating hard; I could barely breathe. "Dad?"

The static persisted, and then came a crackling noise, distant, echoing, as if not of this world.

"Dad? Are you there?"

*Crackle...* "Run..." *Crackle...*

Then there was silence. The call had dropped.

"No." I scowled at the phone. The tiny display read: *Call Ended.*

*"Run?"* I wanted so badly to believe it was my dad, that I'd actually received a call from beyond the grave. If I believed that, I'd believe anything...like my dad knew something I didn't know. Maybe I was in danger that only he could see coming.

*Run?* What did I have to lose?

I ran.

# Chapter Seven

**F**rank was bearing down on his prey, his Crown Vic gunning up the hill and into the cemetery. He scoffed at the statue of Jesus looking over the entrance, welcoming visitors with open arms. He was one visitor the cemetery could do without.

A blur of a Jeep sped by him, a green Cherokee, racing through the exit as if a ghost was on its bumper. Frank blasted the horn then instantly recognized the crazy driver as the bastard he was chasing last night. He checked the laptop and saw the blinking X was now behind him and moving away fast.

"Son of a bitch." Frank executed a 180-degree skid and floored the accelerator, spinning the tires and throwing up dirt and gravel from the shoulder and nearly colliding with a parked car. He wasn't going to let that cell phone get away again. His daughter's future hung in the balance.

\#

I sped out the cemetery exit, periodically glancing at the cell phone that had connected me with my dad. He'd told me to run. I didn't know why nor where I was going, but it seemed logical to put as much distance between me and the cemetery as quickly as possible. Still, I wondered what Dad knew that I didn't, made me think he was really watching me from above. There was no other explanation. I needed to learn more about the dead man's cell phone and executed a quick turn onto the highway ramp and headed for Vericom.

My speedometer needle was bouncing on 80-miles-per-hour so I checked my rearview to be sure I hadn't attracted the attention of the highway patrol, and sure enough, a black Ford sedan, probably an unmarked police cruiser, was speeding up behind me. By the time he was on my back bumper, I thought I recognized the driver. "Crap."

#

Frank was gaining on the Jeep. He turned on the headlights and flashed the brights repeatedly, hoping the son of a bitch would pull over. Instead, the Jeep sped up. "Damn." He gunned the engine and rammed its back bumper. The Jeep fishtailed but corrected. Frank hit him again. The Jeep refused to slow down.

"You want to play this the hard way, huh?" He pulled the gun from his suit coat, motored down the window, and driving with his right hand, he blasted away at the Jeep with his left hand. The gun kicked and wobbled wildly, pummeling the Jeep with hot lead. The incoming wind spat cordite and smoke in his face, but he kept firing. "Pull over, you son of a bitch."

#

I heard the pop, pop, pop of gunfire and the snap and crack of bullets hitting my Jeep. I glanced to my outside rearview and saw the big goon from last night, leaning out the driver's door window, shooting at me, even as his car veered left and right...the Jeep's rearview mirror shattered. "Shit."

I don't know what I was thinking when I slammed on my brakes, a mix of panic and terror, or maybe instinct, but

I instantly regretted it. The black Ford crashed into me, blew out my tailgate window, and sent the Jeep careening into oncoming traffic. A trash truck was headed right for me, brakes locked up and tires screaming. Nearby cars swerved helter-skelter to get out of the way.

I jerked the steering wheel right and sideswiped the black Ford. A bullet shattered my passenger door window, pelting me with shards of glass, but I didn't let up and steered hard right to slam into the Ford again. Metal crunched and scraped as I forced the Ford over the curb and into a pole. Amid all the car parts flying by me, I saw the gun skidding across the pavement. I stomped on the gas, and a quick look to my inside rearview showed me the Ford had a smashed grill and buckled hood. Steam and smoke sprayed into the air. Then, to my horror, like this nightmare would never end, the car reversed, the bumper fell off, and now moving forward, the car ran over its own debris then stopped where the gun had come to rest. The driver jumped out and retrieved his dropped weapon. Now I was sure he was the same black-suited thug who'd tried to kill me last night.

Fighting tunnel vision, I weaved through traffic and pressed on down the highway toward Vericom.

#

Frank picked up his gun lying on the street amid the broken pieces of his Crown Vic. He took aim at the fleeing Jeep, but noticed the crowd of looky-loos gathering and quickly put the gun under his suit coat. Meanwhile, the scumbag with the cell phone was getting away.

He jumped back in the battered car and took up the chase. The car made clunking sounds, and steam from the busted radiator fogged up his windshield with a greasy slime. He hoped to catch the bastard before the car gave out entirely.

#

I kept checking my rearview mirror. As impossible as it seemed, that bent-up black Ford was several blocks behind me, throwing steam and sparks.

*That guy just doesn't give up.*

In a desperate bid to not draw police attention to myself, I maintained the speed limit on the ramp to I-85 southbound, and then accelerated toward the Bronx.

#

Frank drove like a maniac, as he didn't want to lose sight of the Jeep up ahead. It wasn't hard to spot, having no back window and a crumpled back bumper. He turned on the wipers, which only smeared the antifreeze across the windshield. Pedal to the metal, he almost caught up to the Jeep when the V-8 surged and sputtered. A dinging alarm made him check his instruments. The overheat light had popped on. "No. Not now."

A quarter-mile later, the Ford ground to a halt on the side of the highway. As the Jeep receded into the distance, he slammed his fist on the steering wheel. "Fuck."

After stabbing the gun in his suit coat, he shoved open the door and got out, at first to survey the damage, but before he could shut the door, a miracle happened. He couldn't believe his eyes. A roadside assistance pickup truck with flashing yellow roof lights pulled up behind him. *Highway Helper* it read on the door. "I'll be damned."

A young fellow popped out of the cab. He had on coveralls and a ball cap. "You need some help?"

"One second." Frank ducked back into the car and grabbed the laptop from the seat, then approached the man who'd inadvertently found a boatload of trouble. "Thanks. I got it from here." He shoved him out of the way and jumped into the service truck's cab.

"What the hell, man?"

He slammed the transmission into drive and burned rubber out of there. In the rearview, the man tore off his cap and threw it on the ground. Frank wanted to say 'sorry' but there was no time for such niceties.

Running eighty and ninety down the highway, he soon spotted the green Jeep a half mile ahead of him. He was just minutes from catching the prick, putting a bullet in his head, and retrieving the cell phone. Massey would be happy, Chloe would be saved, and he'd celebrate with a fifth of Jack Daniels.

The Jeep took the exit ramp number 7 going west.

Filled with determination, Frank followed, maybe a hundred yards back, made the exit and quickly spotted the Jeep as it turned onto a side street. When Frank turned, he found himself on an access road to Vericom, the cell phone giant housed behind high fences and a heavily guarded entrance where the Jeep stopped. Frank stopped short and watched the driver converse with a guard.

"Shit."

He pulled to the side, parked against a berm of snow a plow had piled up, and shut off the truck. To wait.

#

A cool wave of relief washed over me when I realized I'd lost the black Ford menace. Stopped at the gate to Vericom, I showed my work badge to the guard.

"Mr. Calhoun. What happened to your Jeep?"

It was a mess. The left side rearview had been blown off, the passenger window blown out, and the back end was smashed in. "Uninsured motorist."

"Why are you here on a Sunday?"

"Problems with a phone. Can't wait until Monday." It wasn't a lie.

He opened the gate and I drove into a nearly empty parking lot. On weekends, only a skeleton crew was on duty. I found a spot close to the front door.

Within minutes, I'd used my work badge to key my way inside.

# Chapter Eight

**B**art's fall into oblivion ended with a thud. He bounced once and skidded into a rock wall. The pain felt like every bone in his body splintered into a million pieces. Either the impact knocked the air from his lungs or he could no longer inhale a single breath of life. The air was so hot, his flesh boiled, and he could smell the stench of death and decay. His mouth tasted of bile that had surged up from his guts. If he was dead, he wasn't dead enough.

He squeezed his eyes shut, afraid of what horrors surrounded him. Maybe he'd awake from this nightmare, find himself back in the sub-basement lab with Frank. Only now did he understand the despicable evil Massey had discovered and exploited for his own personal gain. Someone had to stop him.

*Laughter.* Echoing laughter.

"What do you want from me?" Bart shouted.

*"Want from me, want from me,"* echoed back.

"Your soul," a guttural voice bellowed.

More laughter.

Despite the pain, Bart stood and got his bearings. Everything before him glowed red: the rock walls of a tunnel, even the acrid air. The ceiling was on fire as if solid rock could burn as easily as firewood. From all that he'd seen so far, Bart knew anything was possible in the obelisk's world.

Worse, he realized he was completely naked. Every stitch of his clothes had been incinerated, as was all his body hair, right down to his eyebrows. Bald and broiled, he had to escape from this hellhole. There had to be a way, but which way..?

In one direction, a gray light filtered in, as if there was an opening in the tunnel of fire, an exit into the acid rainstorm he'd trudged through only moments ago, but maybe weeks or eons, he couldn't be sure. However, he was sure he didn't want a repeat performance of the maelstrom outside. That left the other direction, which appeared to go deeper into Hell's fiery bowels. That was even less appealing than the acid rain. Every nerve in his tortured body prickled as he elected for the exit and hopefully a way back to the lab.

He took a stagger-step toward the gray opening, which suddenly shrank in size, as if the distance to it had doubled. Another step created the same effect. After another step, the opening became but a gray dot in the distance.

"Awe, come on," he shouted into the hellfire.

*Laughter.*

There was only one viable choice: to move down the fiery tunnel. He staggered forward a step, warily, his eyes scanning the red glow for danger, though he had no idea what that danger could be: a demon, perhaps, or a horde of demons, maybe a monster with sharp teeth and long claws.

"Bring it on, damnit."

*What's the worse that can happen to me? Death? Bring that on, too, ya prick.*

He worked his way along the tunnel until it ended at a drop-off into an abyss. Looking over the edge, he saw darkness so deep that the ceiling of fire couldn't illuminate the bottom. He scanned the width of the hole, maybe a foot or a mile, who knew, but there was no opening, outlet, or ledge to circumvent the pit. The only way to go was down...but how? There were no steps, no rope ladders, no elevators. He had no choice but to jump. What was the worse that could happen? He could die. He'd gladly choose death over existence in this putrid place.

"Geronimo." He jumped.

As he fell, he noticed the darkness break apart, first in tiny embers flashing by, to showers of sparks that melded into a faint red glow just as he hit dead bottom. Did it hurt? Hell, yes, it hurt, hurt like hell, but he was getting used to enduring unfathomable pain.

Ahead lay another tunnel. He regained his feet and stepped forward, less fearful than he'd traversed the last tunnel, but he'd soon find his fearlessness premature.

The ceiling in here wasn't on fire, but everything was bathed in a red glow that revealed a terror his mind couldn't process, could believe, but there they were, bodies, hundreds of them, if not thousands, sinewy and stretched like some godawful gummies, arms and legs and torsos interlinked and stuck to the rock walls that went on, seemingly, forever. Faces stared at him, elongated from foreheads to chins, their toothless mouths oval, and their eyeballs afloat in dark round sockets. They had the skin of mummies, leathery and scarred by boils and burns. The dank and putrid odor of decay punched him in the face, but these guys weren't dead. They writhed in agony and emitted the most despondent moans and cries ever heard by man or beast.

Bart didn't know whether to shit or go blind.

And if that sight wasn't horrific enough, slugs of some kind, slimy green with sucker mouths and eyes mounted on stalks at either side of their heads, slithered in and out of the nostrils and earholes of these poor damned souls, feeding and shitting as they moved about like ants at a picnic of the dead.

A tearing sound drew his attention to the ceiling as one of these condemned souls broke free, one emaciated limb at a time, then dangled, shuddered, and dropped to the floor with a splat. He lay there, excreted like human waste, as the slugs appeared in droves and chowed down this feast on the table of Hell. The other hangers-on watched in abject horror, as if they knew that would also be their own fates one day.

Bart feared that would be his fate, as well.

"Welcome to Hell, my boy."

From out of the red glow, a most horrifying figure appeared, and Bart immediately knew this creature was omnipresent in his subterranean abode. He dwelled in the rock, the fire, and even within the photons of light. Bart wanted to run, but there was nowhere to go. The creature moved toward him with long strides on muscular legs, oddly hairy in this hairless realm, as was the rest of his body, but his head was bald and his eyes brimmed with fury as he loomed over this newcomer.

"Are...are you the devil?"

"Call me Satan. Call me Lucifer. Call me Beelzebub. But my name is Fred."

"Fred?"

"Rhymes with dead."

"Am I dead?"

"Not yet."

"Is that guy dead?" Bart pointed to the heap of feasting slugs.

"His journey through Hell is simply changing stages. Yours is just beginning stage."

Bart was suddenly raised up and flung against the wall. His fellow wall-hangers grabbed him with gooey hands and embraced him in their spidery arms and legs until he couldn't free himself no matter how much he struggled. "What are you doing to me?"

Fred stood back, rubbed his pointy chin with fiery fingers and stared at his newest acquisition, as if Bart were an exquisite work of art on the wall of a gallery. "You should do just fine."

"Let me go," Bart screamed. "I don't belong here."

"That's what they all say."

A sharp pain speared Bart's spine as a steel rod impaled his body through and through, much like a bug pinned on a corkboard, a specimen collected for Fred's own amusement. Bart now knew he was forever trapped in this realm of consequences that he'd fully earned for his life of crime. Cold fear flowed through his bones.

"Ah, yes." Fred blew fire from his nostrils. "You are mine now." He dissolved back into his fiery domain.

Bart hoped for a quick death, but judging from these guys hanging with him, he didn't think that relief would come any time soon.

# Chapter Nine

In the sub-basement lab at Massey, Inc., well after hours, Carlson sat in front of his monitor, crosschecking his calculations as data scrolled down the screen. The server that monitored the obelisk's frequency, gain, and bandwidth had detected a spike in power output, topping out at over 3,000 megawatts, which created a fireworks show as the Cisco server crashed. A similar power spike, but only in the 200 megawatts range, had happened once before, when O'Malley had contacted his deceased wife, Miriam, at this very terminal, before his self-righteous act of thievery. This power spike meant the present holder of the stolen cell phone had made a call, probably transmitted at a longer distance, thus the obelisk required more power to place the call, which overloaded the Cisco's circuits.

This presented Carlson with two problems. Without the server, he could no longer monitor the obelisk's activity, and the secrecy of this project was now in jeopardy. Someone else knew the unique power of the cell phone and would not likely remain silent.

The question Carlson now grappled with: should he keep this information to himself or inform his boss of the latest transmission? Fearing such bad news could easily cause Massey another heart attack, he would stay quiet, for now.

However, that server had to be repaired as soon as possible.

*A power spike?* Such an impossible feat, that a mere stone of crystal, quartz, and granite, could demand amps and wattage for its own purposes and facilitate drawing those electron flows from the lab's power grid. Yeah. That was an astounding accomplishment, to say the least. However, to him, an MIT grad and highly gifted scientist, he knew it was impossible. Even a light bulb could not draw power of its own accord. There had to be a switch to complete the circuit. What was the obelisk's switch? Where was it located? Who or what intelligent force controlled such a switch?

*The power or the switch? What came first. One can't exist without the other. Only the obelisk knew...*

He buried his face in both palms. What came first, the chicken or the egg? This age-old question had always haunted him. Somewhere along the line, one or the other had to have been created out of nothing, which had no scientific basis in fact. One or the other had to have evolved, but neither could exist without the other. Where science couldn't explain it, religion claimed it could, with one word. Faith.

"Bullshit." He stood and walked to the fence in front of the obelisk. It looked mysterious under the spotlights, even majestic in its own geological way. Its rough-hewn granite shell and crystalline nodules revealed no hint of a crack or seam where it had opened to inhale Bart...and most likely the cleaning lady, as well. Science couldn't explain the anomaly. Faith certainly didn't have a leg to stand on, either. Its existence, along with the chicken, couldn't be explained without considering a supernatural answer. The universe was full of unexplained phenomena, including its own existence. The Big Bang. What element or elements exploded to create such a bang? Where did those elements come from? What set off the explosion in the first place? Who or what would do such a thing? And why?

Dilemmas like these kept him awake at night. As a scientist and technician, truth and proof went hand in hand. He'd often said, "Don't tell me something is so and so. Show me. Prove it."

He reached over the fence and touched a crystal. "Take me. I've got to know."

Nothing happened. It seemed as if Bart's bad intention, his attempt to steal the crystal, must've angered the stone as if it were sentient in some way. Yeah. Bart would now know the secrets inside, if the transition hadn't killed him outright.

Carlson needed that cell phone...to call Bart...to see if he'd answer, to hear what he had to say. However, first he'd have to get that Cisco server fixed. Massey must be told it had crashed, for whatever reason. He didn't need to hear an excuse. He didn't need to know everything.

Carlson dialed Massey.

He answered. "Did you get the cell phone?"

"We have a new problem."

"What's that?"

"We've suffered a server crash."

"So? Fix it."

"It's number 1A, sir. The obelisk. I need a Cisco router tech to look at it."

"Wasn't that Arthur O'Malley?"

"Yeah, but Bart shot him."

Massey groaned. "I'll get HR to hire somebody ASAP."

"Thank you, sir."

"Call me when you get that phone."

"Absolutely."

Massey hung up.

Carlson returned his attention to the obelisk, the rock, as mysterious as the first chicken to walk the earth. "You can't hide your secrets from me," he said out loud, which caused him to think he was losing his mind. Talking to a rock? Could he be walking a thin line between science and insanity?

# Chapter Ten

In Woodlawn, Sheila Calhoun, wearing a robe and slippers, walked down the steps to her living room. She was headed for the kitchen to fix something to eat. She didn't know what to fix, but she had to eat, which had become a chore, cooking for one, though she had no appetite for food or life itself. Still, she couldn't starve herself like some prisoner on a hunger strike. She wanted to live long enough to find out who killed Dermot and see his murderer brought to justice.

She stopped at the dining room buffet where their wedding picture, taken in Gaelic Park, had stood for many years. The happy bride and groom were flanked by framed photos taken during happier days: a Caribbean cruise one winter, picnicking on the Blue Ridge during the fall, Sea World and Epcot in Orlando one spring. Then there was Sean bundled up in a cradle, and one of him in his Boy Scout uniform, another of a proud Marine. On the wall above the array of pictures, a crucifix hung, Jesus looking over her family, now broken despite God's divine protection. If not for Sean moving in with her, she might not have survived this long.

*A broken heart is a cruel bedfellow.*

She picked up the wedding picture and cradled it in her upturned palms. Dermot was so handsome in his rented tux, and she looked stunning in her mother's wedding dress, silky and flowing. A lone tear trickled down her cheek as she recalled their honeymoon back in Ireland. She'd met Dermot's family on the farm where he'd grown up. She even fed and milked the cows and swept the barn, just as he'd done when he was young. Ireland enlightened her to Dermot's down-to-earth upbringing, and she'd felt as if she belonged there, too.

Out in the countryside, they drove the Ring of Kerry, past waterfalls and breathtaking mountain views. One journey took them through a valley in Galway, where sheep grazed on the steep grassy slopes as if they had the power to defy gravity.

Their marriage was blessed with so many good memories. And now this nightmare, this house they'd built in Woodlawn, now her self-imposed prison, her escape from a world so cruel that a good man doing his job could be shot and killed with complete anonymity. It wasn't safe out there, not in the Bronx, not down the street, not anywhere in New York City.

She rubbed her temples as if that alone could calm her fears. There was no escape from this house, not as long as Dermot's killer was still out there. If Detective Mullen would do his job, get justice for this family, then, and only then, life might turn a page for her.

With a heavy heart, she shuffled into the kitchen and found leftover Chicken Noodle Soup from Clancy's Deli in the fridge. She heated herself a bowl in the microwave and set the teapot on the stove.

Seated alone at the table, she wished Dermot were with her right now. He'd no doubt have his unshaven face stuffed in an open newspaper, but at least they'd be together.

The microwave dinged. Hints of chicken, parsley, and celery tantalized her nostrils. The teakettle whistled.

She got up and gathered her meal together then returned to the table, alone. Sipping tea, she wondered where Sean was today, what he was doing. Why wasn't he home with her? He'd probably been called in to work...or maybe he was out with his girlfriend, Bridget O'Hare, possibly at the zoo or a Sunday matinee. Wishful thinking, of course, that they would get married and give her some grandbabies. Dermot would like that. Sean was already in his thirties, spent most of his adult years in college and working for Vericom. There would come a day, she knew, that Bridget would take him away from here, to a nest of their very own. What would she ever do without him?

She'd no sooner spooned her soup when someone knocked on her front door. A shot of panic shuddered through her, the outside wanting in. Probably a solicitor looking to make a buck. She sipped hot soup from the spoon. He'd go away.

More knocking, then a woman's voice: "Sheila, we know you're in there. Open up." Maggie's voice.

Sheila didn't want to see her best friend. Not now. She wasn't ready to be social and giggly, as if nothing had gone wrong in her life.

"Sheila."

She got up and crept into the living room to peer out the curtain slat. That was Maggie, all right, her red hair falling in waves over her shoulders, and three other women from the church where they'd played bingo together, during happier times. Thelma, a blonde with a squeaky voice, and

Brenda and Shirley, two brunettes who hadn't missed a meal in years.

"Come on, Sheila. We miss you."

She moved to the door. "Leave me alone."

"Let's have a look at you...make sure you're okay."

"I'm fine."

"Please," blonde Thelma squeaked.

Sheila knew they'd never leave until she made an appearance, if even for a second, at the very least. How long had it been since she'd ventured outside? Eight months? Ten? *All right, a year*, she finally admitted to herself. Maybe it was time she opened the door, but that was all. Open the door. Done.

With trembling fingers, she twisted the dead bolt, and then grabbed the doorknob, but her hand stalled. All she had to do was turn and pull, but some gremlin in her head was screaming, *"No. No. No. Don't do it."*

She thought of her time in Ireland, the freedom she felt on the farm, the courage she'd mustered to feed and milk the cows. Where was that woman now? How could she have let that killer take her husband and destroy her life, as well?

"Sheila, please, come to the door."

*I can't let him do this to me.*

She gritted her teeth, and with sheer determination, turned the knob and pulled the door open. Sunshine spilled across the floor.

"Sheila," Maggie cried. "You're skin and bones."

"What happened to you?" Thelma squeaked out.

Brenda and Shirley saw her much differently. "Good job, girl. What diet are you on?"

Sheila fought to breathe. "As you can see, ladies, I'm still alive."

"You call this living?" Maggie sounded angry. "It's two o'clock in the afternoon and you're not even dressed."

Sheila shrugged. "Cuts back on the laundry."

Her friends laughed.

Maggie said, "You haven't lost your sense of humor."

Oh, yes she had. Grief was not a laughing matter. She stepped outside, onto the porch, much like a ghoul stepping out of a crypt. Frosty air licked at her ankles. She scanned the skeletal trees, the snow on the ground; everything looked so dead and so cold. Her palms felt suddenly sweaty, and her heart palpitated wildly. She felt light-headed, like she'd pass out at any second, and braced herself on the doorframe. "I-I can't do this. I'm so sorry." Stumbling backwards and over the threshold, she lost a slipper but managed to scramble back in the house where she quickly shut and locked the door.

"Sheila," Maggie shouted. "What's the matter with you?"

More pounding.

"Go away." She slid down, and with her back against the door, felt hot tears flood her eyes. How would she ever shed this grief, this terrible phobia of terrors beyond the door, and move on with her life without Dermot?

Her friends finally gave up and left, but she remained slumped on the floor, bawling.

Her soup and tea grew cold.

# Chapter Eleven

I hustled through the lobby at Vericom, a chasm of marble, glass, and crystal lighting, to the control room. My employee four-digit PIN gave me access. During the week, one hundred technicians and operators manned the array of consoles and computer terminals that made instantaneous global communications possible. Twenty big-screen TVs lined the walls, each depicting the smooth flow of digitized frequencies and fiber optic code moving across the country, from ocean to ocean and beyond. Any fluctuation or interruption in these electron and photon superhighways would set off alarms across Vericom's robust network. This Sunday, only three techs were on duty, and they were too busy to pay me any mind.

I sat at my terminal and keyed in my code to activate my computer hub.

*"Welcome, Mister Calhoun."*

I knew management would find out I'd signed in, and they'd probably wonder what I was doing here, as I'd had weekends off most of my career. And I also knew, by opening a window into the company's secure server, I'd probably get fired. However, that secure data wouldn't be easy to access. To open the main menu window, I'd need a work order number generated by a service department manager, and no one would give me such a number just to learn the history of this old cell phone. Company protocol left me no choice but to break into the work order program like a common teen hacker. Doing so would probably get me thrown in jail, but at the moment, I didn't care about the consequences. Only the results.

I typed on the keyboard, which brought up an arrangement of department-server icons linked by lines representing routes into and out of each mainframe. I typed *Service Department.* The arrangement rotated as the computer zoomed in on one icon. I clicked on it. A graphic of blocks resembling a Tetris game opened up in colors of red, green, and blue. I selected green, as that was an admin color, and a menu window opened showing a dozen green blocks that shifted from foreground to background, each department labeled in bold letters. Every shift created the sound of a heavy door closing.

*Work Orders* shuffled to the front.

I clicked on it.

A window popped up that would have normally stopped me cold, but I was hot and on a roll.

*USER IDENTIFICATION REQUIRED TO PROCEED!*

I clicked *OK* and entered my PIN. Now my goose was cooked, for sure.

The next window gave me another menu. I clicked on *Work Order Generator*, which gave me a form to fill out. *Customer Name:* I typed John Smith, *Address:* I typed 101 USA Lane, and so on, even detailed the work I was not going to do, until finally, a work order number flashed on the screen: *1XB2033889.* I copied it to the clipboard and exited the program.

Now for the real-time monitoring tool, ACCESS. It

gave secure access to every cell phone's serial number, its owner history, and incoming and outgoing calls listed by phone numbers and locations. It also gave me the power to track a customer's phone, anywhere, anytime. For these privacy and security reasons, this program was highly restricted. We only used it for tracing network problems, not for snooping around to get personal information on a particular phone. The company's rules were very clear about misusing the program. Again, let them sue me, jail me, beat me with a rubber hose. I needed to know how a cell phone could communicate with the dead.

My heart beat hard as I clicked the ACCESS icon. The array rotated and zoomed in on the opening window.

*WARNING: PRIOR AUTHORIZATION REQUIRED TO ENTER!*

A black text box with a pulsing red border appeared below the warning. I clicked my cursor in the box and pasted the work order number into it, which only appeared as white dots on a black background. I hit ENTER.

The screen changed to a main menu board. I was in. I ran a hand across my sweaty brow then removed the StarTAC from my coat pocket. From an assortment of wires with different plugs, I selected the one that fit the phone and plugged it in.

*SEARCHING* blinked center-screen then: Motorola StarTAC 1 came up. I typed *Display SID*. The serial number came up along with corresponding information:

NO SIM CARD INSTALLED

INOPERABLE PHONE

LAST REGISTERED USER: *Alfred Gonzales.*

*Who was this guy?*

I typed his name into the customer database. Several names came up, but only one who owned a StarTAC. His address and current phone number were listed, but I wondered if they were still valid. On my terminal's desk phone, I dialed Mr. Gonzales.

The phone rang.

*Encouraging.*

The callee picked up. "Hello?"

"Mr. Gonzales?"

"Who is this?"

"I'm calling from Vericom Tech Support about your Motorola cell phone, a StarTAC. Are you missing this phone?"

"That old phone? I used it while I was in college. In fact, it was in a box of junk I'd donated to the Salvation Army...not too long ago."

*Discouraging.*

"Which Salvation Army?"

"The Bronx. On Jerome."

"Thanks for your help." I hung up, Googled the Bronx store, got the phone number, and called them.

At first, the manager didn't want to give me any information, but when I told him I was a Vericom tech looking to track down a lost cell phone, he became very cooperative. A check of their records, which they kept on all incoming electronic devices, revealed a Motorola StarTAC had been donated by A. Gonzales and sold to a C. Carlson...for five dollars.

The manager added, "I told him the old phone didn't even work, but he didn't mind. Said it was for his boss."

"Any idea where I might find this Mr. C. Carlson?"

"He listed his place of employment as Massey, Inc."

I frowned. "Ronald Massey? The New York Billionaire?"

"Yeah. Why would *he* want a five-dollar cell phone?"

"Why indeed. Thanks." I hung up.

I knew a little about Massey, Inc., not because Ronald Massey had amassed a real estate fortune, but because he also dabbled in cellular technology, research and development, more as a hobby and no real competition for Vericom. So I wondered: What did Massey want with an obsolete cell phone? Why were those goons willing to kill to get it from O'Malley? Were they working for Massey? Had Massey figured out a way to call dead people? That certainly seemed to be the case, and I needed to find out how he did it so I could talk to my dad again. To do that, I'd have to pay Mr. Massey a visit.

## Chapter Twelve

**F**rank sat in the stolen *Highway Helper* service truck, waiting for the green Jeep to reappear from Vericom's secured compound. As boredom set in, he turned his attention to the contents of the cab. The air held the oily smell of a repair shop in Harlem, probably due to grease rags that had been tossed on the passenger floorboard. An assortment of papers, work orders and tech bulletins cluttered the dashboard, along with crumpled coffee cups and a half-eaten donut.

The laptop lay on the seat next to him, and next to it, a clipboard with a hand-scrawled note read: *1:05pm, Black Ford, New York – ACB-2134, breakdown southbound.*

"Damn." Frank realized he couldn't get away with stealing the truck, and how would he ever explain his damaged car on the side of the highway? The cops were no doubt looking for this truck. If he got busted in it before he got the cell phone, he might get thrown in the slammer, but his daughter would pay a much higher price for his failure, a life confined to a wheelchair.

He vowed not to get caught, at any cost.

The guard paced the gate with a cell phone to his ear, occasionally glancing at the truck parked a half-block down. Frank wondered if his lurking presence had aroused the guard's suspicions. Maybe he was on the phone with the NYPD.

*Son of a bitch.*

Frank took out his gun, ejected the clip, counted three rounds, plus one in the chamber. There was a spare clip in the glove box of his car, but fat-lot-a-good that did him now.

Impatience gnawed in his guts. He slammed the clip back into the gun and thought to ram the gate with the truck, pop the guard with one round, and save the last three for the clown in the Jeep. Seemed the deeper Frank got into this quest, the more criminal charges he'd rack up, and the further his American Dream would fall behind him.

The laptop beeped. The X was on the move, and sure enough, the Jeep emerged from the exit gate, throwing dust as it sped past him. "Here we go."

Frank started the truck, whipped a U-e, and took chase.

#

I knew I was in the clear as I raced away from Vericom. The black Ford had probably broken down and left my would-be killer walking. So when I noticed the *Highway Helper* truck turn around as I passed, I thought nothing of it.

Within minutes, I was slogging southward on the Bronx River Parkway. My destination was Manhattan, the West Side Highway, and the sprawling complex of Massey, Inc. skyscrapers that overlooked the Hudson River. One thing about driving through New York City, there was no direct route to anywhere, and heavy bumper-to-bumper traffic was the norm. There seemed no difference between Sunday evening and Monday rush hour. I turned the heater to full-blast, as the Jeep's broken windows let in enough winter wind to drop the chill factor somewhere south of zero.

The sun was low, and I spent most of the time in the shadows of buildings. Slowly, in stop-and-go-slow traffic, I approached the ramp to I-95 West, the Cross Bronx Parkway. However, to get to the expressway, I'd have to traverse a half-mile of congested, 25-mph boulevard traffic to get around the West Farms Bus Depot. With daylight waning, there was no way I'd arrive at Massey, Inc. before dark.

Oddly, the *Highway Helper* truck had taken the exit ramp behind me. I guessed there must not have been enough breakdowns on the parkway; he'd have better hunting on the interstate.

The traffic ahead of me stopped at a red light. As I joined the queue, with a bang, my body lurched, and the back of my head struck the headrest. I checked my inside rearview. The service truck behind me had rammed my rear bumper, and I could see the driver's face through the windshield, his gritted teeth...and suddenly I recognized the thug who'd chased me earlier. Frank, as I recalled. Hard to forget the name of the man who'd tried to kill me twice.

My throat seized. "What the hell?" Instinctively. I ducked low in case he started shooting again. There was nowhere I could go to break out of this traffic jam. I was a sitting duck and didn't dare get out to address the accident. If I did, he'd surely pick me off, so I sat low, and as the traffic crept forward, I moved, too, as did the menacing truck.

I could only assume he hadn't started shooting because there'd be too many witnesses to my murder, so I inched forward every chance I got, finally cleared the traffic light and accelerated up the ramp to I-95, looking forward to a high-speed getaway. What I found was another clogged up thoroughfare, and the killer was still on my tail. I forced my way between slow-moving big rigs, tried a few quick lane changes, but the truck stayed on my bumper, its roof lights flashing yellow as if it had some kind of special privilege over everyone else.

By the time I reached the Prospect Avenue tunnel, I still hadn't shaken my pursuer, and the 50mph speed limit was nowhere near attainable, so I took the exit at Third Avenue, hoping to lose him on the surface streets. No such luck. The traffic was atrocious there, too. I squeezed the battered Jeep across crowded lanes, turned right, turned left, took side streets and alleys, but the truck dogged me at every turn.

And worse, the sun had gone down, and the dim light of dusk made details hard to see; pedestrians, bicyclists, and panhandlers were but mere shadows darting out of my way. I turned on my headlights, flashed my high beams, and hoped I didn't hit anyone. My promise to O'Malley, to guard the cell phone with my life, was getting more dangerous by the second.

Before I knew it, I was stopped behind a semi and a garbage truck. My rearview showed me the door fly open on the service truck. Frank was getting out, the gun clearly visible.

"Fuck." In seconds, he'd have me dead in his sights. Fighting sheer panic, I revved the engine and jumped the curb. The Jeep took out a bike rack, a newspaper box, and a bus stop bench before I saw an opening in front of the semi.

I cranked a hard left, blew the red light, and careened down a narrow street that ended at a T intersection.

One Way. Left only.

"Hang on," I shouted to myself.

The Jeep's tires barked in the turn, but I straightened her out on another narrow street lined with parked cars on both sides. To my right, a wrought iron fence bordered a wooded area, a park, most likely. I saw no truck in my rearview, but I didn't get out one second's victory hoot when *Highway Helper* charged from the next side street, nearly t-boning me in the intersection. That's when a terrible truth hit me square between the eyes. Frank wasn't going to stop until he got that cell phone.

*I should give up, stop running, give him the phone, and wish him a happy life.*

I couldn't believe I'd actually thought of such a surrender. Why would I willingly relinquish the one and only connection I had with my dad? Not happening.

The time had come. I'd have to take a stand. Me against the thug, Frank, and his gun. I couldn't keep running. I'd have to go home eventually, and I wasn't about to lead the killer anywhere near my mom's house. So, I had to find a way to put Frank at a disadvantage. It had been over ten years since the Marines. Boot camp, jungle training, and hand-to-hand combat were far too many Guinness pints behind me. I could easily get my ass kicked...or worse.

A break in the line of parked cars on my right revealed a bus stop. The area in front of it was set off with 'no parking' stripes. I took them as an invitation, slammed on the brakes, and screeched to a rubber-smoking stop in front of a bench. The inhabitants sat there wide-eyed in shock while those standing around jumped back in disbelief.

I left the engine running, the lights on, and bailed from the Jeep just as the truck skidded into my fender with a bang. By the time Frank got out, I was over the fence and running into the woods.

The sky was growing darker, and nearby streetlights flickered on. Skeletal trees cast shadows on the ground, like wretched fingers scraping across the snow. I passed a clearing with a snow-covered baseball field, but I stayed among the trees, tripping through bushes as I looked for a place to confront Frank, once and for all. I'd be easy to find if he followed my footprints in the snow.

I came to a shoveled sidewalk that curved around to a stand of trees, but to keep my pursuer on track, I ran straight across a small clearing to recross the circular sidewalk, and placing my feet in as much shadowed snow as I could find, I ducked into the trees.

Satisfied I was as invisible as I could be, I fought to restrain my heavy breathing and waited for Frank to find me. He was already approaching the far sidewalk, head down, following my trail. He had a gun in his right hand and something else in his left, a laptop I could tell as he got closer. I knew how to disarm a gunman, but I hadn't practiced the move since the Marines. Little did I know I'd ever need that skill again.

A woman strolled by on the near sidewalk with a German Shepherd on a leash, the only souls I'd seen brave the cold evening air. The dog seemed to notice me, slowed, but when the woman coaxed him onward, he continued to look in my direction, ears perked and tongue lolling.

Frank reached the stand of trees and stopped on the sidewalk, his dark eyes peering toward me and returning to the footprints I'd left for him. He seemed leery about following the tracks when he couldn't see where they'd lead him.

*Come on, Frank. Don't chicken out on me now.*

He glanced to his left, in the direction the dog lady had gone, then right as if to be sure he was alone, then proceeded forward, finally. As soon as he was an arm's length from me, I stepped out of the shadow, hands up in surrender.

My sudden presence made his eyes grow round, and he jerked the gun up to my face. I had him just where I wanted him. My Marine training kicked in. I swept my left hand down to push his gun arm to my right as my right hand came across to grab the gun and twist it in the opposite direction. That move wrenched the gun from his grasp, but I'd failed to get a solid grip on the barrel. The gun did a pirouette in mid air and flew off into the darkness.

Frank let out a grunt, but I didn't give him a chance to think, kneed him in the gut, which bent him forward, then I kneed him in the chin. I thought that would surely send him to the ground, but instead, he bulled his head into my stomach and rammed my back into a tree.

Hardly able to draw in a breath, I slammed my elbows down on his back, but the big man, driven by some unearthly force, rose up and hit me across the face with the laptop. I went down like the Bismarck. Before I could regroup, he jumped on me, pinned me to the ground, and with sledgehammer fists, proceeded to beat the tar out of me.

"This one's for Bart."

*Wham.*

"This one's for Chloe."

*Wham.*

"This one's for me."

*Wham.*

My lights started blinking out. The spindly tree branches spun in circles above me as my life flashed before my eyes. If only I'd taken a different path, taken Bridget up on her offer to stay with her that night at McGee's, handed over the dead man's cell phone right away. But no. I had to be the hero and grant O'Malley his last wish. Now I was doomed to suffer the consequences for the choices I'd made. On the upside, I did get to hear my dad's voice one more time. Seemed I was on my way to meet him, getting closer and closer with each blow from Frank's fists. Who would take care of my mother now?

What happened next came in a blur. A vicious growl. A guttural scream. And suddenly, Frank flew off me. My bleary vision perceived an impossible sight: Frank on his back in the snow and a dog on top of him, tearing him to shreds. A big dog. A German Shepherd. Frank screaming, "Get him off of me. Get him off of me."

I didn't stick around to make sense of it all, scrambled to my feet, did a couple back skips to be sure I wasn't dreaming, then hightailed it out of there.

## Chapter Thirteen

Spitting blood, I raced through the woods, dodging branches and jumping bushes as I worked my way around the baseball field and back to my Jeep. The bus stop was awash in flashing lights. Police blocked traffic to allow a tow truck to hook up to the *Highway Helper*. Metal made scraping sounds as the truck's front bumper untangled from my fender. I glanced around to see if Frank stood somewhere in the crowd of looky-loos, didn't see him, thought he and the dog might still be getting acquainted.

An NYPD cruiser had pulled up behind my wrecked Jeep, so I couldn't just get in and drive off. I'd have to explain the situation to the cops and hope they'd let me go on my merry way. After wiping blood from my fat lip, I stepped to the police cruiser's driver's door. I could see the cop, a lieutenant, writing on a clipboard. I tapped on his window and stepped back.

His expression was priceless. He rolled down the window. "What the hell happened to your face?"

"That's my Jeep."

He got out of the car. "Who are you?"

I noted his name tag: *Dawson*. "Sean Calhoun."

"Mac," he called to a cop standing with the tow truck driver as he worked levers to drag the truck up on the flatbed, yellow roof lights still flashing. "I've got the Jeep's driver over here."

I put up my hands. "Look, you guys. I was running for my life from that guy." I pointed to the *Highway Helper*. "I bailed out here and ran into the park."

Mac shined a flashlight in my face. "Looks like you didn't run fast enough. Seems he beat you up pretty good. You need an ambulance?"

"I just want to go home...if you'll move this car." I tilted my head to Lieutenant Dawson's squad car.

"Where's the suspect now?" Dawson asked me.

"He had a gun." I dared to touch my swollen eye. Big mistake. "On the other side of the ball field. Dog got him last I saw."

"Must be Frank Coletti," Mac said. "His battered Crown Vic broke down after he'd left the scene of an accident, and then he stole this truck."

I groaned. "If you hurry, you might catch him."

Mac shined the light through my busted out back window. "Why is your Jeep all banged up?"

"Like I said, he was trying to kill me."

"Any idea why?"

"Road rage, I guess. Can I go now? My mom must be worried sick."

"Mac, take a few men and scour the park. See what you can find." Dawson got into the cruiser and backed it up. "We'll be in touch, Mr. Calhoun, get a statement from you later."

"You can get my number from Detective Mullen."

"We'll find you." He indicated my bent-up license plate. "We're not a bunch of amateurs."

Of course. They'd run my plate. "Tell Detective

Mullen that your Frank Coletti was one of the thugs who were chasing me last night. He had something to do with that dead man in the alley behind McGee's."

*Bet you amateurs didn't know that.*

I jumped behind the wheel of my Jeep and backed out of the bus stop zone. Frank would find himself behind bars by tomorrow. My plan to visit Ronald Massey would have to wait until then, as well.

I found Third Avenue and jumped on I-95 to the Bronx River Parkway where I turned north toward Woodlawn. Traffic was tight but moving along. Mom would need supper soon. I hoped she'd find the leftover Chicken Noodle soup in the fridge, because I was in the mood for a pint of Guinness and a shot of Jameson. Seemed this Sunday had been the longest day of my life. Never thought going to work on Monday would be a relief.

I got off on the Yonkers Avenue exit and took the hook going back south on Bronx River Road to McLean Avenue. At the River's Edge Bar, I turned right and drove slowly into Yonkers, past apartment buildings, single-family homes, and a flurry of small businesses and specialty shops, not to mention several well-patronized bars. I was headed to Rory Dolan's at the top of the hill.

Pedestrians bustled by on both sides of McLean Avenue where people stood in front of the Irish Community Center and smoked outside the Dollar Tree. In several places along the route, I had to maneuver around double-parked delivery trucks.

The party never stopped on McLean Avenue. I used to do bar crawls with my friends, after the Marines, before my dad's murder, and before Mom took a bad turn. We'd start at the bottom of McLean, on the corner of Bronx River Road, at the River's Edge Bar, and walk all the way up to Rory Dolan's Irish Pub. The rules were simple. We'd drink one pint per bar and move to the next. Inevitably, we'd meet some chaps at one bar and hold up for a second pint and a round of shots. Yeah. Before we knew it, we were schnockered by the time we reached Rory Dolan's, the most popular bar in Yonkers, and the bartender would cut us off posthaste.

So here I sat in my wrecked Jeep, in the parking lot beside Rory's, nearly freezing, with my memories of better days and a swollen eye to remind me of how dangerous my days had become. I could only hope that, when I walked in, I wouldn't scare the hell out of every one. I can hear them now: "It's not Halloween, Sean. Take off your mask." Or "Does your face hurt? It's killin' me." *Ha. Ha. Ha.* Or "You're ugly enough to make a freight train take a dirt road." Yeah. They'll laugh it up, all right.

I got out and walked to the old-country wooden doors that shouted Ireland, passed an A-frame advertising the day's special: *Dublin Style Fish and Chips - $8.50,* and stepped inside. The twanging strings of an Irish jig filled the air with happiness, and the kitchen aromas seemed thick enough to eat with a fork. Patrons drank and conversed at a long wooden bar and dined at tables draped in white linens. Everyone looked so neat and clean; the staff wore long-sleeved white shirts, thin black ties, and black trousers, whereas my soiled coat and jeans, beaten face, and disheveled hair were more fitting the style of rough-and-tumble McGee's.

I sidled up to the bar, felt the smooth wood surface,

and ordered a tall Guinness. The bartender, she was much too polite to comment on my looks, simply smiled, and slid the pint to me, foaming at the brim. The cold brew felt good on my fat lip and surely washed any blood from between my teeth.

"Sean? What the hell?"

I swallowed hard, turned around, and saw Bridget, all decked out in her white and black uniform, tray in hand and a face full of shock. "Bridget. I didn't know you'd be working tonight."

"What happened? You're hurt."

"You should'a seen the other guy." I lifted my pint to her. "It's been a rough day."

"Are you in trouble?"

"Nothing I can't handle."

She set a gentle hand on my arm. "Come over tonight. I'll patch you up. You can tell me all about it then."

I knew how that would end. A roll in the hay, and then, *stay the night with me,* and I'd decline, *I have to take care of my mom,* and then she'd be mad, *what's wrong with you, you momma's boy,* and then she'd storm into the bathroom, slam the door, and I'd spend the rest of the night talking her out so I could go in and pee.

"Please, Bridget. I just want to enjoy my beer, unwind, and go home. I'll get Mom to patch me up." I wanted to end with, *no strings attached that way,* but elected to take a slug of beer instead.

"Fine." She turned away and went about her business.

*Fine.* Leave it to her to leave me with thoughts of the dilemma I would soon be dealing with when I get home, when Mom sees the mess Frank had made of my face.

# Chapter Fourteen

O fficer Mac Brennen led two officers over the fence to search the park for the car thief, Frank Coletti, and the site of the assault on Sean Calhoun. He immediately found hurried tracks through the snow and followed them around the baseball field where they headed into a stand of trees, stripped bare by the cold of winter.

Meanwhile, Lieutenant Dawson got on the radio to dispatch. "Contact Detective Mullen. Have him call me. I've got a lead on the O'Malley murder."

"Yes, sir."

"Dawson." It was Mac checking in.

"Go ahead."

"We found a witness over here. She says her dog had alerted on something in the trees, so she doubled back in time to see a big guy in a black suit beating another guy with his fists, so she let her dog loose to break up the fight. By the way she described the guy's face, I'd say it was Sean Calhoun. Happened just like he'd said."

"What about Frank?"

"When she called off her dog, he ran toward the tennis courts across Crotona. I've got a man following his tracks, but I'm sure he's long gone. We found a laptop in the snow, and we're looking for the gun the woman said she'd seen go flying. She called 911, so I expect some help any minute."

"Stay on it, Mac."

"Roger."

Dawson's cell phone chimed. It was Detective Mullen.

"What's going on out there, Lieutenant?"

"Do you know Sean Calhoun?"

"What kind of trouble has he got himself into now?"

"Not sure." Dawson waved at the tow truck to clear the scene. "We're looking for a guy named Frank Coletti. According to Calhoun, Frank was trying to kill him, wrecked his car, and stole a *Highway Helper* truck in the process. He's on the run, right now."

"What's that got to do with me? I'm trying to enjoy a peaceful dinner with my wife."

"Calhoun told me to tell you Coletti is involved in your O'Malley homicide case, and he's one of the thugs that were chasing him last night."

"Sounds like Calhoun is in over his head. Did he say why Frank was trying to kill him?"

"He told me road rage, but he's not being straight up. I think you should haul him in for questioning."

"I'll head for the office. Give me five minutes to eat my dessert."

Dawson hung up just as Mac returned with a laptop and a gun, both in plastic evidence bags. "Found this stuff but Frank got away."

"I'll take it to homicide. There might be something here that Mullen can use for probable cause and issue an arrest warrant for Frank Coletti."

\*\*\*

# Gateway

Since Bridget had ruined my mood for drinking, I finished my pint and drove straight home. The windows were dark. Maybe Mom had gone to bed early. In the driveway, I activated the garage door and pulled in next to her Camry, basic white, stock wheels, nothing fancy. I recalled how happy and excited she was on the day Dad brought it home from the dealership. For the past year, it hadn't taken her anywhere. The gas in the tank had probably lacquered up by now. Shutting off the engine, I hoped she wouldn't come out here and see my battered Jeep. My face would be hard enough to explain.

I slipped into the kitchen, dimly lit by the nightlight on the stove. After hanging my coat by the door, I removed the troublesome cell phone, stuffed it in my pants pocket, and made a beeline for the fridge to take out an ice tray. From a drawer, I got out a plastic bag, put some ice in it, and pressed it to my left eye. Man...did that hurt. After returning the ice tray to the fridge, I noticed a bowl of soup and a cup of tea on the table, barely touched. Both were stone cold. I wondered why she hadn't eaten, but I didn't dare wake her to ask why. With any luck, I could duck into my room, get on my computer, and see if I could find any reason Massey Inc would want a five-dollar cell phone. I'd face Mom in the morning.

As soon as I walked into the living room, that plan was blown out of the water. The stove shone a wedge of light across the floor that landed on Mom, sprawled out at the front door. Shock and fear ripped up my spine and made my neck hairs bristle. I dropped the icepack. "Mom." I rushed to her and knelt, put my hand on her shoulder. Her body shuddered. "Mom. What happened?"

"Where have you been?" she cried into her hands.

"Why are you lying on the floor? And your dinner is cold."

"I can't go on like this anymore, Sean. I wish the Lord would just take me."

"Don't say that." I took hold of her arm. "Let me help you up."

"I don't want to get up. I want to lay here and die."

"You're not going to die...now, come on." I levered her up to a sitting position and rested her back against the door.

She just slumped there like a rag doll, head down and her hair all mussed.

"See? You're halfway there. Let's get you to your feet and I'll help you to the kitchen. We can reheat your soup and eat some together."

"The bingo ladies came over," she said to her lap. "I tried, Sean, I tried."

I noticed she was missing a slipper, looked around, didn't see it. My swollen eye wasn't helping any. "Where's your slipper?"

"It's on the front porch, I think."

I looked out the front window and there it lay, right alongside the WELCOME mat. "You were outside, Mom. That's great."

She looked up at me with bleary eyes and red-faced anger. "I told you, I tried."

And just then, the stove light betrayed me.

Her eyes widened in shock. "Oh, my God. Sean. What happened to you...your face...you were in a fight?"

"I ran into a door, Mom. It's nothing."

"Don't lie to your mother."

"Come on." I took her hands and pulled her to her feet. "You need to eat."

I got her to the kitchen and sat her at the table. While I reheated enough soup for two, and got the teakettle started, she asked, "Where have you been all day?"

"I was at the cemetery this morning, stopped by work, and dropped in at Cory Nolan's for a beer."

"Don't tell me you went in there looking like that?"

I sat at the table and pressed the icepack to my eye. "You should have seen the look on Bridget's face when she saw me."

"When are you going to do right by that girl?"

I groaned. "Maybe we should talk about something else."

The kettle whistled. I poured tea and dished up our soup. We didn't talk about anything further.

I cleaned the dishes. Mom settled in to watch the late news on TV.

Upstairs in my room, I tossed O'Malley's cell phone on the bed then sat at my desk. A wiggle of the mouse brought my computer out of sleep mode. I held the icepack to my eye with my left hand, and typing with my right hand, I Googled Massey Inc and found a link to their company website.

"Let's see what you guys are up to," I whispered and opened their homepage. Above an impressive montage of photos: several skyscrapers, the New York skyline, construction sites, and Massey's headquarters building, internal links were listed:

*Real Estate Ventures. Property Management Services.*

*Stock Options. Career Opportunities. Contact Us.*

There was no mention of any cell phone research and development departments. I had a gut feeling the StarTAC wasn't just a gift for Ronald Massey but the key to a greater venture into the afterlife. I clicked on *Career Opportunities* to see if I could glean any hints about what was going on behind the scenes.

First and foremost in bold print: CISCO ROUTER TECH NEEDED.

I huffed. *Right up my alley.* However, I had to wonder what kind of router they owned. Accounting? Rent-Lease? Buy-Sell. Almost every big company needed routers for online commerce, as well. Vericom used Cisco routers to enable cell phone service in multiple ways, but none could route calls from dead people. I had every reason to believe this career opportunity had nothing to do with the StarTAC.

I searched the police blotter and found a warrant for Frank Coletti: Grand Theft Auto and leaving the scene of an accident. I figured Mullen would keep any connection between Coletti and O'Malley close to his vest, for now. If I ever got my say, I'd add assault and battery and attempted murder to the list.

After I put the computer back to sleep, I picked up the cell phone from my bed and stashed it in the top drawer of my dresser, under my socks. I didn't want to take it to work with me tomorrow. That way, if I got any flack over signing into ACCESS, I wouldn't be tempted to produce the phone as evidence in my defense. Besides, who would believe me? A cell phone that can communicate with the dead? I'd be laughed out of the building.

After I showered and laid my head on my pillow, I

thought about Mom's fear of going outside. Agoraphobia. She would have to overcome that fear if she were to get back to normal. That slipper on the front porch was a solid first step.

\*\*\*

Most of the halls and offices were dark when Detective Mullen walked into the 47th Precinct headquarters building on Laconia Avenue in the Bronx. However, the same could not be said for the homicide office, which seemed in perpetual motion 24/7. Phones rang and keyboards clicked. The murder board on the wall had far too many cases listed for this early in the year. Since the O'Malley case was penned in black grease pencil, ten more cases had been added. Murder was big business in New York City.

After hanging up his coat, the next stop was the coffee station where he grabbed a Styrofoam cup and poured bitter brew from a heavily stained pot that was last washed sometime back in the '60s. Normally he'd kill the taste of the coffee with copious amounts of sugar and powdered cream, but tonight he would drink it black. The O'Malley case was heating up, and he needed to be on his best game.

At his cubicle where family photos were pinned to the wall, he saw Lieutenant Dawson perusing through the O'Malley case file. "Lieutenant? What do you got for me?"

"Detective..." Dawson offered him an evidence bag. "We might have the murder weapon here."

Mullen set the coffee down and inspected the evidence through the clear plastic: Glock 22, .40 caliber, clip removed, one live round from the chamber. "Get this down to the lab. Fingerprints. Ballistics. The works. Pronto."

"There's only a skeleton crew—"

"Tell them this case goes to the front of the line."

"I'll see what I can do." Dawson handed him the COE form to record the handoff of evidence, which Mullen signed. "And one for the laptop." He held up a bagged iMac. "Who brings a computer to a fist fight?"

"Might be a clue in it." Mullen signed the COE. "Have computer forensics take a look."

After Dawson left, Mullen sat at his desk and picked up the coffee cup. It was hot enough to burn the face off the devil. He hoped ballistics would match the slugs taken from O'Malley's back, at autopsy, and any fingerprints would belong to Frank Coletti. The physical evidence would be enough to close the case, but why Frank had killed O'Malley was another matter, one he hoped Sean Calhoun could shed some light on.

He picked up the desk phone and dialed Calhoun's home number. He knew it by heart because of Dermot's murder and the following year of calls to update Sheila on his progress with the case, or lack thereof. The phone rang.

"Hello?"

"Sean. It's Mullen. How you holding up?"

"Frank Coletti did a number on me. Did you get him?"

"I'm waiting on lab results."

"More excuses?"

"Can you come down to the station? I've got some questions for you. On the record."

"I'm in bed."

"Yeah. That's where I should be...in a perfect world, but murder never sleeps."

"I'll come in after work tomorrow."

"Fair enough. But one thing. How did you get involved in O'Malley's murder? Can you tell me that much?"

"I was in the wrong place at the wrong time."

"Did you witness the shooting?"

"No."

"Sean. There's something you're not telling me."

"Goodnight, detective." He hung up.

Mullen slammed down the receiver. "God damnit." His only hope: the lab would come up with something worthy of probable cause.

## Chapter Fifteen

In the penthouse office at Massey, Inc., Monday's early light shined through the plate-glass windows. A silver tray of German strudel, flown in fresh from Berlin that morning, sat on the reception table, untouched, along with a thermal carafe of espresso, shipped straight from Caffé Florian in Venice. Ronald Massey wasn't in the mood for such luxuries. He'd expected that cell phone to be in his hands by now. Driven by frustration and angst, he paced in front of the windows with his hands clasped behind him, all the while fighting to remain calm, but that fool Coletti was taking too long to check in.

His desk phone rang.

"That better be Frank," he muttered and picked up.

"Mr. Massey." It was his secretary, Janice.

"What is it?"

"Doctor Santos called. I'm to remind you of your appointment tomorrow."

Massey sneered. "Reschedule it."

"You've rescheduled three times already."

"What's the big deal?"

"He wouldn't say. You should go, sir, find out what's got him all worked up."

"I'll try to make it." He hung up and ran a hand across his sweaty face. His left eye twitched. Anytime he thought about seeing Dr. Santos, the twitching started.

*All he does is nag about everything I shouldn't be doing: No drinking. No smoking. No bacon. No stress, and bug me about all the things I should be doing: Exercise. Vegetables. Vitamins. Rest.*

Massey didn't like anyone telling him what to do, especially Dr. Santos. However, Massey had to give it to him; he'd saved his life after two heart attacks.

His cell phone rang. The display read *Sharon.*

"Yes, dear."

"Have you heard from Frank?"

"I expect him to show up here any minute. What's wrong?"

"It's my niece, Chloe."

"How's she doing?"

"Not good. Clarissa just called. The tumor is getting more and more painful every day. She needs that experimental stem cell treatment. The poor girl is suffering."

"Honey, I made a deal with your brother. I'm sticking to it."

"Please, Ron. I'm begging you. Forget the deal and help this girl."

"Not until Frank upholds his part of the deal."

"Come on. You've got more money than God. Why do you always have to get something in return?"

"It's a quid pro quo world, baby." He hated how cold that sounded, *but it is what it is.*

"Clarissa needs to know when you're going to come through for Chloe. You said you would—"

"I know what I said. When Frank gets here, I'll talk to him."

"Tell him to call me."

"Sure. I've got to get back to work now."

"See you tonight."

He hung up and went back to pacing. Yeah. Frank had asked him for help with his daughter's medical problem. Now Sharon was ganging up on him. The girl had to be in terrible shape for his wife to butt in.

*Why does everyone think they're entitled to handouts?*

Frank should pay for his own daughter's treatments. Nonetheless, Massey didn't think of himself as a scrooge. He gave people opportunity. Bad luck was a part of living. A tumor was Chloe's bad luck. A bum heart was his bad luck. *Shit happens.*

He pressed his lips together. A deal was a deal. Frank had to get that cell phone first. Then he'd help Chloe.

His cell phone rang again. It was Carlson.

"Now what?"

"Frank's laptop is reporting some weird commands. Someone is probing the hard drive, not hacking it, but reading it. I think it's fallen into the hands of the police."

"How's that possible?" Massey felt his face heat up, and he started to sweat. Worse, he felt that ominous ache in his chest. That meant trouble. He paced to the desk drawer and brought out the nitro. "I'll be down in a minute."

If the police had that laptop, it would inevitably lead them to Massey, Inc., and if their forensic examiner was worth his weight in salt, they'd want to know about the cell phone tracking program, and they might even figure out that cell phone had something to do with O'Malley's death.

He put a nitro tablet under his tongue. The pain in his chest eased. He took a deep, calming breath.

The intercom chimed. "Mr. Massey?"

"Yes, Janice."

"Frank is here to see you."

"Frank. By God, send him in."

The double doors opened as Frank pushed his way in. He looked a fright, bandaged here and there, his suit coat torn and dirty like he'd been run over by a truck.

"What the hell happened to you?"

Frank strode directly to the strudel and helped himself to a handful. He must've missed dinner and breakfast, the way he was scarfing down the expensive fare.

"Where's my cell phone, Frank?"

He swallowed. "I ran into a snag, boss."

"It's a cell phone, for Christ's sake. Not the Hope Diamond. How hard can it be?"

Frank poured himself a mug of rich espresso, drank it down like lowly water. "I'm gonna kill that son of a bitch."

"Who?"

"Fuck if I know." He slammed down the empty mug. "But he's a tricky one."

"Where's my laptop?"

"I need another one. And a gun. I lost my gun, too."

"Frank. You'd fuck up a wet dream. We think the cops have the laptop and your gun."

"My fingerprints are on it." Frank stormed to the window and glared out at the Hudson River. "Felons aren't allowed to have guns. I'm going back to prison, but I'll tell you what...not before you get your cell phone and Chloe gets her treatments."

"All right. Follow me." He hurried into the elevator, and they rode it to the sub-basement.

Carlson met them at the opening doors. Massey stormed out. "Do you have a fix on the cell phone?"

Carlson grimaced at Frank's disheveled appearance. "A house in Woodlawn." He gave Frank the address. "Go. Go. Go."

Frank headed for the elevator with purpose in his stride.

Massey glanced at the crashed server, 1A. "Has HR found someone to fix the Cisco?"

"Not since last I heard...and that would be ten minutes ago." Carlson stood there, iPad in hand, looking at Massey, wide-eyed. "Boss?"

Clutching his chest, he dropped to his knees. This wasn't any nitro pill pain. It was a full-on ventricle de-fib.

"Your heart, sir."

Massey stabbed a finger at Carlson. "Get me that cell phone."

The lab became a swirling blur...then nothing.

***

Monday morning. I had to be to work at 8am. It was 6:30. Every muscle in my body ached. My face felt like it was on fire, and my left eye wouldn't open. The last thing I wanted to do was go to work. However, one of my dad's favorite sayings was, *"Never call in sick. If the company figures out they can get along just fine without you, you're good as fired."* No. I was going to work. He'd also said, *"It's better to be early than late."* I'd shoot for 7:30. I'd been called worse than a brown-noser by meaner people than those at Vericom. I spent the first half hour in the bathroom with a cold compress to my eye, finally got it to open. My split lip made my morning coffee a challenge to drink. I managed a quiet breakfast with Mom before I asked, "Can I borrow your car?"

"What's wrong with your Jeep?"

"Broken window." Okay, so I made light of the damages.

"What if I want to go somewhere today?" She'd said it with a deadpan expression.

"Really?"

"Okay. What am I thinking? Of course you can use my car."

I kissed her forehead goodbye with the side of my mouth, grabbed her keys, and headed out. It wasn't long before I was bogged down in traffic but made it to Vericom before 8:00.

My boss, Jack Wagner, liked his employees to be punctual because, if something broke down during the nightshift, the dayshift could follow up immediately. As I entered the lobby, none other than Jack Wagner was waiting for me, arms folded across his chest. He didn't look happy.

Angst walked at my side. "Good morning, Jack."

"Be in my office at nine sharp."

"What's up?"

"Don't put on that you don't know." Jack turned his back on me and walked away.

I furrowed my brows. He didn't say a word about my face. I knew ACCESS had ratted me out, but I was prepared to explain my actions. After pacing across the lobby, I used my ID badge to get into the control room. The place was alive with activity, a far cry from yesterday's quiet-and-peaceful, but a few techs avoided eye contact with me.

Ryan walked by. "Why did you have to go and piss off the boss?"

"Me?"

"We're walkin' on eggshells in here."

"Did Jack say what he's pissed about?"

"No, but he met with a woman from HR earlier."

"HR?" That was troublesome.

"What did you do wrong...besides walk into a door."

He'd noticed my face but I didn't answer. If I did, I'd have to claim the 5th. I stopped at the barista kiosk, got a latte and a bagel, then sat at my terminal, logged in with my passcode, and got an unexpected message. ENTRY DENIED blinked on the screen. I must've fumbled the keys, typed again, got the same message. Jack had locked me out. It suddenly became apparent that yesterday's foray into ACCESS would have the exact consequences I feared.

Steeling my nerves, I ate my bagel and drank my coffee and watched the message blink at me. 9:00 sharp, I knocked on the door to Jack's office.

"Enter."

I opened the door and stepped in, surprised at the trio awaiting my presence. Jack Wagner, to be expected, pressed and polished; Jenny from HR: she wore a blue business suit, had her hair up in a bun, and a laptop sat in front of her; and our union rep, Chuck Felton. He was a big man with a flat-top crew cut, and he wore an official Communications Workers of America red shirt. It felt reassuring to have representation, though I was guilty as sin.

"Close the door," Jack said. "And have a seat."

The three of them sat on one side of the table, across from a lone chair that was meant for me. I sat with my back straight and both feet planted firmly on the floor, half expecting a cone of light to beam down on me. "What's this all about?"

"Don't worry," Chuck said. "We'll sort this out in no time."

I glanced at stern faces staring at me. "What's to sort out?"

Chuck turned to Jack. "Really? After Mr. Calhoun's twenty years of service to this company, you want to can him on a technicality?"

"Can me?" That was a gut punch.

Jack leaned toward me. "You broke the rules, Sean."

Jenny typed on her laptop.

"Bet he's got a good explanation," Chuck said.

"You think?" Jack drilled me with a piercing glare. "Let's hear it then."

Jenny stopped typing, looked at me expectantly.

I couldn't tell them I had a dead man's cell phone, that I got wrapped up in a murder investigation and needed to know more about that phone, and to do that, I needed access to ACCESS to access the metadata.

Why? They'd ask. Oh didn't I tell you? Wait 'til you hear this. It can call dead people. No really. My dad called me on it. He's been dead a year. He warned me a guy was coming to kill me, for no reason other than I had the cell phone and he wanted it back. And he almost succeeded, and if not for a German Shepherd, I might not have gotten away with my life.

*Sure. They're gonna believe that.*

Might as well throw in how a StarTAC set a record in the annals of telecommunications history for the longest cell phone call ever, an out of this world call from the afterlife.

*I'm so screwed.*

Jack put his hands up. "We just want the truth, Sean. Say something."

I decided to give them the short version. "I found a cell phone, just wanted to give it back to the owner."

"You came in on a Sunday. Logged into your terminal, broke into two secure programs, all for a lost cell phone?"

"I thought I'd do someone a favor."

"We're not in the favor business here, Sean."

"Look." I leaned forward. "I knew what I was doing. I knew it was against the rules. I did it. I admit it. But it was for a good cause."

Jenny was typing like mad.

Chuck said, "See how simple that was? He explained it. I ask you to reconsider terminating him."

"So..." Jack said. "Did you return the cell phone to its rightful owner?"

I shrugged. "It was an old StarTAC. He didn't want it."

"You knowingly risked your job for nothing?"

"Life doesn't always work out the way you want it, Jack."

"You're not getting off scot-free. Sets a bad example for the others." He looked at Chuck. "Thirty days suspension, without pay."

"With pay," Chuck countered.

"No way will the board approve that."

"I'll file a grievance. Tie you up in court and lawyer fees for a year, at least. What do you think the board will say about that?"

Good old Jenny kept typing.

I ping-ponged between them. Either way, I'd keep my job.

"All right," Jack said. "Two weeks suspension without pay."

"One week," Chuck countered.

I'd heard Chuck was a tough negotiator. It was magic watching him in action.

"One week without pay." Jack looked at me. "Deal?"

"I'm sorry I broke your trust, Jack. It's a deal."

Chuck stood. "My work is done here."

Jenny closed her laptop and smiled at me as if she didn't see anything wrong with my face.

Jack stood. "Hand over your ID badge."

I dug it out of my pocket and missed it as soon as I gave it to Jack. After twenty years, I felt naked without it.

"See you next Monday, Sean."

I hoped they wouldn't learn they could get along just fine without me.

## Chapter Sixteen

A bright light shined in the distance. *Go into the light.* He walked toward the rising glow, his feet padding across sand, a gentle surf licking at his toes. Palm trees, laden with coconuts, swayed in the breeze, and from somewhere came the strains of reggae and giggling.

He sat at a Tiki bar, on a wooden stool, under a thatched eave, its shade cool and refreshing. He wore a Hawaiian shirt, all flowers and leaves, Bermuda shorts and sunglasses. Next to him sat a long-haired woman all leggy and lovely.

Bart tended bar, shaking a shaker. "Welcome to paradise, Mr. Massey." Red liquid poured into a tall glass and a little paper umbrella popped up on the rim. He set it before Massey and produced a similar drink of his own. "To your perfect heart."

"I feel great." Massey drank the most wonderful drink he'd ever tasted, spicy and smooth going down. "Where am I?"

"In the obelisk, sir."

The obelisk. "My link to the afterlife...where is everyone? Hitler, Jimmy Hoffa—"

"Over there." He pointed to the ocean's horizon where dark clouds boiled up from the water and roiled the sea in whirling fury.

Gateway

Massey gulped. "Hell is over there?"

"Some say there can't be a Heaven without a Hell...or vice versa."

He glanced at the woman sitting next to him. "Who's she?"

"You don't recognize your cleaning lady?"

"That's right...she...and you...you both disappeared into the obelisk." He noticed a group of beautiful young women frolicking in the surf, splashing each other and waving at him. "Who are they?"

"Seventy-two virgins."

"It must be true. The obelisk is Heaven's Door...but what am I doing here...and you? You don't belong in Heaven. For all your crimes, you should be over there." He pointed to the storm. "In Hell."

Bart took away Massey's drink. "It's time for you to go."

"Go? I want to stay here."

"That's what they all say."

A hurricane wind swirled around him.

"No. No. No."

"Clear."

*Thump!*

Paradise turned black and faded to ever-lightening shades of gray.

"We've got a pulse."

White light surrounded him and his eyes opened to see doctors and nurses standing above him. A heart monitor was beeping so fast, it was about to blow a fuse. He looked around, saw the familiar surroundings of a hospital room. No beach. No Tiki bar. No gorgeous virgins.

Jim Keane

Massey felt startled at first, then recognized his situation. He'd landed back in the hospital, no doubt in the coronary ward, Mt. Sinai West, five city blocks from his headquarters.

Doctor Neil Santos probed Massey's chest with a stethoscope. "We lost you there for a few minutes."

"I was dead?"

"As a doornail, they say."

Tubes ran from his arms, wires from his chest, and he heard the welcome sound of a slowing heart monitor. Someone had stripped him of his thousand dollar suit and replaced it with a hospital gown. The bedrails were up so he wouldn't fall out. Yeah. This wasn't his first rodeo. Heart attack number three had killed him, but he was still alive.

He had to laugh out loud.

An I-V bag with a clear liquid dripped above him. He wondered how long Dr. Santos would keep him laid up this time.

*I have to get up. I'm fine.*

He tried to sit up, made it a few inches when a bolt of pain punched him in the chest. He winced and dropped back down.

*Okay. Maybe I'm not in good shape.*

Dr. Santos was all decked out in his holier-than-thou white lab coat over his dress shirt and tie. He sported a full head of hair and a healthy tan face, Bahamas, no doubt. "Mister Massey." The nurses left and he closed the curtain. "That was a close call. It's time to get serious about your heart disease."

"Did they find the Mack truck that hit me?"

He sat on a swivel chair beside the bed and examined a chart. "When are you going to start listening to me?"

"Hey. I ate my vegetables and still ended up back here." Massey grimaced when he inhaled. Those defibrillator paddles really packed a punch.

"Let's be straight with each other."

*Here he goes again. I've heard it all before.*

"You've suffered another heart attack."

"No shit, Sherlock."

"Be brash if you want, but this time you're not as lucky as you were the last two times. Now you're left with myocardial ischemia."

"I'm supposed to know what that means?"

"Heart muscle damage. Your left ventricle is enlarged due to lack of oxygen, stretched like a balloon, which thinned the heart wall. It could burst at any time. I've warned you about this."

Cold fear flushed through Massey's bones. His youthful resistance to a healthy lifestyle had come back to haunt him now. "What's the prognosis, doc?"

"Your job is killing you." Santos flipped through the chart. "Eating vegetables? That ship has sailed. Eat all the bacon you want. Your diet isn't your worst enemy now. It's stress. If you don't stay away from the office, consider yourself a walking dead man."

Beeping from the heart monitor ticked up a notch.

"But I have a company to run. I can't just walk away."

"I've got you on Captopril for your blood pressure but it's still higher than your penthouse office. Your total cholesterol is off the charts. You have critical afib. That's why I have you taking Coumadin to thin your blood and hopefully prevent a stroke. Still, your heart is a time bomb just waiting to explode. So don't give it a reason to do that. Stay away from stress. Relax. Get plenty of rest or kiss your ass goodbye."

"Yeah, yeah, yeah. I get it. I'll take it easy."

"All your money is no good if you're dead."

"Can I go home now?"

"We're going to monitor you overnight."

"What about tomorrow?"

"If you don't get some rest, you won't see tomorrow."

It couldn't be that bad. The doc's bedside manner really sucked. There was too much at stake back at the lab. He needed to know what was going on at all times. "How about visitors?"

"No."

Massey was all about control. Now it appeared his life was spiraling out of control. "Where's my phone? I can have my cell phone, right?"

"No phone. Just rest. If you want to live, that is." Santos stood. "I'll check on you in the morning."

There was no sense in arguing. Besides, he couldn't just get up and walk out. Hell, he couldn't even sit up. The quicker he felt better, the sooner he'd be out of there. Then he'd call Carlson, find out what's happening with the obelisk, the Cisco router, and that stolen cell phone. Just thinking about all those problems ticked the heart monitor up another notch.

He took in a painful breath. "All right, doc. Thanks."

Santos checked the heart monitor and shook his head. "I'm not happy with this." He ducked out the curtain slat. "Nurse."

"Yes, doctor?"

"May I have a word with you in the hall?"

*What's he got up his sleeve now?*

The nurse came in with a syringe and stuck the needle into his I-V tube. Pale liquid dripped into his veins.

"What's going on?"

"Your heart rate is too high. This will slow it down, help you sleep, too."

His eyes fluttered and his vision blurred. A floating sensation took flight, and he soared into a dark sky of nothingness.

Massey dreamed of the paradise he'd seen during his near-death experience...until the sunny beach exploded in a blast of white light.

A nurse had opened the curtains. "Good morning, Mister Massey."

"No," he screamed at her. "No."

"Try to stay calm. You had a bad dream."

His chest felt as if it would explode. "It was a beautiful dream."

"Dr. Santos wants a CT scan of your chest."

"What for?" He started to hyperventilate, couldn't catch his next breath. "I gotta get out of here."

"You need to calm down, Mr. Massey."

"The obelisk. Where's the obelisk?" He wanted to go back to paradise. There was nowhere else he'd rather be.

*** 

A few hours later, after being shot up with some kind of isotope and run through a machine from the USS Enterprise, Massey saw Dr. Santos enter the room. He always looked professional in his white lab coat and stethoscope.

"Mr. Massey. I hear you had a rough night."

"Come on, doc. It was a rude awakening. What torture are you planning for me now?"

He pulled up the swivel-stool and sat next to the bed.

"You're going to die."

"Aren't we all?"

"I know this is iffy, but you need a heart transplant. At the very least, I need to get you on a waiting list for a donor."

"What are the odds?"

Santos grumped. "Of finding a donor or surviving the surgery?"

"That was my next question. Can you guarantee—"

"If you want a guarantee, buy a toaster."

Massey shuddered. He was living on borrowed time, as it was, but to push his luck with major surgery he might not survive, that wasn't acceptable, not until he got that cell phone back and talked to someone in the afterlife.

"Do you want me to put you on the list?"

"I don't know, doc."

He stood. "Think about it."

"When can I go home?"

"When I say so." He walked out.

Massey had all the money in the world. He could buy a heart, ten of them, but he couldn't risk the surgery. He had to get back to the lab, and if Frank came through with the cell phone, he'd call Bart. Massey had to know, if while he was dead for those few moments, had he experienced a beautiful dream, or was paradise really waiting for him.

# Gateway

\*\*\*

With no job for the next week, I sat slumped behind the wheel of Mom's Camry in the Vericom parking lot and stared at the tremendous building where I'd worked the past twenty years, first as a trainee, then an associate, then finally a fully certified Cisco technician. I knew every room, every server, every inch of cable and fiber optics in that place. My specialty was troubleshooting faulty circuit boards and motherboards that kept the servers and routers buzzing. I'd also designed and installed state-of-the-art CCTV security cameras and programmed the network to perfection. This time my ingenuity had bitten me in the ass. I was lucky to have gotten off with a week's suspension without pay.

For all the pride I felt and the memories I held dear, that giant building felt distant and abandoned. My boss and my peers had alienated me. The root of this bump in the road of my career stemmed from Massey, Inc. and a cell phone with extraordinary communication powers.

So now what? The day was still young. I decided to visit Massey, Inc., as Frank Coletti had interrupted my last attempt with deadly intent. I touched the swollen lip he'd left me as a souvenir and wondered where he was now and if he'd show up as unpredictably and violently as he had before.

I started the engine. Guess I'd find out soon enough. Traffic on the expressway would be impossible, so I decided to take the train. I drove down to the waterfront and parked at the Metro-North station. The posted schedule noted the next train to the city would arrive in five minutes.

I could make it to the platform in time.

The northbound train blasted its horn and pulled out of the station on track number one. I carded a ticket machine for the southbound train and took the footbridge to track number four. An express train rattled through, non-stop, on track number two. Even at this hour, commuters stood shoulder to shoulder on the platform. The train rattled in, stopped, and multiple doors slid open. Passengers debarked, and then the rush was on to press inside and get a good seat. Two minutes later, I was on the Hudson Line train heading south to New York City.

In Grand Central Terminal, as soon as the doors hissed open, I was the first to hurry out and rush up the ramp to the lobby where the four-faced clock read 11am.

After a quick jaunt to the subway, I was headed to the west side of Manhattan. I got off at the Lincoln Center Station, just a few blocks from Massey, Inc. Dodging pedestrians left and right, I arrived at Riverside, and the first of a long row of tall buildings owned by Massey Inc. My jaw dropped in awe of how one person could own so much property. I felt as though I was standing among giants whose reach would go on forever. There was only one building with a lighted *MASSEY* sign on the top floor, so I stepped up to its enormous glass doors. When I pulled on a handle and entered the foyer, a doorman stopped me, any wonder by the looks of my face.

"May I help you, sir?" He glared at me as if I were some sort of riffraff off the mean streets.

"I need to see Ronald Massey."

"You got an appointment?"

I'd need a good reason to get past this guy. The Cisco

tech opening came to mind. "I saw a job listing on the website, came to see him about it."

"You have to apply online. We don't take walk-ins."

"Come on. I traveled all the way from Woodlawn."

His neck muscles took on the shape and stiffness of tree roots. "Then travel all the way back."

"Please. It's cold out there."

"Are you going to make me call security? Those guys aren't as nice as me."

*Shit.* I'd come all this way for nothing.

## Chapter Seventeen

**B**ack at the Calhoun homestead in Woodlawn, Sheila sat at the kitchen table, gripping a letter from the MTA in her shaking hand. It was the third appeal to the company's insurance carrier for compensation from Dermot's pension.

In bold letters it read: DENIED.

Dermot died on the job. He died protecting his passengers. He'd paid into his pension his entire career, but because he didn't check the box for spousal benefits and pay the extra premiums, she would get no monthly income to live on. The company's worker-compensation paid for his funeral and a one-time payout, but because they had no minor children, no further financial assistance was allotted.

She set her forehead on the table and cried. This was so wrong. The household bills kept coming in. Sean paid them as quickly as he could, but he couldn't support her forever. She'd stopped working after Dermot's murder. Her accounting office was patient at first, *take all the time you need,* but after a couple month's absence, they let her go. Eventually, she'd need to get a job, but that would mean leaving the sanctity of her home, and she couldn't find the strength or will to venture back out into the world.

*What can I do? How will I survive?*

If it weren't for Sean, she'd be doomed. Her savings were meager—

A muffled ringing sound resonated throughout the house, interrupting her thoughts. It reminded her of the old landline phones with that monotone *ring, ring, ring.* She stood from the table and followed the sound to the living room. It was coming from upstairs, but there was no phone up there...unless Sean had installed one, but why would he do that? They both had cell phones. She climbed the stairs and discovered the ringing emanated from Sean's bedroom. She pressed her ear to the door, and sure enough, a phone was ringing in there. Curiosity drove her to open the door, something she'd never normally do, as his room was his private domain.

Once inside, she scanned the desk and nightstands. No phone. As she walked in farther, she passed the dresser and noticed the sound changed tone, and it was now behind her. Back at the dresser, she opened the top drawer. The muffled ringing instantly became louder, but she saw no phone. It had to be in here. Why would Sean stash a phone in his drawer? She rummaged through his socks and shorts until she uncovered the ringing phone. It was a cell she'd not seen before, a flip phone, she knew, with a short antenna.

She picked it up and wondered who would be calling Sean. Whoever it was, the caller seemed desperate to let the phone ring until he answered. She decided to take a message for him and flipped the phone open. The display showed *no service*. Obviously it was broken. She set the phone to her ear. "Hello?"

All she heard was a distant crackling noise from static or interference. She pulled out the antenna to its full length and tried again.

"Hello? Is anybody there?"

Mixed in with all the background noise she heard a faint voice call her name. "Sheila? Sheila?" the voice said. "Is that you?"

Tiny cold fingers skittered up her spine. "Sean?"

*Crackle...*"It's Dermot."*...Crackle.*

Her heart lurched when she finally recognized the voice. "Dermot?"

"I'm sorry...*crackle*...I left you so soon."

Her knees threatened to send her to the floor. "What is this, some kind of sick joke?"

"Don't hang up." More static.

She always hung up on robocalls and telemarketers, but this caller was beyond cruel. He didn't want to sell her something; he wanted to rip out her heart. Hadn't she been through enough?

Dermot's haunting voice emanated from the static. "I know you've been suffering."

"Did my son put you up to this?"

*Static.*

"I know you miss me, as I miss you."

"You're not Dermot. He's dead."

"I don't know where I am...*crackle*...but I still love you, my little Irish rose."

That took her breath away. Not even Sean knew of Dermot's sweet nothings in the privacy of their bedroom. Staring up at the ceiling as if she might see all the way to Heaven, she placed her hand behind her to locate the bed and slowly sat down. Even as her brain tackled the impossible, her heart took in every word. "Dermot? It's really you...but how can you be talking on a phone when you're dead?"

"I don't know...I hear your voice...all around me."

Her eyes broke out in tears. "Dermot. I've missed you every second—"

"I know...I wish I had one last chance to thank you...for sharing your life with me."

"We didn't get to say goodbye."

She clutched the cell phone as if it were his outstretched hand. Earth and Heaven had come together and brought him back home, and her mind blossomed in visions of the green valleys of Ireland, the cows, the sheep, this home in Woodlawn, the birth of their son, and how precious their time together had been, living as if life would never end. He was her gift, on loan from God, to love, honor, and respect until God called him back, and for all that, she shouldn't mourn, but celebrate.

Now she sobbed out loud.

"Don't be sad...we will be together again...someday... Until then...live your life to its fullest...*crackle*...I'll be waiting...*crackle*...Sheila...Sheila...

"Dermot? What is it?"

*Crackle*...Sheila...you must go now...get out of the house...run, run, run...

Silence.

"Dermot?"

Nothing. She looked at the display. *Call Ended.* Her soaring emotions took a dive.

*He's gone. Dermot, no. Call me back.*

Just then, a big man in a black suit burst through the bedroom doorway. "Give me that phone."

Even as terror clawed through her chest, she held the

phone behind her back and shouted, "Get out of my house."

He didn't stop. He didn't back down. He bulled toward her with teeth clenched and fists balled. "I'm not playin', lady."

She dropped to the floor and scooted to the corner, but she couldn't put distance between herself and the intruder, and in less than a second he was on her with fists and fury.

\*\*\*

Cold air bit into my pores as I hurried out of the Metro-North train station and trudged up the hill to the parking lot. I jumped into my mom's Camry and fired up the engine. Her perfumed scent lingered in the car, even after all those months since she had parked it in the garage, unused. Merging into the flow of traffic, I figured I'd be home before dark, get online to Massey's website, apply for the job, and then fix dinner for Mom. The hard part would be explaining to her why I wouldn't be going to work for the next week.

I had to get that job at Massey, Inc. I wondered how many other techs had applied. With my luck, they'd take two weeks to vet me and schedule an interview. That could create problems at Vericom. Jack would have a fit if I told him I needed time off to track down the cell phone that had already caused such a ruckus.

I drove past McGee's, thought to stop in for Happy Hour, and on any normal evening, I'd have done just that, downed a pint or two and unwound from the day's tensions. Not today. I was on a mission. As I passed the alley where O'Malley had lost his life, a shot of adrenaline heated my veins. It all started down there, on the ground among the shattered glass and dirt, where I had to run for my life to keep that cell phone from falling into the wrong hands. O'Malley was dying, but he welcomed death because he knew what awaited him on the other side. Miriam. He had spoken to his dead wife on that cell phone, same as I had spoken to my dad. The big question facing me was how could I reconnect that call to him in the afterlife? The answer was at Massey, Inc.

As I drove into the driveway, I punched the garage remote, and as the door rolled up, I noticed the front door was open. "What the hell?" I shut off the engine and bailed out of the car. "Mom?" She would never leave that door open. When I got to the porch and stepped over her slipper, I discovered the doorjamb was splintered, the lock bent and ruined. My heart jumped. Had a burglar broken in? "Mom?" What terrible fate had befallen her?

My stomach was a tight fist as I stormed through the front room, noticed the TV still in its place, to the kitchen where I hoped to find her. "Mom?"

No answer. Had someone kidnapped her? Had her friends finally dragged her out to play Bingo? I couldn't think straight over the jackhammering of my heart. I checked the bathroom and the back room. No Mom anywhere. "Mom, where are you?"

I pounded up the steps, two at a time, checked her bedroom, the master bath, and then I saw my bedroom door was open. An icy fist punched my chest. She would have never gone into my room, not even if it were on fire. I rushed to the doorway, and what I saw was beyond my comprehension. My top dresser drawer was pulled out, my socks and shorts scattered around, and sure enough, the cell phone was gone. Frank had been here. I'd made a grave error. Somehow, he'd been able to track the phone, though it had no SIM card. How could the impossible be possible? And that meant Mom had come face-to-face with O'Malley's killer. My blood ran cold.

"Mom?"

I turned around, scanned my bedroom, and as tunnel vision set in, I saw blood spatter on the far wall. "Oh, God, no." I rushed around my bed, and my worst fears were suddenly revealed. On the floor. My mom. Lying there. Motionless. Blood drenched. "Mom," I screamed, ran to her side, and knelt next to her body. I was afraid to touch her, to feel for a pulse and not find one, to touch the cold flesh of death. Please, God, let Mom be okay. Wherever the courage came from, I didn't know, but I touched her neck, felt a pulse, noticed her chest rise with a shallow breath. Nothing else mattered anymore. Not the cell phone, not my job at Vericom, not Massey, Inc. She was alive, but for how long? I fumbled my cell phone from my pocket and dialed 911.

"What is your emergency?"

"My mom...she's...she's been attacked."

"Is she breathing?"

"Yes."

"Help is on the way."

I collapsed next to her, held her hand, and fought back tears that couldn't help the situation. I had to be sharp. I had to be strong. I had to figure out where I went wrong and how to make amends. She didn't deserve to get caught up in the mess I'd gotten myself into. She must've been terrified when Frank broke in, a defenseless old woman against a hardened criminal. Why did he have to beat her up? What was she doing in here? Was she trying to get him out of my room? None of it made any sense.

"Mom, I'm so sorry."

Frank must have honed in on the cell phone, ripped open the top drawer of my dresser, tossed out my shorts and socks to get to it. Just the thought of him invading our home, invading the privacy of my underwear drawer, and attacking my mom sickened me. All I wanted to do was find him and kill him with my bare hands.

What a fool I was to leave the phone in the house, to think a phone capable of contacting the afterlife somehow worked the same way all cell phones worked. What was I thinking? Now, my mistake could cost my mom her life.

*Damn, damn, damn. It's all my fault.*

Approaching sirens wailed in the distance.

"Help is on the way, Mom. You're going to be all right."

Seconds later, emergency vehicles stopped out front. I didn't want to leave her lying here by herself, but I had to go downstairs and show them inside, show them where she was lying upstairs, where I'd failed to protect her, where I'd let her down. The good son, as Clancy had called me, wasn't so good, after all.

I ran down the steps, knowing Frank had trod these very stairs with malice in mind. Meanness and murder. Like he'd done behind McGee's to O'Malley. I'd let him down, too. Now his cell phone was in the hands of the bad guys.

Outside, the neighborhood was ablaze with flashing lights. First responders were scurrying around an ambulance and a fire truck. A police car was racing in from down the block.

"She's up...upstairs." My strained voice caught in my throat. "Hurry."

The EMTs, toting cases of equipment and supplies, fast-stepped toward me, and I moved aside to let them pass. Several firefighters followed them inside while two medics removed a gurney from the Montefiore ambulance in preparation to transport her to the hospital. I felt helpless. I had to let these guys do their jobs. Still, I followed them upstairs and stood in my doorway. I couldn't believe how many men in heavy green uniforms fit in my room. They'd moved the bed aside, shoved in my dresser drawer, and made floorspace for all their gear.

"Sean Calhoun," a voice said behind me.

I turned to see Lieutenant Dawson.

"What the hell is going on with you?"

"It was Frank again. I know it was Frank."

"How do you know that?"

"He found where I lived and beat my mother half to death."

"Why?"

I couldn't tell him about the cell phone, how Frank must've tracked it to my house, how he'd kill to get it back. All I could say was, "I don't know," but I knew he worked for Ronald Massey. I had to get to my computer and apply for that job before somebody else got it.

The men gathered around my mother and lifted her off the floor. She had been strapped to a yellow backboard, neck in a white brace...the bandage around her head was already stained with blood. They'd fixed an oxygen mask on her face and, as a team, carried her and their equipment down to the front doorway. I couldn't believe our lives had come to this.

Dawson pulled me aside, as I was too shocked to move. "Are you all right?"

"I want to ride with her to the hospital."

"Give us five minutes to stabilize her," a medic said.

*Five minutes.* There was nothing I could do for her. She was in good hands.

After the men got her down the stairs, Dawson followed them. I now had a clear path to my computer. *Five minutes.*

I sat at my desk, woke the computer, and went directly to the Massey, Inc. website. *Career Opportunities.* The job was still listed in bold letters. I clicked on it, got an employment application. Simple enough. Though I struggled with trembling fingers, I filled in the blanks: *name, address, phone, email,* and then typed a pitch into the text block labeled *Qualifications*:

*I'm a certified Cisco router technician, with over twenty years of experience, on temporary leave from Vericom, available as a sub-contractor to repair and consult as needed.*

That would have to be enough to get me in, to confront Ronald Massey, maybe even get that cell phone back. I logged off and raced downstairs. The EMTs had just lifted the gurney into the back of the ambulance. I was about to climb in when Lieutenant Dawson stopped me.

"Looks like a robbery gone bad. Did you notice anything missing?"

I shook my head. "Can we talk about this later?"

"If Frank Coletti did this hospital job on your mom, he had to have had a reason."

I stabbed a finger at Dawson. "Find him, arrest him, and ask him yourself." I jumped into the back of the ambulance. Firemen closed the doors. Under the fluorescent ceiling lights, my mom looked a frightful mess, black and blue and bloodied. Frank had worked her over something fierce, like he had done to me, but she didn't have a dog to save her. She got the full force of Frank's rage. Something very personal had driven him to such madness.

"Buckle up," the paramedic said.

I sat in a jump seat and buckled the belt. Two medics rode with us, one strapped in at a console of machines and meters while the other hovered over my mom, hooking up wires and a blood pressure cuff. The air smelled of antiseptic mixed with the coppery odor of blood.

Someone double-slapped the back door, and the driver accelerated from the scene, siren chirping. To say it was a smooth ride would have been a lie. The truck weaved and bobbed over rough asphalt and leaned heavily into the turns. It would slow down and speed up erratically, and sometimes the siren changed its tone to a warble and a horn blast. The oscilloscope lines and throbbing meter needles on the wall told me my mom was still hanging on.

Within minutes, the siren cut off and the ambulance roared to a stop under the portico at the emergency room entrance. The back doors flew open. A nurse in scrubs jumped aboard and helped prepare the gurney for offloading. It took less than a minute before I was dashing down a hallway behind the gurney, its wheels rattling with speed. They rolled my mom through doors marked *TRIAGE*, and a paramedic broke away to stop me from going any farther.

"Wait out here."

"But she's my mom."

"They'll tell you when you can see her."

I glanced around the hallway, saw an open area with rows of chairs and a television mounted high in the far corner. Mom was on her own, and I could only wait to learn her fate and struggle with my own failures, as my mind seethed with thoughts of revenge. Someway, somehow, Frank Coletti would pay for what he did to my mom.

# Chapter Eighteen

At the 47th Precinct station, Detective Mullen paced the homicide office, from his desk to the door to Interview Room 1 where Frank Coletti should have been awaiting interrogation, but the BOLO had come up with zip, so far. It was dinner time, and again the O'Malley case kept Mullen from a meal with his family. "Spaghetti," his wife had said, "and garlic toast," his favorite, but tonight he had to settle for a stale cup of coffee and a day-hardened donut.

The forensic report was due any minute. He hoped the fingerprints on the gun would prove Frank Coletti had assaulted Sean Calhoun in the park, and he hoped ballistics would match the slugs taken from Arthur O'Malley's back.

*I'll finally solve the O'Malley murder.*

Unsolved cases haunted him, like the murder of Dermot Calhoun. A year's work had yielded no leads, and the Calhoun family was no closer to getting justice now than they were the night of the murder. He remembered one of his training sergeants saying, "You won't solve them all," but he'd neglected to mention the sense of failure that would walk with him on every case thereafter. A good detective soldiered on to the next murder. "There'll always be another case to work, another broken family waiting for justice." And with the sergeant's words in mind, Mullen had crafted his career, one murder at a time, solving those he could, and holding the unsolved ones close to his heart. He'd become the definition of a good detective.

His desk phone rang, and he ran to grab it, hoping for a break in the case. "Mullen."

"Got something for you," Rodriguez said. He was the swing shift lab tech supervisor.

"Lay it on me."

"Good prints on the gun. Ran them through the DCJS Latent Print Lab, got a hit right away. Came back to a Frank Coletti, a one-time inmate on Riker's Island."

"And ballistics?"

"It's not a match to the O'Malley slug."

"Shit." Mullen sank to his chair. The murder weapon was still out there...and O'Malley's murderer, as well. "What did you find on the laptop?"

"Coletti's prints and an unknown. We sent it to computer forensics, see what they can find."

"Keep me posted." Mullen hung up and ran a hand across his stubbled chin. Back to square one on the O'Malley case, but something didn't make sense. Coletti's criminal file was phonebook thick, but after his release from prison, nothing. Nothing for ten years. And now this armed crime spree. Had the guy gone nuts? Why would he go back to a life of crime? A felon with a gun? That alone would put him back in the slammer for a decade. Motive. He had to have a reason to go bad. Money? Maybe he'd racked up a debt with the mob, or maybe his house fell into foreclosure. Something had triggered his fall from grace, and what did that something have to do with Sean Calhoun? He was a straight-up guy, but somehow he'd gotten himself tangled up in Frank's mess.

Mullen's cell phone rang. It was Dawson.

"What's up?"

"You're not going to believe this."

"Try me."

*After the O'Malley case setback, how much could it hurt?*

"It's Sean Calhoun again, up to his ass in alligators."

"What happened this time?"

"A break-in at his mom's house. She's in pretty bad shape. Transported to emergency."

"And Sean?"

"He came home and found her, swears up and down Frank Coletti did it, got no proof, though, and he didn't tell me why Frank would break into his house and beat up his mom."

"Get CSI in there. Scour that house. Get me one hair, one fiber, one skin cell, one fingerprint. Give me anything that ties Frank Coletti to that crime scene."

"We're on it. Did forensics report back on the laptop and gun?"

"Coletti's prints on both."

"Score one for the good guys. Go home and get some sleep."

"Not until I write up an affidavit for an arrest warrant on Coletti. I'm sure the District Attorney will see I have enough evidence to take a warrant to a judge."

"Let me know when it's signed. I'll find the son of a bitch."

"Stick with the house. I'll get the CAT to track him down."

"Yes, sir."

Mullen hung up and leaned back in his chair. The O'Malley case was starting to stink to high heaven. If Frank had broken into Sean's house, what for? Why risk getting busted for a home invasion...breaking and entering...burglary? Either he had a death wish or there was something in that house he wanted, and he wanted it bad enough to beat it out of Sheila. Seemed odd for Sean to point the finger at Frank without proof or motive. Mullen's years of experience told him Sean wasn't being forthright about his accusation. What was he hiding?

*How does the Calhoun family fit in to Frank's crime spree?*

More likely, it was a random break-in, some doper looking for cash to buy his next hit, his next high, but even that theory didn't jive with the facts. As much as he didn't want to put Sean under more pressure, he was already dealing with enough misery, it was time Mullen ordered patrol to bring him in for questioning.

\*\*\*

In the sub-basement lab at Massey, Inc., under the fluorescent lights, Carlson typed on his keyboard in an attempt to break into Mt. Sinai Hospital's database and get an update on Massey's condition. Phone calls had gleaned no information, as the nurses he'd spoken with wouldn't answer his questions. "How's Ronald Massey doing? May I speak to him, please?"

"Are you family?"

"No, but he's my boss—"

"Family only."

The doctor had issued strict orders that Massey was

not to be disturbed, especially by anyone from his company. To make matters worse, they'd taken his cell phone away. Carlson had even tried dropping in on him, with flowers and a get-well card, no less, but the nurses had run him off.

"No visitors."

He was desperate to get information to Massey about a promising applicant for the Cisco tech position because fixing the connection to the obelisk was of the utmost importance. HR wanted to set an interview for next week, but Carlson couldn't wait that long. He needed that server fixed right away. It would take an order from Massey himself to push for a more immediate appointment.

Breaking into the hospital's server was like cracking the lock on a safe. A brute force attack, like dynamite to the combination dial, would do more harm than good. He didn't want to overwhelm the hospital's server with a blitz data dump of random passwords, so he had to be subtle, like a safecracker's nimble fingers on the dial and a keen ear on the door.

He began his masked attack on the server by writing code to the data stream that flowed through the hospital's network. He typed:

*cmd/copy/utilman; cmd/remove/utilman/bak; install/ utilman2; cmd/reboot/wpeutil; execute.*

The computer beeped.

*Access Denied*

"Shit." He slammed a fist on the console. The mouse jumped. He tried another series of commands.

*Execute.*

*Working...* displayed on the monitor.

While he waited to see if this hack would work, he scanned reports from the bank of servers in his lab. The one that caught his eye, 2B, the server tracking the stolen cell phone, showed a spike in frequency output that had lasted three minutes, two seconds. His eyes widened and his heart rate jumped. The cell phone had received another call. With the Cisco server down, there'd be no data recorded, as the obelisk was offline and couldn't be monitored. Still, there was no mistake; someone had taken that call. Frank, maybe? Did he have the phone? Did it ring? Did he decide to answer it? If so, who did Frank speak to? What gave him the right to interfere in this project?

Carlson's face heated in anger. He switched to the satellite map, and sure enough, the phone was on the move, heading into the Bronx. A quick calculation told him the frequency jump happened twenty-eight minutes ago, but Frank was twenty-five minutes away from the address where the phone had been located. He couldn't have answered the call. But who?

His mouth dropped open as icy fingers crept up his spine. The obelisk knew, but its secret could not be revealed until that Cisco server was up and running.

With his elbows on the console, he rubbed his temples.

*This makes no scientific sense.*

As he mulled over the permutations of possibilities that the obelisk's frequency could be transmitted without the server, his brain hurt. He was again trying to solve an impossible puzzle. What came first: the obelisk or the frequency?

His eyes darted to the obelisk then back to his

monitor. The cell phone's frequency, oscillating on the screen, seemed to be reaching out to the obelisk...like the outstretched arms of a baby to its mother. He saw movement in his peripheral vision. Startled, he shifted his gaze to the obelisk.

*Did it just move?*

He gazed at it, daring it to move again.

*"No way. I'm just a rock."*

"You moved. I saw you."

*"I did not."*

*What's the matter with me? I'm having a conversation with a rock.*

He shook off his idiotic musings, got back to his current dilemma: What came first, the obelisk or the frequency? One could not exist without the other existing first, or vice versa. Maybe the obelisk had always transmitted the frequency, but how was it connected to the afterlife? Maybe the voices of those dearly departed souls were also on that frequency, but it all meant nothing without a receiver. The old StarTAC cell phone, with the help of science and technology, became the receiver for that frequency, thus opening a line of communication and revealing what lay beyond death. Like cracking open an egg resulted in an omelet or the premature death of a chicken.

*Chicken or the egg? Chicken or the egg? What came first? The chicken or the egg? The obelisk or the frequency?*

"What the hell is the answer?" he screamed at the obelisk as it stood there stoic as any rock. Unamused. Uncaring. Then it laughed at him.

"What are you laughing at?" He got to his feet and held up his own cell phone to the rock. "Call me. Tell me. What are you? What have you done with Bart? Where's the cleaning lady?" He stormed to the fence and showed the rock his fist. "Talk to me, damn it."

Nothing.

He stalked back to the main terminal and shoved his swivel chair toward the silent obelisk. With the crack of splintering wood, the chair broke through the fence and slammed into the obelisk.

The obelisk appeared to grow and pulsate as if angered by the chair, the missile it had become. Of course, Carlson knew it had to be a delusion spawned by twelve-hour days, sitting at the terminal, observing the obelisk as if it were a newborn babe, watching it grow and change... As soon as his thoughts materialized, and as soon as he recognized the lunacy thrashing about in his head, he heard the murmur of voices all around him, though no one else was there.

*"Can you hear me now?"* the obelisk said in a haunting, gravelly voice. *"I'm alive, as you can see."*

Carlson swallowed a boulder, got it stuck in his throat. He slapped a hand on his forehead. "You're alive. I knew it."

*"I can answer all your questions."*

His heart thudded against his ribcage as he mustered the most provocative question of all time. "What came first, the chicken or the egg?"

*"But not that one."*

"No," he screamed. "You're a phony, a fraud, a conman. You don't know a damn thing. You're just a fucking rock."

The obelisk grew bigger and taller, and as it touched the ceiling, the entire lab trembled as if the rock had set an earthquake upon all of New York City. He closed his eyes and expected the building to come crashing down on him. His stomach churned up bile. It was the end of days.

Then silence.

He opened his eyes. The obelisk stood before him, as plain as a lamp on a table.

*What the hell just happened?*

Ah, but he knew how to find out. He retrieved his chair and rolled it back to the main terminal, where he sat and opened the video security program. He rewound the recording two minutes and hit PLAY. There he saw it all play out on the monitor, the obelisk stoic, him throwing a fit, screaming at the rock, and rolling his chair into the fence, but not a word came from the obelisk. It didn't grow to the ceiling. The lab remained still. No earthquake.

Gritting his teeth, he hit STOP and looked up at the obelisk. "Oh, you are a crafty devil."

The computer beeped.

*Mt. Sinai West - ACCESS DENIED.*

\*\*\*

Ronald Massey lay in his hospital bed, as incapacitated as a common lab rat with electrodes and tubes invading its body. The omnipresent heart monitor pinged an irregular beat. A curtain surrounded his bed. A tray-table with a dish of red Jell-o and a sippy cup of water had been positioned above his lap.

*What the hell is this crap? Where's my filet mignon*

*and a nice bottle of Opus One?*

Hospital policy was geared to maintaining control. Control over what he ate and drank, and when he slept and peed.

*Don't the people in this place know who I am?*

He was Ronald Massey, a multi-millionaire who could buy their damned hospital.

However, he needed to remember the reality of his situation. A third heart attack could have been akin to, *Strike three. You're out.* Santos had saved his life again. Now he felt pretty good and wanted to get out of here before the nurses started wooing him for his money.

There'd been so many questions on his mind. Where was the stolen cell phone? Had Frank come back with it yet? What was Carlson doing about the crashed server? Did he find a tech to fix it? Carlson should have called him, at least stopped by to fill him in. The hospital made him feel as if he'd landed on the moon and got cut off from the human race.

*Santos must have given the staff strict orders: Don't let anyone talk to Massey.*

*And where did they put my cell phone?*

It had to be with his clothes in the closet. He rolled the tray-table aside and peeled the electrodes from his chest. The heart monitor wailed a steady tone. He was sure an alarm would sound at the nurses' station, as well. They'd respond quickly, so he had to hurry. As he got out of bed, his foot kicked a bedpan, and the slosh of its contents made him groan.

*That's gonna stink.*

Wearing an open-back hospital gown and feeling

naked without an Armani suit, he peeked out through a slat in the curtain to make sure the coast was clear.

*All right.*

He hustled to the closet, rifled through the pockets of his suit coat, and came up with the cell phone, just as he'd suspected. Hospitals were so predictable.

He hurried back to bed, slipped under the covers, and stashed his phone under the pillow. It wasn't three seconds later when he heard frantic footfalls enter the room.

"Mr. Massey?" A nurse bulled through the curtain slat, and when she saw the dangling leads, she frowned. "Mr. Massey, were you out of bed?"

He shrugged. "I must've rolled over in my sleep."

She glanced at him sideways as she reapplied the electrodes to his chest. "You need to be more careful."

"Yes, dear."

"I'll be back later to check on you." She left through the curtain slat with a flurry.

"What's for lunch?"

No answer. He was alone again.

He turned on the television, set the volume high enough to mask his voice, and then retrieved the cell phone and dialed Carlson.

"Boss. How are you? They wouldn't tell me squat." His voice sounded surprised and happy simultaneously.

"I'm still alive."

"Are you getting out today?"

"Still working on that. I need updates, now."

"Yes, sir. HR found a suitable candidate for the Cisco tech position, but they say they can't interview him until next week. I can't wait that long. We need your okay to expedite. Thursday morning would be great."

"By all means. Bring him in. I'll text HR, tell them we'll take care of the interview on our end. Did Frank get the cell phone?"

"He's got it but hasn't brought it in yet."

Massey clenched his fist. "What's he waiting for, damn it?"

"Now don't get yourself worked up, sir. Your heart. Remember?"

"You let me worry about my heart. How's the obelisk?"

"It did something strange."

"Strange?"

"I believe the cell phone received a call, three minutes, two seconds in duration."

Massey sat up, and his eyes darted to the left and right. His breaths quickened. "But without the server, you don't know where the call came from."

"I know it sucks, sir, but it's strange that the obelisk would transmit something when no call was initiated. The frequency of the cell phone jumped all on its own. There's something going on I don't understand."

"Worse than Bart and the cleaning lady?"

"Sir, if this thing gets out of hand, the obelisk can wreak havoc on the world. I've seen a preview."

Voices emanated from the hallway.

"Someone's coming. I have to go. I hope to get out of here tomorrow."

"Feel better, sir."

Massey hid the phone under his pillow. His mind raced with ideas about who had called and from where, the afterlife, he was certain. However, proving it was a different matter, and he couldn't do squat from this hospital room.

*** 

On Wednesday afternoon, a nurse wheeled multi-millionaire Ronald Massey into the lobby at Mt. Sinai Hospital. In his lap lay a prescription bag of anticoagulant and blood-thinning medications, along with his discharge papers and instructions from Dr. Santos. It was about time he was getting out of this hellhole.

A long black limousine idled outside.

The hospital doors opened with a whoosh. Massey inhaled a cool breeze that felt good in his lungs. It smelled like freedom. His heart pounded with excitement. He was wearing his thousand-dollar suit, albeit his tie was undone, and his shirt needed a fresh pressing. He had undergone a traumatic experience. No one could expect him to always look perfect.

The limo driver pulled his lanky frame out of the driver's seat then marched to the back passenger door, opened it then stood regally by the rear fender. The bill of his chauffer's hat shielded his eyes from the sun.

The nurse wheeled Massey out to the limo. "Don't forget to take your medicine."

"Yeah, yeah, blah, blah."

"We don't want to see you back here."

Massey's legs were noodles as he got up from the chair, and his throat tightened as an army of newshounds rushed to the open door.

"Mr. Massey. Mr. Massey."

"Stand back," the driver ordered the mob.

Massey grabbed the handhold and lowered himself into the plush rear seat. The nurse rolled the wheelchair back to the hospital.

"Mr. Massey, how are you feeling?" a reporter asked.

"Like a million bucks." He sat up straight with his shoulders back and head held high.

Carlson sat on the far side of the seat with an iPad on his lap. He furrowed his brow and shook Massey's hand. "It's great to see you, sir. We have a lot to talk about."

"I'm looking forward to your update."

Reporters crowded the doorway, arms stretched toward him with microphones in their fists to get every word on tape. "Are you still eating fast food?"

Massey laughed. "I've been on a strict diet. Lots of fruits and vegetables. Damn near killed me."

Another reporter asked, "Are you going to run for mayor?"

"I've got enough on my plate. Mayor Allerton is doing a great job. I support his plans to keep guns off the street, but leave the hookers alone, by golly."

"I hear some of your properties are tax delinquent. What are you going to do about that?"

"No comment. Thanks everyone for your concern. Now, I must go. Driver, take us home."

"Yes, sir." He pushed the reporters back and closed the door.

"Mr. Massey..." another reporter shouted.

The driver got behind the wheel, and seconds later, they were gone.

Massey's thumping heart slowed and he exhaled. He

set the bag of medicine on the seat next to him. "Did you get the cell phone?"

"Not yet, sir."

"Have you heard from Frank?"

"Nothing, but he's got the phone. I tracked it to his house in the Bronx. I think he's lying low. Cops are looking for him."

"Did you hear from the new Cisco technician?"

Carlson nodded. "He's coming in for an interview in the morning."

"Good, but don't send him to HR. Takes too long with all their background checks and red tape. Get him downstairs and put him to the test right away."

"Test, sir?"

"Tell him this...if he fixes the server, gets it up and running, the job is his."

"Seems fair enough."

"We need that server online by the time Frank brings in the cell phone. Then we'll get rid of them both."

Carlson scowled. "Frank, too, sir? What about his daughter?"

"Life is full of disappointments."

The limo turned into the parking garage under Massey, Inc.

# Chapter Nineteen

In the ICU ward at Montefiore Medical Center, I sat slumped against my mom's bed and buried my face in my hands. The steady beep of her heart monitor echoed ominously throughout the room. I couldn't believe what the doctors had told me about her condition. They had to drill a hole in her skull to relieve the pressure from her swelling brain, a common occurrence with blunt-force trauma. She'd also sustained a busted eye socket and a broken nose. Dear God, it was a miracle she'd survived Frank's brutal assault.

I had paced the hallway near the operating room, watched the clock tick away the hours, not knowing if she'd live or die. When the nurses wheeled her into the ICU, her head and face were wrapped in bandages. "She's in a drug-induced coma," they told me.

My knees buckled as grief and guilt squeezed tears from my eyes. How could I have let this happen?

I raised my head slowly, my eyes bleary with tears, but I could see the wires that snaked up under her gown, and the tubes stretching from sentinel machines to her arms and into her mouth. A ventilator pumped air into her lungs, breathing for her with a *hiss-thump, hiss-thump*. The machines seemed more alive than my mom. She looked so frail. I wasn't sure if she would ever regain consciousness again.

It was all my fault. My stomach twisted into a tight

knot. What a fool I was to bring that phone into the house. Obviously, Frank had a way to track it, though it didn't have a SIM card. I still didn't believe it, I didn't want to believe that I could have been so wrong, but the reality of my mistake lay broken before me, broken beyond belief.

The thought of Frank Coletti bludgeoning my helpless mom senseless made me clench my tear-soaked hands into fists. Woodlawn was a safe neighborhood; break-ins were as rare as solar eclipses, but Frank had changed all that. Mom wasn't even safe in her own home anymore.

Hot rage seared through my veins. I remembered the power in Frank's fists, his weight on top of me, the blows that exploded on my face, how I thought I'd never survive his brutality. Yeah. I'd disarmed him of his gun...maybe that's why he didn't just shoot my mom and be done with her.

I took hold of my mom's hand, knowing her encounter with Frank could have turned out much worse. "You're going to be okay, Mom. We'll get through this...just like we've done before, with what happened to Dad and all." I wanted to tell her I'd spoken to him, on the cell phone Frank took from my dresser drawer, the cell phone he'd beaten her to get back for his boss, Ronald Massey. Hell. If she could hear me, she'd never believe me, same as Mullen would never believe it. Who would ever buy such a fantastical story? It was up to me to solve the O'Malley case and find out why he gave his life to keep that cell phone out of Massey's hands.

A doctor walked in with a clipboard in hand. If he were over twenty-one, I would have been surprised. He had slicked-back black hair and olive skin, possibly from India.

"Mr. Calhoun..." He offered me his hand. "I am Doctor Kavor." His accent came from India, as well.

I shook his hand, but there was little grip in his handshake, as if his fingers were accustomed to the finesse of working a scalpel on delicate tissues, and not the macho delivery of a masculine greeting.

"What's the prognosis, doc?"

He flipped through pages on the clipboard. "According to her chart, she is holding her own, good blood pressure, normal pulse, but it was, in the operating room, touch-and-go. Brain swelling, it is a dangerous condition." He frowned with concern as he looked at my mom. "She has suffered more trauma than a WBA boxer."

"When will she wake up?"

"When the swelling is down, we will bring her out of it."

"Can she hear us?""

"Not at all."

I slumped my shoulders in resignation. "I understand."

"Go home, Mr. Calhoun. Get some rest. We will keep an eye on her."

"I can't...I just can't leave her. I should have been there...to protect her."

"Looks like to me you have taken a beating, as well."

I touched my broken lip. "We've both had a tough day."

Kavor scowled, shook his head, and stepped out, leaving me alone with my mom and the incessant beeping and hiss-thumping of the machines.

I held her doughy hand. My breath shuddered as I

squeezed it, hoping she would squeeze mine in return, but there was no response. My lips quivered. I wanted to tell her how sorry I was, but she wouldn't hear me. I looked up to the heavens...well...the ceiling. Why did bad things happen to good people? Why Mom? Why me? Why did Frank come into our lives? God, please, what is your game plan?

The clouds didn't part; the sky didn't open up; no grandfatherly voice answered my questions. I thought of Dad's funeral and shivered, how all of our questions went unanswered then, as well. Why Dad? Why did you have to take him, God? What are we going to do now? The priest didn't know the answers, either. Mom and I stood at Dad's grave, holding each other tight, and heard how God loved us, His children, how He's called Dermot home to be with Him, how we'd see each other again someday, and we found no solace in those words. Just pain, anguish, and tears. Mom didn't deserve to go through all the torment Dermot's death had laid on her. I needed to tell her that he was all right. The only way she'd believe I'd talked to him was to let her talk to him herself. I just had to get that cell phone first.

My phone vibrated, announcing a new email in my inbox. I let go of Mom's hand to check the sender. It was from HR at Massey, Inc. My throat tightened as I read the message.

*Mr. Calhoun. We've reviewed your application and would like you to come in for an interview tomorrow morning at 9am.*

I emailed back: *Thank you. I'll be there.*

I pumped my fist. Now, I had a way into Massey, Inc.

I could find out what was going on with that cell phone, which I was sure was back in Ronald Massey's hands by now. Problem was, how many questions would HR ask, especially the one about where I worked last? And how long would it take for a background check? Could be, I'd have to be back at work at Vericom before I got a foot in the door at Massey, Inc.

Timing was everything.

Footfalls approached the room. I whirled around, expecting to see Frank charge in to finish the job. To my relief, it was Detective Mullen. He glanced at my mom lying there in dire straits and made the sign of the cross on his chest. "I'm sorry about your mother."

Everyone was so damned sorry about my mom, but what was anybody doing about it? "Did you arrest Frank Coletti?"

"Why would he break into your house?"

I frowned. "Isn't it your job to figure that out?"

"My job is to catch O'Malley's killer."

"I told you Frank did it. Go get him."

"We need evidence, beyond-a-reasonable-doubt evidence. The DA won't file charges on your word alone. CSI dusted your place for prints. Nothing. No fibers. No hairs. Nothing to prove Frank had anything to do with the assault on your mom. And you say nothing was stolen."

*Except for the cell phone. I should tell him everything. Let the police handle it before I get in over my head at Massey, Inc.*

However, I couldn't do that. If I told Mullen and he raided Massey, Inc., Ronald Massey could shut down his cellular operation, deny knowing Frank Coletti, and buy a million lawyers to make it all go away. I would never learn how my dad could talk to me from the grave. No. I had to stay on course. "I didn't see anything missing."

"If Frank broke in," Mullen pressed, "why ransack your dresser unless he was looking for something? What was he after?"

"I don't know. Are you going to drag your ass on this investigation like you did my dad's, or are you going to get out there and do what the police are supposed to do? Arrest the bad guy, or do I have to give him to you on a silver platter?"

"This isn't my first rodeo, Calhoun. You're not telling me everything you know."

"I know Frank damn near killed my mom. Isn't that enough?"

"Stay away from the house for the next twenty-four hours."

"Why?"

"I'm going to have CSI take another look, turn up every board and brick, if they have to. I'm on your side, Sean, but I need proof. Same with your dad's case. No proof, no arrest."

"Okay. I get it. I'll stay here with my mom, but I'll need a change of clothes for work tomorrow."

"I'll leave CSI a note. Call me when you're ready to tell me what the hell is going on." Mullen walked out.

I put two chairs together and lined them up next to Mom so I could hold her hand. The life-support machines beeped away mechanically. If there was any change in her condition, I wanted to be the first to know. As long as those machines kept up their steady tones, I could take solace that she was still alive. To lose one parent was heartbreaking enough, but to lose two parents would be unbearable. Hot tears spilled from my eyes. I released my mom's hand, wiped the guilt from my cheeks, and wrapped my arms around myself. She had to survive, she just had to.

I'd dozed off for a bit, woke up to a nurse's voice. "Mr. Calhoun. Care for some supper?" She held a tray with a silver dome covering a plate. "Turkey, stuffing, potatoes, gravy, and mixed veggies. What do you say?"

I couldn't remember the last time I'd eaten. "Sure, thanks." I sat up straight.

She set the tray on my lap. "Enjoy."

I took a sip of tea then dug in. Not bad. Hospital food got such a bad rap.

\*\*\*

My cell phone alarm went off at 6am. I woke up, surprised to find a blanket over me. I yawned, rubbed my eyes then shuffled to the bathroom to wash my battered face, wet my hair, and comb it back with my fingers. A toothbrush would have come in handy. I used my index finger and hot water.

The nurse came in. "Did you get some sleep?"

"A couple hours." I dried my hands with a paper towel. "Thanks for the blanket."

"No problem. You hungry?"

I stepped out of the bathroom. "Starving, but I wish my mom could eat something."

"Me too. I'll order you some scrambled eggs, toast, and apple juice."

"Sounds too good to be true."

The nurse looked over the bedside machines. "The doctor will be in to see her soon."

"I have to leave, but I'll be back later. Call me if there are any changes."

"Absolutely." The nurse left.

A few minutes later, an orderly brought in a tray.

I ate breakfast at my mom's bedside, then after I finished, I kissed her on her bandaged forehead. "Get better soon, Mom. I love you."

I called a cab.

\*\*\*

As the cab drove up to the curb, I was prepared to see a cop standing in front of the house. However, there were no police officers in sight, just the yellow crime-scene tape flapping in the breeze. The investigators must've taken a breakfast break. I ducked under the tape and opened the unlocked front door. Hopefully, nobody had burglarized the house while the cops were gone.

I saw splintered wood on the carpet and fingerprint dust everywhere. Who was going to clean up this mess? Me, I was sure. In the kitchen, Mom had spread bills out on the table; she must've been fretting over them when Frank broke in. I climbed the stairs to my room where the cops had made another mess with their fingerprint dust. Sections of wallboard were cut out, same with the carpet and curtains, probably to collect blood spatter evidence for the crime lab. My bed was upended; my dresser drawers were tossed, but my computer desk was untouched.

As I looked around, a cold chill prickled my neck hairs. This was where the assault occurred. I pictured my mom's horrified face as Frank confronted her, probably interrogated her about the cell phone. She wouldn't have known what he was talking about, must've suggested he look in my room. He might have dragged her up here to keep an eye on her while he rifled through my stuff.

*So he finds the phone...why did he beat her up? Why didn't he just leave?*

I hoped to ask him that question directly, as soon as Mullen had him in handcuffs.

I showered and dressed for my interview then headed out in the Camry to the Metro-North train station, caught the southbound toward Manhattan.

As I rode the train, I sat hunched in the seat, my hands clasped to keep my nerves in check. It had been over five years since I'd applied for a job. I wasn't sure I could pull it off. I didn't need a full-time position, maybe a part-time consulting job, just enough time to get access to their network and see what I could find out about that cell phone. However, with Frank in the mix, I could be walking into a mobsters' lair. He'd probably kill me on the spot, but getting that cell phone and talking to my dad again was worth the risk.

# Chapter Twenty

I got off the Metro-North in Grand Central Terminal and hustled through a sea of commuters toward the subway tunnels. The four-faced clock read 8:30am. They didn't call Grand Central Terminal the crossroads of the world for nothing, as every person here had a particular path they were following. Mine would hopefully lead me to the cell phone and another conversation with my dad. All I had to do was get inside Massey, Inc. without getting killed in the process.

My heart thumped with dread.

I wondered if Frank Coletti was hiding among all these people, looking to pop out of the crowd and shoot me dead. I was sure Mullen hadn't arrested him yet. He didn't have any proof. Proof my ass. How much proof do the cops need when it was unquestionable who'd pummeled my mom half to death? I'd survived encounters with him earlier. Next time, I might not be so lucky.

I arrived at the subway terminus as brakes screeched and brought the train to a gentle stop. Hot, stuffy air hit me like a slap in the face. My route was firmly implanted in my brain. The Times Square shuttle would take me west to Times Square, a one-minute ride, and then the B Way would take me northwest to the Lincoln Center, a five-minute ride. From there, I'd catch a cab to Massey, Inc., a three block drive. I'd be there in plenty of time for my job interview.

I raced to get aboard and turned to face the platform to see if I could spot Frank among the commuters. He was nowhere in sight. My immediate angst settled to a slow boil.

A lingering odor of sweat and urine made me wonder when the subway car was last cleaned. The floor was littered with trash: drink cups, fast food wrappers, even a Pampers diaper added to the reek. I moved to stand near an air-conditioning vent before anyone could crowd me out. A bell chimed and an announcement came over the speakers. *"Please stand clear. The doors are closing."* I swear, ten more people crammed themselves into the car before the doors rattled closed. A second later, the train rumbled forward.

I gripped the handhold above me and thought about the interview that awaited me. What would HR ask? What would I tell them? More importantly, how long would it take before they decided to hire me? I needed to access their computers as soon as possible.

A minute later, the train arrived at Times Square, the doors opened, and I surged out with the crowd. On the mezzanine, a man was playing the flute in one corner, and a woman down the way belted out a soulful ballad. Both entertainers had a tip jar set on the floor in front of them. I blew by them on my way to the B tracks where I caught the northbound to the Lincoln Center. Five minutes later, I pounded up the steps to the surface street where I inhaled the February fresh air, thankful to be out of the ever-present stifling heat and stench in the bowels of New York City. I licked my dry lips and dabbed sweat off my forehead with my coat sleeve.

The cacophony of blowing horns replaced the hiss, squeal, and rattle of trains. Buses lumbered by while cyclists darted in and out of traffic. A queue of taxis awaited their fares. I jumped into the open door of the front taxi. "Massey, Inc."

The driver, bespectacled and gaunt and wearing a turban, turned to me. "Buckle your seatbelt, sir."

I settled back for the short ride and watched the meter roll over like a Vegas slot machine. I noticed an empty McDonald's cup on the floor, but otherwise, the cab was a far cry cleaner than the subway cars. Hints of a woodsy musk cologne lingered in the cab.

I gazed out the window at the people all caught up in their lives. None of them had a clue that I'd recently received a phone call from my dead dad. As the tall buildings swallowed the sky, I folded my arms across my chest. My inner voice shouted, *"What are you getting yourself into?"* I ignored my better judgment, but my angst loomed higher as the cab got closer to Massey, Inc. I needed that cell phone. I needed to know how it worked. I needed to talk to my dad one more time.

The driver pulled into the loading zone at the front doors to Massey, Inc. on Riverside Boulevard. "Here we are, sir."

I swiped my credit card to pay the fare. "Thanks for the ride."

"Thanks for the tip." The cab pulled away.

I looked up the side of the massive building made of glass and steel. Grey clouds lumbered above, and I shivered from a gust of wind. The briny smell of the Hudson River whipped around in the air. On the sidewalk, a wire-haired terrier sniffed a fire hydrant while a woman held the leash and waited. A young boy wearing a Yankees hat stood by her side. People bundled in parkas rushed past me, and a family of four hopped a snow berm and hustled down the block. A couple pushing a stroller passed me, and an old woman carried a grocery bag into Massey, Inc.

Yeah. The bustle of New York City had no clue why I was here and what risks I was willing to take for one more phone call with my dad.

I entered the foyer where a familiar doorman stood with his arms folded. "What are you doing back here?"

"I have a job interview."

"Are you Sean Calhoun?"

"Yes, sir."

"Follow me."

As I followed the doorman across the foyer, I took note of the security cameras and the layout. The floor was made of white marble inlaid with gold, and set off on my right, tropical plants marked the perimeter of a waiting area with plush couches and chairs.

The doorman spoke to the concierge behind a desk. "Tell Carlson he's here."

The concierge made a phone call and the doorman turned to me. "Have a seat and someone will be with you soon." The doorman marched back to his post.

I strode to the couch and sat on the plush cushions, back straight and left ankle set atop my right knee, professional, confident. Hints of white tea and fig overpowered my nose and I sneezed. So much for first impressions. As I glanced around, I wondered if Frank was somewhere nearby, perhaps watching me on a security camera. If so, I was a sitting duck. I felt flashes of heat on my face, my throat tightened, and my mouth suddenly tasted like sand.

A white lab coat clad man approached me, an iPad tucked up under his arm. He could have been in college by the looks of his unkempt hair, Yankees shirt, jeans, and sneakers. "Mr. Calhoun?"

I stood to meet him. "Yes, sir."

"I'm Carlson." He extended his hand to me.

I accepted his handshake. It felt warm and firm, confident.

"What happened to your face?"

"Oh." I touched my bruised cheek. "It's nothing."

"Looks sore."

*Yeah, thanks to Massey's thug Frank Coletti, who beat me up and damn near killed my mom. You probably know him. Tell the bastard I said hello.*

"Are you from HR?"

"I'm the lab supervisor, and I'll conduct the interview. This way."

That surprised me. No HR? I might get in faster than I'd imagined.

Carlson led me through a vast lobby of high ceilings and tall pillars. To my left, subdued chatter and soft music emanated from a restaurant and bar. *The Real Deal.* To my right stood a row of chrome elevators beneath neon signs that read: *RESIDENTIAL SUITES, BUSINESSES, SPORTS CENTER.* We passed the security desk and a window marked: *VALET.* Next to the leasing counter, rows of bronze mail slots lined the wall.

My jaw dropped at the sheer size of this lobby. And one person owned the entire building, as well as many more like it. My dad, who'd busted his ass just to put food on our table, had taught me to be humble and to appreciate everything we had, not to flaunt our good fortunes. Without even having met Massey, I already disliked him.

Then there was this lab tech, Carlson. Obviously, he was just a grunt for Massey. I wondered what he knew about the cell phone, if he'd helped develop it, or perhaps he wasn't involved, maybe more of a paper pusher. Did he know Frank Coletti and his murderous means? I had to go on the assumption they were all in cahoots with each other, so I'd better not let my guard down. To not seem apprehensive, I tossed out a compliment. "This place is amazing."

Carlson stopped at a large black elevator marked *PRIVATE*. "Mr. Massey has put a lot of work and pride into his company. I'm proud to work for him, as perhaps, you will be, too." He pushed the down button.

The elevator doors slid open. Carlson let me go in ahead of him. When the doors closed, he pressed the *SB* button. With a bump, the elevator began to descend. That sent a jolt of alarm through me. I expected corporate offices would be upstairs. Instead, we were heading down below street level. I doubted there were any exit doors in the basement. The mirrored elevator walls closed in around me, and my neck hairs prickled. "Where are we going?"

"To the lab." Carlson tapped on his iPad. "We're going to do your interview a little differently."

I tweaked my brow. "How so?"

"It's easy to claim to be an expert, another thing to

prove it entirely. Just stay focused on the interview. I really do want you to pass our rigid requirements."

"How soon do you expect to hire somebody?"

"We have a Cisco server that crashed. I need it fixed without delay."

I rubbed my chin. "I can handle that problem."

"If you want the job, you'll need to get it up and running."

"I see. Kind of a test, huh?"

Carlson tucked the iPad under his arm. "HR says you claim to be qualified for the job."

"Did HR tell you I worked at Vericom?"

He looked surprised. "No. What happened to that job?"

"Temporary leave. I'd like to make it permanent." I lied.

"We'll see."

The numbered floor lights above the door indicated SB, and the elevator slowed. A terrible thought crossed my mind. If HR checked with Vericom, they'd know they suspended me for unauthorized access to a secure program, which was exactly what I intended to do here. They might not let me anywhere near their network terminals. For now, as long as Carlson was oblivious to my employment history, I'd leave him in the dark.

The elevator stopped and the doors opened. With wide eyes, I scanned the expansive white room before me. Clusters of flatscreen displays sat atop a long console, much like the terminals in a NASA control room, where technicians sat on swivel chairs and typed commands into computers that flashed sequenced LEDs on their control panels and beeped out responses. Other technicians monitored a bank of servers, moving down the line from one station to another, checking this and that. The air smelled ionized and hummed to the tune of electronic cooling fans.

I wanted to ask Carlson what they were up to down here, but I elected to act nonchalant, as if this environment was totally the norm for me.

"This way," Carlson said.

I followed him to a massive terminal positioned in front of the servers, much like a conductor before an orchestra. While he typed on the keyboard, I noticed looms of cables running from the servers to the far end of the room where a strange sight met my gaze. A blue tarp covered an object of some kind, maybe ten feet tall, a bit pointy at the top, fat around the bottom, egg-shaped I guessed, and surrounded by a four-foot wooden fence. The server cables disappeared under the tarp.

Crinkling my brow, I wondered if Massey had built some kind of supercomputer, something the techs had to program, but why cover it? What were they hiding? Did it have something to do with the StarTAC phone's unique ability? A quick glance around me revealed video cameras positioned strategically around the lab and in the steel girders above me. If I had to bet, I'd bet Ronald Massey was watching me this very minute. The thought gave me the creeps.

"What's all this equipment for?" I asked over Carlson's shoulder.

"It's our data center for the entire company. On top of that, our tenants' computers are linked to this network, as well."

"It's quite extensive. I'm impressed."

I was being facetious, of course. For a multipurpose building, Massey had installed a lot of supercomputers and employed a lot of people working at a high level. He didn't need this much juice to manage his finances and real estate holdings. It also made no sense that Massey's business tenants would link their computers to the servers down here. Something else was going on, and Carlson wasn't being forthright with me, for whatever reason; either it was none of my business or I didn't yet have a need to know. Perhaps this network had something to do with the gizmo under that tarp, but instead of asking him about it, I stuck with the plan of getting the job. Then I'd be in a better position to get answers to all my questions.

Carlson hit the ENTER button and turned to me. "All set. We're ready to see what you got to offer us."

"Let's do it."

"Look at his main terminal in front of us. Decipher the data stream and tell me what it means."

"May I sit down?"

Carlson extended his hand to the chair. "By all means."

I took command of the swivel chair and examined the data stream. It was running in a loop, repeating the same data, menial log entries, a restaurant shopping list, I determined. I ran a debug command so I could filter out all the individual items and reveal the critical background operations. I found the 'loop' command and typed, 'end loop.' The data stream stopped, allowing me to enter a command of my own: SERVER CHECK.

"What are you doing?" Carlson asked.

A critical event reported all the interfaces for the Cisco server at the time it had crashed. I tried to ping their IPV6 addresses but couldn't reach them. Then I saw what killed this server. The message appeared on the monitor: CC OVERLOAD.

I turned to Carlson who was looking over my shoulder, breathing down my back. "The Controller Card took a voltage spike."

"Spike?"

"Overload. What the hell is this server linked to?"

"Never mind that. Can you fix it?"

"I'll need to replace the CC."

"Over here." Carlson led me to a Cisco server.

I'd seen this type before. There were twelve circuit boards inserted into the mainframe from left to right, and the two middle slots were for the CCs, the Controller Cards, which among other duties, allowed access to this server via a management cable. Once remote access was lost, the only way to relink it to the network was with a management cable. Then I could communicate with the server directly, but only if I had a laptop with the proper program.

I sat in a chair in front of the dead server and smelled the first problem right away: burnt electrical circuits, a smell no tech would ever forget. Next, I saw there was only one controller card. Its status lights were out. Usually, redundancy was built into a server, so if one card went down, another card could take over. I wondered what happened to the second CC. Maybe the last tech only installed one. Still, it must have taken a lot of power to fry the lone CC. I had to believe the culprit lay hidden under the blue tarp. "Carlson. I need a new CC, a screwdriver, and a laptop."

"Right here." With a foot, he slid a briefcase toward me. "Should have everything you need in here."

I leaned over, opened the lid, and took a quick inventory. Laptop. Screwdriver. Controller Card. Blue management cable. "I'll give it my best shot."

"If you get the Cisco up and running, you've got the job." Carlson walked back to the main terminal.

I pulled the laptop from the case and fired it up. After I connected the management cable to the laptop, I plugged the other end into the CC maintenance USB. The laptop chimed, and the *SERIAL SYNC+* program loaded. It gave me the server's IP address: 192.168.1.1., which I would need to ping the CC once I'd restored connectivity. I typed *CONNECT*.

The laptop beeped. *NO DEVICE DETECTED*. That I expected.

Before I tackled the problem, I checked my cell phone for any news from the hospital. No message meant no change in Mom's condition. I had to pocket my disappointment, along with the phone, and get back to work on the server.

In the search bar on the bottom left side of the screen, I typed in *cmd* to bring up the command line. A black box appeared. I typed in: *ping - t 192.168.1.1*. This command would continually ping the IP address. When the CC detected the address, I would hear a tone.

I hit ENTER to activate the ping command, and to no surprise, the response was *NO REPLY, destination host unreachable.*

While the steady ping was active, I first tried rebooting the faulty controller card. This trick I'd used several times when troubleshooting a hardware problem. I removed the mounting screw, pulled out the card for thirty seconds, and reinserted it into the slot, hoping the card would wake up and respond to the ping.

Instead of the status lights blinking on, the laptop response remained: *NO REPLY.* That was disheartening. However, I was now convinced the overload damage was insurmountable. I removed the entire card and observed the fried circuits, far worse than anything I'd ever seen before.

I saw Carlson peek over at me, figured he was monitoring my progress on the main terminal. From the Cisco briefcase, I pulled out a replacement controller card. It was sealed in an anti-static bag, so I knew it was a new part. Since static electricity could ruin a circuit board, I found a grounding strap in the Cisco case, clipped it to the server's frame, and looped the other end around my wrist. This ensured I was grounded so any static electricity would dissipate through me and keep the card safe while I handled it.

I slowly slid the new controller card into the slot. Immediately the status lights blinked on steady. I screwed the card into place and checked the laptop. *NO REPLY.* I knew I had to be patient while the ping command searched for its destination address.

"Having trouble?"

To my surprise, Carlson was standing over me with his arms folded. I glanced up at him. "Give it time."

"You've been dicking around here for more than an

hour. Do you know what you're doing or not?"

*Don't let this guy get under my skin. Think of the big picture. Remember why I'm here.*

The laptop emitted a chime.

I watched the new controller card's lights start blinking. The ping command came back with the message: *REPLY FROM 192.168.1.1.* The cooling fans hummed on, and banks of circuit lights flashed up and down the server.

I removed the grounding strap from my wrist. "It's working."

Carlson frowned as if I hadn't convinced him I'd earned the job. "I should login to make sure we're good."

"You'll have to use the default password then reinstall your own."

Carlson's brow furrowed. "Ah, sure."

"You don't know the default password, do you?"

"Forgot it."

"Allow me." I typed the factory login and password: *admin/admin.* The welcome screen popped up on the laptop. I was in. I performed some *SHOW* commands to make sure everything was up and running. *NO ERRORS.*

I stood and ceremoniously wiped my hands together. "Guess that means I've got the job."

"Mr. Massey will be pleased."

*I bet.*

Carlson grabbed my hand and shook it enthusiastically. "You're now our Head Technician."

"What happened to the last one?"

His face blanched. "You clean up around here. I'll change my password and login." He rushed back to the main terminal.

I put the faulty CC in the anti-static bag and packed up the tools. Carlson could send the CC in for repair or replacement later. Right now, I needed an excuse to get in here tonight and search for the cell phone data. Looking at the burned CC, I came up with an idea. "Hey, Carlson."

"What?"

"You only have one Controller Card for this Cisco. Leaves you with no redundancy. There should be two. Active and standby. If this new CC burns out, your server will crash again."

Carlson's brow furrowed. "I can't have that. What do you suggest?"

"Let me get you another card. I'll even install it tonight...if you can get me access to the lab after hours."

"Yeah, sure. I'll leave your name at the security desk. I need the server in tip-top shape and dependable for tomorrow."

*By tomorrow I won't need this job, anyway.*

"See you in the morning, then?"

"Of course. 9am. I'll tell HR to put you on the payroll." Carlson went back to typing at his terminal.

On my way out, I took note of the video cameras. I'd need to disable them so I could use the main terminal, though I was sure it wouldn't take long for security to respond to the blackout. I'd also need time to take a peek under the tarp. I knew I'd be taking a big risk sticking my nose into Ronald Massey's business, but for any chance to talk to my dad, the risk would be worth the reward. I'd have to be careful if I didn't want to end up like Arthur O'Malley.

# Chapter Twenty-One

In the penthouse office, Massey was perched on the edge of his seat in front of the security monitors on his desk, watching Carlson in the lab with the job applicant, Sean Calhoun, who'd just replaced the Controller Card in the Cisco. While it spooled up, Massey drummed his fingers on the desktop. Lights on the server started flashing, and he heard the hum of cooling fans kick on. He leaned back in his chair and exhaled.

*Now all I need is that StarTAC phone. Frank had better show up with it pretty damn soon.*

With the Cisco working and the cell phone in hand, he'd finally be able to speak with someone who'd died and learn what awaited him in the afterlife. However, who would he call? Arthur O'Malley? *No. That call would just piss me off.* What about Jimmy Hoffa? No. He'd save that call for later, once the system tests were completed and he could invite the media without fear of a flopped demonstration. Maybe Miriam or Bart...or the cleaning lady. He hoped one of them would confirm the paradise he'd seen during his near-death experience in the hospital.

The vision was like the fleeting kiss of a woman.

He glanced at his medications lined up on the desk. They were a constant reminder that he was only one heartbeat away from death.

On the monitor, Calhoun stood and wiped his hands

together, as a man who'd completed his work. Carlson's voice came over the speakers. "Mr. Massey will be pleased."

"Nice work, guys," Massey muttered.

His secretary spoke over the intercom. "Sir?"

"Yes, Janice."

"Frank Coletti is here."

*It's about damn time.*

His cheeks heated. "Send him in."

"Yes, sir."

He paced to his window, looked down at the people below, scurrying about, small as ants. None of them realized he held the key to the mysteries of the afterlife within his grasp.

The door flew open and Frank stormed in. He wore a fresh suit and sunglasses. "Sorry I'm late, boss."

"What took you so long?"

"Ran into some trouble getting the phone. Some little old lady wouldn't give it to me...had to beat her up to get it. Cops are looking for me. It's been a rough night. Stopped by MSK Kids hospital this morning to see Chloe. She's in a bad way, boss."

"Did you bring the StarTAC?"

Frank patted his pocket. "Right here."

"Give it to me." He forcefully held out his hand.

Frank surrendered the phone. "I want to thank you for helping Chloe. How soon can you get the money to the hospital?"

"Let's stay focused on the phone."

"But they need the money before they can start the experimental treatments."

Massey rolled his eyes. "Keep your shirt on. It can wait."

"The hospital won't treat patients without prior insurance approval. This is no different."

Massey focused on the monitor.

"She needs your help right away."

"Look. I'm all broke up about your little girl, but—"

"She's all I have. Please take a minute to write a check for the fifty grand they need."

"I'm not giving you a check."

"Then send it to the hospital by courier."

Massey's gaze never left the monitor.

Frank looked over Massey's shoulder. "What's so important..." He gasped. "That's him."

"Who?"

"The guy I've been chasing all over hell-and-gone. He took the cell phone from O'Malley's dead body. What's he doing here?"

"New employee."

"You've gotta be shittin' me."

"He fixed the Cisco, got it up and running."

Frank backed away from the desk. "He works at Vericom."

"How do you know?"

"I followed him there. Boss, I smell a turd in this toilet."

On the monitor, Carlson and Calhoun shook hands. Then Calhoun got on the elevator.

Massey wanted to reach into the monitor and grab him by the throat. "What's he doing here...spying for Vericom?"

"It's the cell phone. He's after it. I'm dead certain he's a threat to the entire operation."

The lobby monitor captured Calhoun leaving the building.

Chills broke out on Massey's neck. "He's getting away. Frank, catch him before he screws up everything."

"You want me to kill him?"

"Bring him back here. Alive. He's got a lot of questions to answer."

"On it, boss."

Massey followed him into the elevator. Frank pushed the *lobby* button. As the elevator descended, Massey adjusted his tie via a mirrored panel while Frank stood facing the door, watching the floor indicator digits count down. He had no idea how lucky he was right now. The plan was to kill him after he brought the cell phone back, but now Massey needed him to get Calhoun.

*His change of fortune is going to cost me fifty grand.*

Frank turned to Massey and scowled. "It's not fair."

"What?"

"You got more money than God and can't even take the time to write a check for my daughter?"

Massey's first thought was to shut him up with a bullet to the brain. Just a hint of that satisfaction made his heart rate jump.

*Remember, no stress. I don't want another heart attack.*

"This isn't the right time, Frank, so drop it. Get Calhoun back here...then we'll talk."

"I got you the cell phone. That was the deal. Now you're stalling?"

"Just do your job before I alter the deal further."

"Why you..." Frank reached into his suitcoat, stopped short and blanched.

"That's right." Massey stood him down. "Cops got your gun, not to mention my laptop and SUV. You're a goddamned screwup, Frank, so don't get ballsy with me."

Frank stepped back. "You promised, sir."

"Sue me."

A ding announced the lobby floor. The elevator bumped to a stop, the doors opened, and Frank stormed out. He rushed out the front entrance and scanned the sidewalk left and right. No Calhoun. The crowd had swallowed him whole. "Damn." It had been one setback after another with Massey and his so-called deal. After he eliminated Calhoun, what would he want next, a moon rock?

Meanwhile, Massey pushed the *sub-basement* button, and the elevator continued its descent.

*Breathe, dammit.*

He inhaled deeply to slow the hammering in his chest then held the cell phone close to his heart. Whatever Calhoun had in mind, he wasn't getting his hands on it again.

The elevator stopped, doors opened, and he stepped out to see Carlson typing at the main terminal. He looked frazzled: hair unkempt, lab coat wrinkled, like a mad scientist on a mission. The Cisco server hummed, lights flashed, and data scrolled down his monitor, a language Massey found as foreign as the gibberish spoken by the Rwenzori Mountain natives as they prayed to their stone monolith in homage to their ancestors in the afterlife. He stepped up behind Carlson. "What are you doing?"

"Systems check, sir. Our new employee did a fine job fixing the Cisco."

"Yeah. About him. He's the worm in a rotten apple."

Carlson turned in his chair, his brows canted with confusion. "What are you talking about?"

"Frank says he's the guy who had the cell phone all along. Stole it off O'Malley's dead body." Massey set the phone on the console. "We think he's pulling some kind of covert operation to get it back."

"Damn. I knew that guy was too good to be true."

Massey scanned the lab and noticed all the vacant work stations. "Where is everybody?"

"I gave them the day off."

"How come?"

"I don't need them for the cell phone tests." Carlson plugged a management cable into the StarTAC and connected it to the main terminal's serial port. The Cisco reported back with a message on the monitor: *DEVICE CONNECTED.* "Perfect."

Frank stormed out of the elevator and approached Massey. "Sorry, boss. He's long gone."

Massey scowled. "Get back out there and find him. He could destroy everything we've worked for."

"Screw Calhoun. He could be anywhere by now. I need to get Chloe's treatments started, so how about that check...right now...before I beat it out of you."

"Look, you cockroach. I'm not some little old lady—"

"I have an idea," Carlson jumped in. "We don't need to find him because he's going to come to us."

Massey grumped. "I'm listening."

"Calhoun's coming back tonight to add a backup

controller card to the Cisco, so it won't crash again." He pointed to the cell phone on the console. "We'll leave it right here, in plain view, and when he takes the bait, we'll lock down the lab and trap him like a rat."

Frank grinned. "Then I'll finish him for good."

"Problem solved." Carlson swiveled his chair to face the monitor. "I'm going to run some diagnostics on the phone, pull up the call history, see what's been going on since O'Malley flew the coop with it."

Massey nodded. "Let me know when you're ready to make a phone call. I want to be here."

"I will, sir."

For the first time in days, Massey felt relieved that the cell phone was back in good hands. "I'll be in my office. Frank, cool your jets and come with me. We'll wait for Calhoun upstairs."

"Meantime, you can write the check."

Massey led him to the elevator. "We'll talk about it."

"Damnit, boss..."

The doors closed, leaving Carlson to his work.

The lab, now specter-quiet but for the underlying hum of cooling fans, was again under Carlson's lone command. He punched on the keyboard: *commence diagnostics*. The servers probed the inner workings of the StarTAC to test and evaluate the phone's connectivity and call history. Shadows lurked throughout the lab as the results scrolled down the screen.

Working alone in the bowels of Massey, Inc., he felt like a forensic linguist deciphering languages and conversations from long-forgotten civilizations. He imagined blowing the dust off a cave wall and discovering how the ancient tribes communicated with each other.

Carlson caressed the phone as it lay on the console, communicating with the servers that would reveal its secrets. Like a purring kitten, it vibrated to his touch. His super-analytic mind couldn't fathom how the phone could communicate across the universe and probe the mysterious depths of the afterlife.

Then something amazing happened. The blue tarp covering the obelisk rippled with a pulsating rhythm. The ancient stone was alive, feeding on the cell phone's energy, and that haunting voice invaded his mind:

*"Ah...The cell phone...it's home...finally."*

Goosebumps rose on his skin and prickled. He rubbed his neck. "Just be quiet. Let me do my job."

*"I am the guardian of the secrets of the universe. A mere scientist like you cannot comprehend the things I know."*

"You don't know jack shit, not even what came first, the chicken or the egg."

*"The egg, you fool."*

"Oh, yeah? Then what laid the egg?"

*"The chicken, you fool."*

"You're driving me crazy." Carlson ran a hand through his hair. "We're not having this conversation."

The tarp started flapping like a torn sail broken loose from its mast in a stiff wind. He ran to the stone and fought to secure the ropes, but the storm was too fierce, and the tarp blew away.

The computer chirped.

He found himself back at the main terminal, staring at the monitor with wide-eyed wonder. There it was, the ones and zeros translated into Arabic, the last number dialed just like any person would text a message: M-I-R-I-A-M. O'Malley had dialed it, but it couldn't be that simple. The call was connected via the obelisk to a destination...huh? The coordinates were beyond anything he'd ever seen. No receiving IP address. No longitude. No latitude. However, it could have been some multi-dimensional trig-geometric grid-point beyond the universe, if he had to guess. He pressed his lips together.

*I don't believe it.*

The tarp fluttered. *"Believe it, Carlson. It's not as difficult to understand as your chicken or egg dilemma. It's as easy as one, two, three, pushing buttons."*

Carlson thought the tarp had blown away, but there it was, still securely in place. He jammed his hands over his ears like a man going mad in his own skin. "It can't be that simple."

*"You're a scientist. Test the hypothesis. Call Bart."*

"Call Bart?" He swore the obelisk had said that, but the idea must've been his own, conjured up in his mind as a way to solve a scientific mystery, as any good scientist would do. However, what did it matter who came up with the idea? He was on the brink of a discovery that would change all of humanity.

He lifted the cell phone from the console and left the management cable connected. A sudden angst rattled him. Massey wouldn't want him to make the first call without him.

*Might cost me my job.*

*"Do it,"* the obelisk demanded.

Gritting his teeth, he flipped the phone open, saw the

keypad, and felt as if he were face-to-face with the Holy Grail, a mere human with the power of God in his hands. His fingers tingled as he multi-tapped B. The keypad beeped. A. *Beep.* R. Beep. T. *Beep.* He held his breath then pressed *send.*

Cooling fans in the Cisco hummed louder. The Controller Card lights flickered with a new fury. On the monitor, a message flashed: *CALLING.*

Hand shaking, he held the phone to his ear. His breath shuddered at the enormity of this moment, as if he were about to contact an ancient civilization, long dead to the world but about to rise from the depths of the unknown.

Static crackled over the line, loud as lightning on a stormy night just before the boom of thunder. Amid the humming of server fans, a voice screamed from the phone. "Hello? Hello. Is somebody there? Help me. Help me."

Carlson's breath hitched. "Bart, is that you?"

Eerie moans and bellows followed...then a squeal like a wounded animal spilled into his ear.

*Crackle.*

His heart thumped with dread, but he had to stay the course, even as demonic screams shrieked from the phone. "Bart...where are you?"

"In pain... So...much...pain."

Carlson shifted his gaze to the obelisk, its tarp waving with fury, straining against the tie-down ropes as if some evil were trying to escape. "What's wrong with him?"

The obelisk remained silent.

"No more," Bart begged, sobbing amid a cacophony of screams all around him. "Please, I beg you."

In the background, a guttural voice reverberated like

distant thunder. "You reap what you sow."

Cold fear flushed through Carlson's veins. "Bart, who was that?"

"The devil...*crackle*...Who are you?"

"Carlson."

"Carlson, you little prick. I hear you...but I can't see you. Where are you?"

"In the lab. Are you inside the obelisk?"

"I'm in Hell, you idiot. Tell Massey...*crackle*...it's worse than advertised."

Carlson's mouth dried. "Why? Is he going to Hell?"

Screams echoed in the background. "Tell Massey to change his ways...to do something good with his money...something unselfish... Tell him to help other people...*crackle*...or he's going to find himself burning in Hell...right beside me."

"You can talk to the devil himself?"

"Not if I don't have to."

"Ask him a question for me. What came first, the chicken or the egg? I've got to know."

Guttural laughter thundered from the phone.

Bart screamed. "Help me. Someone, help me."

Carlson stood and shouted, "Ask him, damnit."

Screams and howls came next. The tarp was writhing and thrashing. The Cisco started smoking. Cables sparked and sizzled. Carlson feared another system crash was at hand. "Bart, I've got to go." He closed the flip phone with a sharp snap. The Cisco quieted, stopped smoking, and the monitor showed a message: *CALL ENDED.*

An icy hand broke into Carlson's chest and squeezed his thumping heart. "Son of a bitch." He set the phone on the console and turned his attention to the obelisk. It stood stoic on its platform, its tarp calm as could be, as if nothing had happened. "What the hell have you done?"

*"Done? Oh...I'm just getting started."*

# Chapter Twenty-Two

**M**y mouth was dry as I walked out the front doors of Massey's building. The doorman even nodded to me, respectfully, but my hands were shaking. I'd pulled off an impossible feat, fixed the Cisco server, got the job, and I was coming back tonight. A glass of whiskey was what I needed to calm down and stay on track.

Dozens of pedestrians walked up and down Riverside Boulevard, most with cell phones pressed to their ears. Yeah. There were billions of these phones in the world, but only one that could connect with my dad. I wanted to talk to him again so badly my chest hurt.

*Patience,* I told myself as I fast-stepped toward Lincoln Center where I caught the inbound subway to Grand Central Terminal. I'd be back tonight with a controller card for the Cisco, and figuring there'd only be a skeleton crew on duty, I could easily mask my incursion into the network and search for data on the cell phone O'Malley had died trying to defend. I also wanted to take a look under the tarp to see what technological wonder Carlson and his team had created.

As the subway rumbled forward, I settled into my seat and pondered over the StarTAC's amazing ability to take a call from someone in the afterlife. My dad had called me. *Does that mean there are cell phones in Heaven? In Hell?* The absurd thought made me grimace. At Vericom, we handled millions of cell phone calls a day, all meticulously routed through a vast network most folks never contemplate. It just worked. Dial mom; talk to mom. That simple. I shivered. What supernatural network could traverse Heaven and Earth to connect loved ones who'd long passed?

At Grand Central, I made the connecting northbound to Woodlawn, stared at the scenery rushing past the window, and thought about McGee's, wondering if Bridget would be there.

She was an awesome young woman, bright and cheery, and for some strange reason had her sights on me, for the long term. I couldn't keep blowing her off, but I had so much on my plate: Mom, for one, my job at Vericom, and the mess I'd gotten myself into when I met O'Malley in that dark alley. My life had been upended since Dad was murdered, and I didn't want to get Bridget involved, but her devotion to me never faltered.

I remembered my dad saying, "Make time for the essential things in your life, son. Tomorrow is never guaranteed." He was right. Bridget had proven she was one of those essentials, standing in the wings, waiting for me to get my act together. I had to chuckle as I envisioned how she strutted through Rory Dolan's, all moxie and full of attitude, serving drinks as Irish fiddles romped from the speakers. She'd do any man proud.

*Don't mess up a good thing, Sean.*

I got off the train at Woodlawn, and dodging passengers and panhandlers, I rushed out to the Camry. From here, it was a quick drive to McGee's where I ordered a Jameson on the rocks to calm my frazzled nerves. The whiskey was warm and smooth going down my throat.

Two patrons played darts while a white-haired man played a flute on a small stage in the corner. My thoughts wandered to the interview I'd just aced. It could have gone several ways: been tied up in background checks or derailed by competition from other applicants. However, my experience working at Vericom had paid off, even while Carlson gave me a hard time. I still had to wonder why I didn't have to speak to anyone from HR. They would have asked me about my termination at Vericom. The first thing a prospective employer did was check with the applicant's former boss. Carlson was able to hire me on the spot. Very strange. Left me with a lot of questions. How much did he know about the phone that was responsible for O'Malley's death? Did Carlson know Frank was a killer? Were they in cahoots? What plans did they have for the cell phone? Did the gizmo under the tarp have something to do with it, like maybe it was some kind of super router?

I took another sip of Jameson, thinking I was lucky Frank didn't show up while I was at Massey's. The interview would have become a matter of life and death.

A firm hand gripped my shoulder and I whirled.

"Easy there, stranger." Bridget smiled as she held a pool cue. "You're kinda jumpy today."

My throat tightened. "Oh, Bridget. Sorry. I was just thinking, is all."

"That shiner you got is looking better, but it'll be a while before I'll kiss that fat lip."

I put my finger on my lip and winced.

She tapped the butt of the cue on the floor. "Are you going to tell me what's going on?"

"It's nothing."

"You're in some kind of trouble, aren't you."

"I don't want to get you involved in my problems."

"Why won't you give me a chance to help you?"

"It's nothing I can't handle. I'm fine."

Her eyes narrowed. "You don't look fine."

I slugged down the rest of my whiskey, and while the grainy scent of the drink lingered on my breath, I wanted to loop my arms around her, pull her in close, and kiss her like a woman deserved to be kissed, fat lip or not, but, of course, I didn't. I just stared at my empty glass.

Bridget sighed. "Well...I got to get back to my game."

As she turned toward the pool table, I whispered, "Hey, wait."

She stopped. "What do you want, Sean?"

"I apologize...ah..." My thoughts tripped all over themselves.

"For what?" Her brow furrowed.

"For being a dick."

"Which time?"

"I've been under a lot of stress lately."

"You can handle it. Remember? That's what you said."

"I lied."

"So you're going to tell me—"

"Let's just say I'm getting close to fixing my problem."

"You can't trust me. Is that it?"

"I'll make it up to you."

"Are you serious? You walk all over my heart...how do you make up for something like that?"

"I don't know. I'm figuring this out as I go."

"Don't be messing with me, Sean."

I inhaled then decided to spell it out for her. "It's Mom. She's in the hospital. Montefiore, ICU."

Her eyes grew wide. "What happened?"

"The guy that did this to me..." I pointed to my face. "He did the same to my mom. I don't want you to be next."

She took a step back. "Me? He knows about me?"

"I don't know for sure, but he's out there somewhere. Detective Mullen is looking for him. He's wanted for murder."

"Murder? What-who?"

"Now do you see why I didn't want you involved?"

"This is supposed to be a safe neighborhood."

"No place is safe anymore."

She stepped in close and put her hand on mine. "Come over tonight. We can watch a movie. Share a bottle of wine. Catch up on lost time."

Hints of her perfume embraced me. "That sounds great, but..."

Her hopeful expression flatlined. "But what?"

"I have to work tonight."

She released my hand. "Jesus, Sean, you're killing me."

"Tomorrow, okay?"

"You know how lame that sounds?"

"Yeah. How about this for lame?" I stood from the barstool, gathered her up in my arms, and kissed her, a kind of side-lipped kiss, but I let her have it good. The pool cue clacked on the floor. She threw her arms around my neck and kissed me back. It had been a long time...damn it felt good to be back in her arms. The bar crowd started hooting and clapping. I hated to break away, but my lip felt like it was going to fall off.

She whispered in my ear, "It's about time you let me back in."

I pulled away and gazed into her eyes, surprised to see them a bit teary. "I'm working on it."

"Hey," one of her girlfriends shouted from the pool table. "What about our game? It's your shot."

"Keep your panties on," Bridget shouted back then winked at me. "I gotta go."

I retrieved her pool cue from the floor. "You watch your back, you hear?"

"You too, mister. Good luck with your mom."

Yeah. Good luck was what I needed. Especially tonight, when I get back to Massey's.

*Get in, do my job, get the cell phone data, and get the hell out of there.*

I signaled the bartender.

"Another whiskey for ya?" He grabbed the bottle of Jameson.

"Just the check."

"Coming right up."

While I dug out my wallet, I wondered what dangers awaited me tonight. I was lucky I hadn't run into Frank the first time. Tonight, I might not be so lucky. If Frank had his way, I was sure I'd never be seen or heard from again. Mom wouldn't last long knowing her husband and her only child were both dead. My chest tightened, and my frayed nerves simmered under Jameson's loving touch. I needed a backup plan, an ace up my sleeve, and for that I decided to call Detective Mullen.

As the phone rang, I drummed my fingers on the bar. The call went to voice mail. I rolled my eyes. "Detective, this is Sean Calhoun. I have a lead in the O'Malley investigation. I'll call you when I've got proof Frank Coletti was in on it."

I paid the bartender. "Keep the change."

He nodded. "Thanks, Sean."

As I was leaving, I noticed Bridget chatting with her girlfriends by the pool table. "See ya, Bridget." She turned and gave me the *Call Me* hand sign.

One of her friends asked, "Who is that hunk?"

My cheeks flushed. I was more of a nerd than a hunk, but as I left McGee's, I was smiling. The sun was getting low. I had to go see my mom, get a controller card from my spare parts collection at the house, and return to Massey's by 7:00.

*Make time for the essentials. Easier said than done.*

\*\*\*

My hands gripped the wheel with angst as I drove to Montefiore Medical Center. Nobody had called me from the hospital, so I had to guess there was no change in Mom's condition. She just had to get better. How much more could she go through and still cling to the will to live? I let out an exasperated sigh. Would I ever talk to her again? Would she be a vegetable for the rest of her life? The *essentials* had a way of slipping through my fingers without prior notice or care.

I parked in the emergency room lot, and I was out of breath from running by the time I got up to her room. She didn't look any different, still couldn't see her face. I found a nurse nearby, waved her into the room. "How's my mom?"

"She's holding her own." The nurse straightened the edge of my mom's blanket. "Her brain has stopped swelling. That's a good sign."

I needed that glimmer of hope, something I could cling to, instead of feeling so full of dread.

"There's been some elevated brain activity."

"That's good, right?"

"But not good enough for us to bring her out of her coma. She's still critical...could go either way."

I lowered my head, looked at the floor, and felt small as an ant. "It's all my fault. I should have been there."

*But no. I was on a wild goose chase for a cell phone with impossible powers.*

"Don't be so hard on yourself." The nurse checked the I-V drip. "What doesn't kill her will make her stronger."

Hoping she was right, I collapsed in the chair at Mom's bedside. The incessant beeping and *hiss-thump* of the machines were worse than slow torture. I could barely bring myself to look at her as she lay there, so lifeless.

"You're going to get better, Mom. It's not your time to go yet. You've just got to keep fighting your way back."

Her body shook. I jumped. Had she reacted to what I'd said, or was it just a random tremor? The beeping continued at its same monotone pace. She was hanging on by a thread. If only I'd taken that cell phone with me to work...

*Oh, God, what have I done?*

## Chapter Twenty-Three

**U**p in his penthouse office, Massey, with his arms folded on his desk, monitored Carlson's movements in the sub-basement lab. He appeared to be studying data on the screen in front of him, but when he caressed the phone like a pet hamster, Massey frowned. "What is he doing?"

Carlson's voice shouted from the monitor's speakers. "Just be quiet. Let me do my job."

Massey leaned forward. *Who's he talking to?* He panned the camera but saw no one else in the lab. *What the hell?*

"You don't know jack shit, not even what came first, the chicken or the egg... Oh, yeah? Then what laid the egg..? You're driving me crazy... We're not having this conversation."

A chill ran down Massey's spine. Carlson was talking to himself? Arguing? *Is he going mad?*

The computer chirped. Carlson jammed his hands over his ears. "It can't be that simple... Call Bart?" He glanced at the obelisk then picked up the StarTAC.

Massey clenched his jaw. *What's he going to do, make a phone call? He said he was just running tests.*

The keypad beeped four times.

"That son of a bitch." Massey tightened his fists as Carlson hit *send*.

*This is bullshit. I told him I wanted to be there for the first phone call. Carlson had smarts, but no common sense.*

Massey thought to run down to the lab and stop him, but he'd never get there in time, so he decided to wait it out here.

Cooling fans in the Cisco revved up. The Controller Card lights flickered with fury. Static fizzled and crackled from the speakers...moans and screams, then: *"Hello? Hello. Is somebody there? Help me. Help me."*

Massey's breath hitched as he recognized Bart's voice.

"Bart," Carlson shouted. "Is that you?"

*Crackle.*

"Bart...where are you?"

*"In pain... So...much...pain."*

Massey couldn't believe Carlson had connected with Bart in the afterlife.

*"No more,"* Bart begged, sobbing amid a cacophony of screams all around him. *"Please, I beg you. I can't take anymore."*

A guttural voice reverberated from the speakers. *"You reap what you sow."*

"Bart," Carlson shouted, "who was that?"

*"The devil..."*

Fear heated Massey's veins.

*"Who are you?"* Bart cried.

"Carlson."

*"Carlson, you little prick. I hear you...but I can't see you. Where are you?"*

"In the lab. Are you inside the obelisk?"

*"I'm in Hell, you idiot. Tell Massey...crackle...it's*

*worse than advertised."*

"Why? Is he going to Hell?"

Screams echoed in the background. *"Tell Massey to change his ways...to do something good with his money...something unselfish... Tell him to help other people...or he's going to find himself burning in Hell...right beside me."*

"What?" Massey couldn't breathe.

Guttural laughter thundered.

Bart screamed. *"Help me. Someone, help me."*

Sparks flew from the Cisco and smoke swirled.

"I gotta go." Carlson hung up.

Fighting panic, Massey slammed a fist on the desktop. "I'm not going to Hell," he shouted at the monitor. "I'm going to Paradise. I saw it for myself." Then reason took hold.

*If Bart's in Hell, why did I see him tending bar in Paradise?*

Massey's neck hairs prickled.

*Now I'm talking to myself...like Carlson. Are we both going mad?*

Carlson's monitor showed a message: *CALL ENDED.* He set the phone on the console and turned to the obelisk. "What the hell have you done?"

Massey stood, and leaning forward with his hands on the desk, realized Carlson was talking to the obelisk. Was it talking back to him? *Impossible. It's a rock.*

He shivered as Bart's warning echoed through his mind.

*I can't go to Hell.*

No. There was still a chance to save himself. Chloe,

Gateway

Frank's daughter... Salvation was already at hand.

He mashed the intercom button. "Janice."

"Yes, Mr. Massey."

"Where's Frank?"

"In the lounge on the phone with the hospital."

"Get him in here."

"Yes, sir."

He reseated himself and stared at the monitor where Carlson was typing at the main terminal, running system checks on the network, from the looks of the data on his screen. That call damn near crashed the Cisco again.

The doors swung open and Frank burst in. "Yeah, boss." His eyes widened. "You look like you seen a ghost."

Massey stood and faced Frank. "How's Chloe?"

Frank frowned. "The pain is getting worse. She's in bad shape. Another day's delay and she may never walk again."

"Then I suggest we get right on it." Massey sat down, pulled open his top desk drawer, and took out a checkbook. "Fifty grand, you say?" He picked up a pen. "Is that all?"

Frank's eyebrows rose. "For one treatment. She needs at least five."

"So, two hundred fifty thousand." He scribbled on the check as easily as if he were signing a Christmas card.

"Thank you, sir."

"It's the least I can do to help the poor girl, by God."

"You're a class act, Mr. Massey."

"A deal's a deal, right? You got me the phone and I held up my end." He looked up to the ceiling. "You hear that, God? I'm one of the good guys."

Frank tweaked his brows. "You okay, boss?"

"Never better."

Frank leaned forward with his hand extended. "I'll get it to the hospital right away."

"Not so fast." Massey put the check back into the drawer and closed it.

Frank scowled. "Hey, what gives?"

"Patience, my boy." Massey leaned to the intercom. "Janice, how fast can you get some reporters up here?"

"Reporters?"

"The Times, The Journal, CBS, NBC, CNN, Fox...all of them."

"I'll call around right away."

"I want them here in one hour...and a lawyer from the legal department."

"Anyone in particular, sir?"

"Someone who looks good on camera."

"How about Miss Duffy? Sharp. Professional."

"Fine. And get my wife up here too."

"I'll see if I can find her."

"Try the beauty salon. One hour. Everyone in the conference room." He tapped the off button and turned to Frank. "Get Clarissa to join us. The girl's distraught parents will play well for the media."

"Sir. I don't think she'll leave Chloe's side."

"She will if she wants the money. Tell her to bring a doctor and a bigwig from the hospital. It's showtime."

Frank gave Massey a thumbs up and left the office.

Massey returned his attention to Carlson on the monitor, who was typing at his terminal. The anger he felt for his super-tech waned. He called him on the direct line to the lab and watched him stop typing to pick up the desk phone.

"Boss, don't be mad." There was panic in his voice. "I should have called you...just got caught up in my excitement. This is incredible. Unprecedented. That call will go down in the annals of communication history...forever, sir."

"Save it, Carlson. I want to thank you for contacting Bart like you did...his message from Hell...was a godsend for me. Eye-opening. You have saved me from spending eternity with that bone-brain."

"He scared the hell out of me."

"Me too. Is the Cisco all right?"

"Perfect, thanks to Calhoun."

"It's a shame Frank's going to kill him." Massey disconnected the call and rubbed his forehead.

*I dodged a bullet, for sure. Now I'm going to assure my place in Paradise.*

*** 

An hour later, reporters swarmed Massey's conference room. Cameras on tripods towered along the back wall, and a technician tapped microphones clumped together on the conference table: *FOX, ABC, CNN, CBS, NBC.* "Testing...*thump-thump*...testing." Reporters with satchels strapped to their shoulders and Nikons in hand vied for front-row positions. The air was abuzz with chatter and hints of French vanilla coffee and fresh Boston cream donuts.

Massey, his chest swelling with pride, settled into a highbacked chair at the head of the conference table and examined the contract Miss Duffy had hurriedly drawn up:

*Concerning Chloe Coletti and MSK Kids Clinical Genetics and Pediatric Cancer Program; five experimental stem cell treatments; yada yada.*

Sharon sat to his right, dressed to the nines. Frank and Clarissa sat to his left. A bespectacled doctor and a hospital administrator sporting a bow tie flanked them.

Massey clacked a gavel. "Shall we get started?"

The chatter quieted. Camera shutters clicked. A sharply dressed reporter wearing a *NYTIMES* badge asked, "What's the big announcement, Mr. Massey?"

"Are you running for Mayor?" another threw in.

Massey held up his hands. "Gentlemen, ladies, this meeting isn't about me. It's about a sick little girl who needs our help. Her name is Chloe Coletti."

The reporters drew closer. "What's wrong with her?"

Massey extended a hand toward the physician in attendance. "Doctor Bradshaw, I'll refer that question to you."

He stood for the cameras. "Miss Coletti is suffering from a tumor that's pressing against her spinal cord so severely she cannot walk. It's inoperable." He sat down.

The administrator stood. "We at MSK Kids Clinical Genetics have available an experimental treatment for Chloe, however, it's expensive, and insurance companies don't cover the costs. We've been lobbying Congress to change that, but we've had no luck convincing those in power to save so many children like Chloe. I beseech everyone listening to contact their representatives and encourage them to enact legislation...for the kids." He sat down.

Frank and teary Clarissa leaned into each other and

hugged.

"Chloe is lucky," Massey put in. "I, my wife Sharon, and Massey Incorporated are hereby donating one-quarter of a million dollars to go toward her treatments."

"What's the catch?" a reporter asked.

"It's the right thing to do, the charitable thing to do, and I encourage all corporations across this country to do the same. Get out your checkbooks and help children in need."

Sharon squeezed Massey's forearm and smiled at him. "That's my husband. He's a saint."

Miss Duffy handed him a pen. He signed the contract. She picked it up and strode to the hospital administrator for his signature. Massey presented the check to Frank, who passed it to the doctor. "Use this money to make our Chloe walk again."

He nodded and accepted the check.

Applause broke out among the reporters and camera crews.

Massey grinned. His seat at the Tiki bar in Paradise was now assured.

## Chapter Twenty-Four

At MSK Kids Hospital, in a room decorated with childhood heroes: Mickey Mouse, Buzz Lightyear, and Captain America, Frank stood at Chloe's bedside and swallowed hard. Finally, she'd get the help she needed, experimental stem cell therapy, thanks to Ronald Massey's generosity. All anyone could do now was hope to the stars the treatments would work and that she would walk again.

Clarissa stood next to him and sobbed. Nothing could quell her angst, not Snowball, the stuffed dog on Chloe's lap, not the balloons with smiley faces floating above the bed, not the sparkly sign posted on the wall: WE LOVE YOU, CHLOE. GET WELL SOON. LOVE MOM AND DAD.

Frank's heart banged around in his chest. Arthur O'Malley had to die to make this day possible. It took madness and mayhem to retrieve the stolen StarTAC. He was sure he'd eventually land back in prison. Only time would tell if his relapse to a life of crime would pay off for Chloe.

A clear plastic tube dripping fluid from an I-V bag was connected to a needle in Chloe's arm. "Daddy, I'm scared." She clutched Snowball.

Frank held her hand. "Don't worry, sweetie. These doctors know what they're doing."

"I don't want to have an operation."

Clarissa wiped away a tear and sat next to Chloe on the bed. "It's not really an operation. Just a tiny needle hole in your hip."

"Well, I don't like it."

"You want to walk again, don't you?"

"Yes," she muttered.

Frank stood and tousled her hair. "All you have to do is go to sleep and let the doctors do the rest."

"Will it hurt?"

"So what if it hurts? You're a tough little girl, right?"

Chloe rolled her eyes. "Can I bring Snowflake with me?" She smiled at her stuffed dog.

"Absolutely. Snowflake will keep you safe."

Dr. Bradshaw strode in. "It's a go from admin."

An orderly wheeled in a gurney, followed by a nurse wearing scrubs.

Frank's heart skipped. "That was quick."

"Massey's check didn't bounce. Everything is ready."

Chloe's eyes shifted to Frank. "Will you be here?"

"The whole time." He looked down at his feet, felt a strangling grasp on his throat for telling her a lie. *I can't tell her I have to go back to Massey, Inc. and kill Sean Calhoun. That bastard has bested me at every turn, but I will have my pound of flesh. Hopefully, I can get back here before she wakes up.*

"Mommy?"

"Yes, dear. I'll be here too." She stood.

The nurse bent to Chloe. "Hey, princess. Let's go for a ride."

Frank picked up Chloe and carried her to the gurney,

where he laid her down gently. "Do what these nice people tell you."

"Okay." She hugged Snowflake.

The orderly wheeled her out. Dr. Bradshaw and his nurse followed.

A knot tightened in Frank's stomach. He was always the guy who got things done, with either his bare hands or a gun. Now he felt useless.

*I need to trust the doctor.*

Frank held Clarissa's hand and led her into the hallway where reporters surrounded them and shoved microphones up to their faces.

"You're Chloe's parents, right?"

"How does it feel to have Ronald Massey's support?"

"Is your daughter going to walk again?"

Cameras snapped pictures of the startled couple.

Frank clutched Clarissa under his arm to protect her from the vultures. The mob forced him to stop. "Let us through."

A buxom blonde in a red dress and heels stepped up and turned to face a camera. "This is Rebecca Grimes reporting live at MSK Kids with our top story. I'm here with Chloe Coletti's parents, benefactors of millionaire Ronald Massey's charity." She turned to Frank, "How's Chloe doing?" and pointed her microphone at him.

Frank gaped at the amount of press coverage Massey had mustered. Now his face would be on every television across the city, and every cop would know where to find him. *Screw them all.* "She has cancer. How do you think she's doing?"

"Stem cell therapy is groundbreaking technology. Is

she expected to walk again?"

His muscles tensed, fists clenched, and he wanted to slug someone. Chloe was being wheeled into surgery, and these clowns could be in the way of a last goodbye.

"How's Chloe taking it?"

"She's scared out of her wits and hugging her stuffed dog."

"That's so sad."

"Now let us pass before I say something you'll regret." He stepped forward but Rebecca blocked him.

"Are the stem cells a permanent cure for Chloe's cancer?"

"Move."

Clarissa chimed in. "Leave us alone."

Rebecca's showy smile never faltered. "We're rooting for you guys."

Frank muscled through the crowd to the surgical department's waiting room where he led Clarissa to the vacant seats against the far wall. The horde of reporters milled about, conversed with each other, and kept keen eyes on the double doors to the operating rooms.

Clarissa dropped into a chair and ran a hand across her face. "I can't wait for this to be over. That poor girl..."

Frank sat next to her. "There's nobody tougher."

She wrung her hands. "Yeah, you're right about that."

Frank leaned to her ear and whispered, "I've got to go now."

That set her aback. "Our daughter is in surgery and you're leaving? What's wrong with you?"

Frank shook his head. "Keep your voice down. I've got to go back to work."

"Are you out of your mind?"

The reporters looked at them.

"Inside voice, please. It's Massey. He's expecting me."

"What's so important that you would leave me alone with these jackals?" She used her outside voice and nodded toward the reporters for emphasis.

"It's business."

"It's bullshit." She folded her arms. "You're not leaving."

"I still have a job to do."

Clarissa's jaw dropped, then: "Give it a break, Frank."

"I'll be back before she wakes up."

"Don't bother."

"Come on, Clarissa. What gives?"

She turned to face Frank, eye-to-eye. "You're not the same man I married...since Chloe got sick, you've been gone a lot, doing whatever you do for Ronald Massey. Who knows what kind of trouble you've gotten yourself into? He didn't fork out all this money because he likes your looks."

"I earned that money."

"I think there's more to it than that."

"What do you want from me? I got the money. Chloe is going to walk again."

"At what price, Frank?"

"Who cares? I handled it."

"I wish you'd go back to fixing cars, work eight hours a day...come home at night...like you used to..." She sobbed.

He took her hands and squeezed them, as if their bond could never be broken. She was right, of course. He didn't even recognize himself anymore. Some force inside him wouldn't let it rest. Sean Calhoun had to die. Maybe then he'd find peace again, probably in an eight-by-ten cell on Riker's Island. Didn't matter. Chloe was all that mattered.

"Frank?"

"Look...Clarissa." He breathed. "This shithole I've got myself into is deeper than you can imagine. You should thank me for keeping you out of it...but I'll make it right. After tonight. You'll see."

"Frank. No. Don't go. Stay here with me. Please. Whatever's out there...it's not worth it."

"Ah...but it is. A man's got his pride."

She yanked her hands from his grasp. "Pride goeth before the fall, Frank."

His stomach sank as he stood. "I've got to go." He lowered his head, shoved his hands in his pockets, and turned to push through the crowd toward the exit.

\*\*\*

In the washroom outside Operating Room Ten, Dr. Bradshaw scrubbed his hands. The water was hot but not scalding, and the antimicrobial soap was lathered up to his elbows and smelled like his grandmother. His thoughts shifted from hospital bureaucracy to his quarter-million-dollar patient lying on the table in the next room. He'd done this procedure countless times. Some successes were greater than others; some failures were heartbreaking but inevitable. He had no idea which way the scale would tip for Chloe Coletti, but he'd made a mental promise to her: "I'll do my very best."

While the scrub nurse helped him into his latex

gloves, he repeated his mantra to himself: *repair, regenerate, restore.*

Hands held up as to not touch anything, Bradshaw pushed his back against the swinging door and entered the operating theater. Chloe lay on the table, attended by an anesthesiologist, two nurses, and one intern, all decked out in their surgical garb. The nurses turned Chloe on her left side and arranged blue cloths to expose her right hip area. She looked so small and vulnerable under the gigantic overhead lamp.

A cardiac monitor beeped out Chloe's heart rhythms. Dr. Bradshaw looked over her vitals, and satisfied she was stable, moved to an instrument stand where small bowls, bone marrow needles, scissors, and sterile towels lay at the ready. He looked over his team. "Let's get to work."

\*\*\*

In the surgical waiting room, Clarissa paced the floor; every nerve in her body prickled. Hospital staff hustled by, and reporters lounged about, waiting for the scoop on Chloe's condition, but she felt so alone. Abandoned. How could Frank leave her at this critical time? She hated him for that and wanted to scream.

After another lap, she flumped back into her chair, stared at her knees, and pressed her elbows against her side. Part of her wanted to make herself smaller and invisible. She felt barren as a tree in the dead of winter.

*It's not fair.*

She dug her fingers into her temples. The worry over Chloe's condition had brought her to tears many times. However, this wasn't one of those times. With Frank gone, she had to be strong for Chloe. The treatments might not be successful. She may never walk again. Pain could be her constant companion. To see her daughter trapped in a wheelchair for the rest of her life... the heartbreak would be unbearable, not for herself, so much, but for all the experiences Chloe would miss: dancing at her prom, walking down the aisle at her wedding, hiking and biking, and everything else life had to offer ambulatory people. Clarissa felt a chill deep in her chest. The thought of pushing Chloe around in a wheelchair seemed overwhelming, but if that came to pass, they'd both survive. She was strong. Chloe was strong. Frank? Who knew if he'd even be around, especially when they needed him the most, like today, right now. His steady hand would be of some comfort, a shared dread they'd face together. But no. He had to go back to work for Ronald Massey.

Once Frank got something in his head, it was impossible to change his mind, and that was his greatest strength, after all, he'd do anything for Chloe. However, Massey had turned that strength into a weakness. He'd used Chloe to compel Frank to do whatever Massey ordered him to do, and that loyalty was too much for her to comprehend. Now Massey had turned Chloe's illness into a media circus that fed his millionaire ego. She feared they'd never be free of his influence on them.

She wished Frank had never quit his auto repair job. How simple their lives were before Chloe's horrible diagnosis, before Ronald Massey, before the media shined a spotlight on their troubles. They didn't need a lot of money to be happy. Their happiness was their togetherness, and now they were apart.

Jim Keane

*I love you, Frank, but you're driving me away.*

***

Back in Operating Room Ten, Dr. Bradshaw turned to the procedure at hand. Pressing his gloved fingers on Chloe's small pelvic bone, he felt for an adequate place to extract bone marrow aspirate concentrate, BMAC, which would be rich in stem cells. These stem cells had the ability to assimilate themselves to other cells within an organ, replace defective or cancerous cells, and alleviate pain or other maladies. He'd worked on the cutting edge of these new technologies, knew their potential benefits and shortfalls, and hoped the best for this little girl.

"Right here looks good. Marker." He held out his hand.

A nurse set a black marker in his upturned palm while the other nurse prepared an antiseptic wipe.

He marked the girl's pale skin, set the marker aside, and accepted the wipe, which he used to sterilize the immediate area.

The intern stepped in closer.

A nurse handed him the bone marrow needle, an odd-looking instrument with a narrow steel needle and a blue plastic 'T' handle, much like a corkscrew handle but with a screw-on cap in the center. He unscrewed the cap and retracted the inner rod that stabilized the needle to prevent bending.

"Looks good." He reinserted the rod and tightened the cap.

The intern didn't miss this safety step.

Bradshaw glanced up at Chloe's masked face, made

~204~

eye contact with the anesthesiologist, who nodded, and satisfied she was sedated properly, placed the needle tip on the mark and shoved it in until it stopped when metal struck bone. A trickle of blood escaped past the needle.

A nurse dabbed at the wound with a fresh antiseptic wipe.

"All right," he muttered and moved the tip across the edge of her pelvic bone to be sure he was centered then twisted the 'T' handle back and forth while applying firm pressure on the bone. Over the years, he'd developed a feel for how far the needle penetrated the outer shell, when it broke through to the marrow, and how deep to go before he stopped applying pressure. Kids were a tough call, as it would be easy to run clear through the bone. He felt the faintest loss of resistance and stopped. "Got it."

He released the instrument. It held firm as he unscrewed the cap and removed the long rod. Now the needle could bend to the inner contour of bone without poking through it.

The nurse took the rod from his hand and replaced it with a threaded plastic syringe. He screwed it onto the 'T' handle threads and retracted the plunger. The syringe began to fill with BMAC, a dark red liquid more precious than gold. He pushed the needle in a little farther to assure the tip remained implanted in the rich fluid. Once the syringe filled, he unscrewed it from the handle. The nurse traded him for an empty syringe, with which he repeated the procedure then placed the second filled syringe on a tray next to the first one. "It's all yours," he told the nurse.

She left the operating room and headed for the sterile lab where the BMAC would be placed in a centrifuge that would separate the stem cells from the platelets and other blood-matter.

Bradshaw pulled out the bone marrow needle and set it aside before stepping away from the operating table. The remaining nurse cleaned the wound and applied a bandage.

The intern stepped up next to him. "How long before the poor girl recovers from this procedure?"

"The bandage can come off tomorrow, and she'll be sore for a few days, but that's not the half of it. We still have to introduce the stem cells to the tumor on her spine."

"Then what?"

"We wait for a miracle."

*** 

In the waiting room, Clarissa sat alone and sniffled as she held her cell phone and looked at a picture of Chloe on a swing in the playground. She remembered carefree days, pushing Chloe higher and higher while her giggles and sunshine warmed a mother's heart.

However, that ended with the blare of a siren, a frantic ride in an ambulance while Chloe screamed in pain. Her back hurt and she couldn't walk.

Then came the analgesics, the doctor appointments, the test, x-rays, IMRs, and CT scans until Chloe was more like a zombie than a little girl. Now she'd been in the operating room for two hours, and Clarissa was trapped in the waiting room under the reporters' watchful eyes. Loneliness felt like abandonment. Minutes crept by like days in a week, months in a year, and years in an eon.

"Where are you, Frank?" she muttered. He should have been back by now.

A sudden image slammed into her mind: Chloe sprawled on the ground next to a toppled wheelchair. *Mommy, I can't walk. My back hurts. Help me, Mommy. Where's Daddy?*

She shuddered at the vision and closed the photo app.

Rebecca's heels clopped on polished tile as she approached. Odd that she wasn't holding a microphone, and no cameraman followed her. "Mrs. Coletti..."

Her jaw clenched. "What do you want now?"

"Can I buy you a coffee at the cafeteria?"

"Why? So you can get your big scoop on my daughter?"

"I'm a mother, too."

"Then you understand why I'm not leaving this seat."

"I do. How about I bring you a cup?"

"That would be nice."

"Meanwhile, you can freshen up a bit...for Chloe."

"I must look a fright."

"The treatment should be finished soon."

"I hope so."

"Everything's going to work out. You'll see. I'll be right back." Rebecca walked out, her stride confident in those heels as the reporters moved aside to let her pass.

Clarissa ducked into the ladies room, looked at her worried face in the mirror, and thought there was no hope for her. She dabbed water on her face, fluffed her hair, and walked back to her seat in the waiting room.

Rebecca returned with coffee in a lidded Styrofoam cup. "It's not Starbucks, but it's something."

"I appreciate it."

"No worries. If you get an update, please let me

know."

She nodded. "Sure."

*Maybe they're not all a bunch of jackals.*

Rebecca returned to her huddled comrades.

Clarissa took a sip of coffee. It was scalding hot and bitter on her tongue. She set it on the side-table, fearing she couldn't eat or drink anything as long as Chloe lay in the operating room.

Dr. Bradshaw pushed through the doors and waved off the reporters charging toward him. "Give me some space."

Clarissa's bloodstream took a shot of adrenaline. She stood. "How's my baby?"

"She's fine. Come with me." Bradshaw led her to a private examination room and closed the door.

"Please tell me you have good news."

He sat on a swivel stool. "Take a seat." He indicated an armchair. "Relax."

Her heart galloped. "Easier said than done, doc." The cushy chair didn't ease her anxiety.

"Where's your husband?"

"Working. He should be back soon."

"Shall I wait—"

"No. Please. How did it go?"

"The first treatment went well."

She held back a breath of relief. "Is she going to walk again?"

"I hope so. She has four more treatments to go, so only time will tell, however, her pain should diminish within a few days."

"That'll be a big improvement. Thank you so much."

"I'm glad I could help."

"Can I see her now?"

Bradshaw shook his head. "Not yet. The nurse will come get you when Chloe is ready for visitors."

"I can't wait to see her."

"She'll be happy to see her parents, as well." His brow furrowed. "Maybe her dad will be back by then."

Clarissa's face heated, a little from embarrassment but a lot more from anger.

*What's taking him so long?*

# Chapter Twenty-Five

At the 47th Precinct station, Detective Mullen sat at his desk, typing up a report on the O'Malley case. He glanced at the vacant interview room where he should have been grilling his prime suspect, Frank Coletti. As of yet, nothing had come back on the BOLO. Frank was in the wind.

It was suppertime and Mullen couldn't blow off another spaghetti and garlic toast dinner with his family, especially since tonight was his son's birthday party. He'd really be in the doghouse if he missed that one.

He sipped on stale coffee. The DA was expecting this report within the hour, and then he could go home. Better late than never. He rubbed his temples and wished he had good news about a break in the case.

Sergeant Ray McNulty, team leader of the Criminal Apprehension Team (CAT), a brown-bearded man in a camo Kevlar vest with *POLICE* imprinted on the front, camo jeans, black boots, and a Yankees hat on backwards, entered the squad room and strode to Mullen's cubical. "You got a minute, detective?"

Mullen pushed his chair back from the computer. *I hope he has good news.* He stood and shook Ray's hand. "Any sign of Coletti?"

"My team has been canvassing the area where Coletti was last seen. We got his house staked out, but nobody's been home all day."

"Shit. He couldn't have just disappeared."

"He'll turn up, make a mistake, and we'll be ready to pounce."

"Then why are you here and not out there pouncing?"

"I hoped you'd have a record of his recent contacts. Friends, accomplices, anywhere else we can look."

"It's all in the file, Ray. Frank's been off the radar for ten years, and suddenly, he hasn't reported to work for a month."

"I talked to his boss at the auto shop. He's no help, and his sidekick, Bart Marconi, nobody's seen him, like he fell off the face of the earth. Got any ideas?"

"I can't help you." Mullen flumped into his seat. "I gotta get this report done for the DA. He's chomping at the bit to issue a murder warrant, but I don't have any proof Frank had killed O'Malley. I'm hoping he'll talk when you bring him in."

Ray set a hand on his holstered Glock. "We don't expect him to come quietly."

"I want him alive, Ray."

"That isn't up to me. It's up to Frank." He executed a military about-face and marched out.

Mullen leaned back and looked at a potted plant wilting on his desk. It was dying, just like the O'Malley case, just like his hope to get home in time for dinner. He scooted forward and went back to typing his report.

*Leads have dried up, but I've got a CI out there working an angle on Coletti's connection to O'Malley. CAT is looking to pick him up. I'd like to interrogate him before going forward on a murder charge.*

Forensics tech Rodriguez walked up behind him. "Got something for you."

Mullen stopped typing. "I hope so. I'm just spinning my wheels here."

"Got a handle on the laptop recovered at the park."

Mullen's heart pumped faster as he turned to the tech. "Let's have it."

"Belongs to Ronald Massey."

Mullen raised his eyebrows. "What would a millionaire's laptop be doing at a crime scene?"

"Interestingly, we found some encrypted software that appears to have tracking ability, and based on GPS coordinates, Frank must've been using it to follow Sean Calhoun."

Mullen's mind churned with questions. *How can a person be tracked? Did he have a device with GPS, like his phone, but why would Frank track Sean's phone?* He ran a hand through his hair. *What was the GPS tracking? What's the connection between a common thug, Frank Coletti, and the big-shot millionaire, Ronald Massey? Was Coletti working for him? Did he have a beef with Sean Calhoun?*

Rodriquez asked, "Are you okay, detective?"

"Oh...yeah." Mullen cleared his head. "Thanks for the update."

"You need some rest, sir."

"Is that all?"

Rodriguez took the hint and headed for the break room.

*I guess I better go to Massey, Inc. and ask a few questions. Tomorrow. I got a birthday party tonight.*

As Mullen added the final touch to his report:

*Sincerely, Detective Tom Mullen, NYPD Homicide,* a ruckus erupted in the break room. Rodriguez ran back in, wide-eyed. "Mullen, you gotta come see this."

"What is it?"

"Coletti's on TV. How stupid can he be?"

Mullen shot out of his seat, confused but curious, and sprinted with Rodriguez into the break room.

Ray McNulty stood in front of the television with his arms folded, surrounded by other detectives and cops. On the television, a news reporter everyone knew as Rebecca Grimes pointed a microphone at none other than their fugitive Frank Coletti. "How's Chloe doing?"

A sign on the wall behind Frank read: MSK Kids. "She has cancer. How do you think she's doing?"

Mullen dropped his jaw. There was more going on with Frank than murder and mayhem.

Ray turned to Mullen. "Like I said, he'd make a mistake, and this one is a doozy."

Rebecca carried on. "Stem cell therapy is groundbreaking technology. Is she expected to walk again?"

A camera framed Frank Coletti's face better than any wanted poster ever could. "Now let us pass before I say something you'll regret."

"His kid has cancer," Rodriguez put in. "How sad."

"I'll send in a CAT team to apprehend him." McNulty grabbed his radio mike. "He'll be behind bars in a New York minute."

"Stand down, Sergeant." Mullen felt a father's empathy. "Bad PR. He's got a sick kid in surgery. Imagine we roll in to MSK Kids with guns drawn to take down a felon while all of New York sees him as a concerned father. The press will eat us alive. We'll get him later."

McNulty frowned. "Later? We've been bustin' our asses—"

"We know he's connected to the laptop, and we know the laptop is connected to Ronald Massey. Sooner or later, he'll turn up at Massey, Inc."

"Come on, detective. We've got him dead to rights on vehicle theft and assault, not to mention a felon in possession of a firearm. We know where he is. What are you waiting for?"

"Proof of murder. That'll put Coletti away for good. He'll be just as guilty tomorrow."

*Murder is worth waiting for.*

"Hold on," Rodriquez jumped in. "His gun wasn't the murder weapon. That's a problem for your case."

"You think I don't know that? There's a missing piece to this puzzle, and I aim to find it, but right now, I've got a birthday party to attend." Mullen returned to his cubicle to send the report to the DA, get his coat, and turn out his lights.

The desk phone rang.

Dread stabbed his heart, cold as any blade. He picked up. "Detective Mullen."

"You want proof that Frank Coletti killed Arthur O'Malley? Meet me at Massey, Inc. I'll be in the sub-basement lab. There's a black elevator. Take it down and bring backup."

"Sean, don't go in there alone. Wait—"

*Click.*

"for me." Mullen slammed down the receiver. "God

damnit." *There goes the birthday party.* He grabbed his coat. "McNulty. Gear up. We're going in."

\*\*\*

I hung up the phone and hoped reinforcements would arrive before I got myself killed. Cold night air prickled the sweating pores on my face. I was a block away from Massey's building, gripping a satchel that carried a refurbished CC for the Cisco, a leftover from a Vericom job that I'd collected, along with other electronic parts that would have been trashed. Controller Cards were a dime a dozen in my world of technology but priceless in my bid to retrieve the StarTAC and talk to my dad again. My stomach lurched. What price would I pay in the end?

My gaze darted to the pedestrians nearby, the shadows broken and scattered by somber streetlights and passing headlights. Was Frank Coletti nearby? Was he waiting somewhere to shoot me on sight? I'd been lucky the first times we'd tangled. Would I be as lucky this time? Every muscle in my body tensed on high alert.

*Relax.* I exhaled. I had it all figured out. I'd get in, install the controller, shut down the video surveillance, then with any luck, find the cell phone. I had to talk to my dad again, somehow, someway. How many other people could say they'd talked to a loved one who'd passed away? There was so much I wanted to tell him: how I missed our Yankee games together, steak dinners, trips back to Ireland...how much mom missed him. How much our lives had changed since he was murdered, but most of all, I wanted to say goodbye, thank him for taking good care of us over the years, and say *I love you* one last time.

I'd walked the remaining block to Massey's headquarters and now stood before the lighted entrance doors. People walked in and out, going on their merry ways with no clue of what I was about to do. I wanted to tell myself I would risk my life for my mom, for Bridget, and for our future, but I knew it was more about me and that horrible emptiness I felt as I waited for my dad to join me at McGee's on that fateful night. Some punk had ripped out the last chapter of our story from the book of our lives, and no phone call could mend the torn pages but only put a period on the last sentence of our time together.

Filled with determination, I pulled the door open and stepped inside.

# Chapter Twenty-Six

**W**hen I entered the expansive lobby of Massey, Inc., dark fear spread through me like the wings of a raven. I clutched a satchel that carried the Cisco Controller Card and inhaled the zesty smell of lemon wax on the glistening marble floors. A cleaning crew was busy at work, polishing Massey's shrine to his riches. The security guard, a brute I'd not seen before, sat behind the security desk and inspected me with dark, hooded eyes. "Can I help you?"

"I'm Sean Calhoun." I lifted the satchel. "Got a part for a computer in the lab downstairs."

"Sean Calhoun, you say?" The guard checked the screen in front of him. "Here it is. Seven o'clock. You're right on time."

"Pays to be punctual." I glanced around for any sign of Frank.

The guard looked up. "Okay. You're all signed in."

"Thanks."

Relieved the guard hadn't given me the third degree, I strode to the black elevator. Within the hour, I should have the StarTAC and, hopefully, talk to my dad again.

As the doors closed and the elevator propelled me toward the subterranean depths of Massey's building, a frightening scenario shot into my mind. *The elevator stops. The doors open. Frank is standing there with a gun pointed at me. "You're dead meat, Calhoun."* Bang! *Fire. Smoke. Darkness.*

My heart thrashed, and I fell against the back wall, grasped the rail, and gulped air. If my fears materialized, I'd be trapped in this death chamber with nowhere to go. I had to hope the thug wasn't down there.

Another terrible notion crept into my brain. What if I never left this building alive? My poor mom. What if she had battled for her life, only to recover and learn that her son was dead? Shot to death. The loss, along with Dermot's, would bury her in despair so deep she would never survive.

And what about Bridget? What about us? Our future would be lost, as well. Yeah. The stakes were high. I'd come this far. There was no going back. I inhaled shallow breaths to steel my nerves. At least I had one thing going for me. The cavalry was coming. However, until Mullen and his men arrived, I'd have to stick with the plan. The elevator stopped. I stepped to the door to await my fate.

As the elevator opened, I raised the satchel to my chest as a shield and clenched my teeth, fully expecting Frank to shoot me.

When I realized I was alone, my shallow breathing returned to normal.

I stepped into the lab and called out, "Carlson? Are you here?" My voice echoed back from the void, but there was no answer, only the hum of electronic cooling fans and the squeak of my shoes on the polished tile as I ventured forward. I glanced down the row of servers, their status lights flickering in the shadows.

"Carlson?"

No answer.

On the far wall, beyond all the computer terminals, loomed that ten-foot-tall object concealed under a blue tarp. What kind of gadget had Massey and his minions developed? Some kind of super router capable of communicating with the dead? How did it tie into the StarTAC? The nerdy geek inside me had to know. I stepped toward it, determined to lift the tarp and see for myself, when I noticed the surveillance cameras positioned around it, their *active* green lights blinking. I'd have to disable them first, so I turned to the main terminal, where I set the satchel on the countertop. There, to my shock and amazement, lay the cell phone that had nearly gotten me and my mom killed. I couldn't believe it. Why was it lying here as insignificantly as a paperclip? Did Massey want me to see it? They had to know why I was here. I looked up at a camera pointing down at me, its green light winking. They had to be watching. The hairs on the back of my head prickled.

*Stick to the plan.*

I opened the satchel and removed the Controller Card. It was crowded with microchips, micro-relays, and micro LEDs. As it was refurbished and used, it wasn't protected in a static-proof envelope, which was okay, as I didn't care if it worked or not.

I caught a motion in the shadows down the server aisle and saw Carlson step into the light, head down as he eyed his ever-present iPad. My heart took a jolt of surprise. "Damn. You scared the shit out of me."

He looked up, a bit wide-eyed, as well. "Oh, Calhoun. Nice of you to make it. I thought you might not show."

"I didn't think anybody was here. Why didn't you answer when I called your name?"

He paced up to me, cool as could be. "Obviously, I didn't hear you come in."

That didn't seem possible, but I didn't let on that I didn't believe him.

He patted one of the servers like a proud father. "Just making sure these babies are okay." He peered at the cell phone on the countertop then looked back at me. "Do you have everything you need?"

"Oh, yes." I held up the CC as evidence. "I was just about to get started."

"Then I'll leave you to it." He strolled to the elevator. The doors opened and he stepped inside. "See you tomorrow." The doors closed.

"Damn." I needed that elevator down here...for a quick getaway. Now, when I grabbed the cell phone, I'd have to wait for it to come down.

Looking at the StarTAC, I felt like a mouse tempted by a piece of cheese in a trap that would break my neck. I gulped.

*Stick with the plan.*

\*\*\*

In the penthouse office, Massey sat in front of the security monitors on his desk, watching Sean Calhoun install the CC in the Cisco. Massey was no tech. He wouldn't know if Calhoun was inserting it correctly or upside down. What he did know, the StarTAC was clearly visible on the countertop and he would soon witness Calhoun's attempt to steal it.

Frank was looking over Massey's shoulder. "I hate that guy."

Carlson entered the office and joined them at the desk. "Anything?"

"Not yet," Frank muttered.

"How's your daughter?" Carlson asked.

"I don't know. Probably fine, but my wife is pissed. I should be there with her, but no, I gotta kill this shithead." He pointed at the screen. "Once he takes the bait, he's all mine."

"I like the way you think," Massey said, eyes on his prey.

"I can't wait to have a couple minutes with him." Frank slammed a fist into his open palm. "I'll toss him around like a rag doll, punch him in the gut, break some ribs, and stomp on his face, then kill him with my bare hands." He made claws with his fingers and closed them into hard-knuckled fists.

Massey slid open his desk drawer and took out a gun, a Sig Sauer .45, and set it on his desk. "Here you go, Frank. I hate to ruin your fun, but this will be quicker."

"A bullet is too good for him."

"Plug him and toss his body into the obelisk."

Carlson huffed. "I don't think it works that way."

Frank took the gun and snarled. "I don't care how it works. I want to be done with him and get back to my family."

***

The cell phone was so close...I wanted to snatch it up and get the hell out of there. However, I needed to focus on the job at hand, which was to install the Controller Card, disable the security cameras, peek under the tarp then grab the phone and get to the elevator, posthaste.

I sat in front of the Cisco server and opened the panel to reveal the bank of CCs. One of them was missing. Cooling fans hummed inside the frame, blowing air on my face that smelled of warm electrolytes. Normally, I'd ground myself with an anti-static wristband to safeguard the card against any unwanted shock, but this time I didn't bother. I held the card with both hands and lined it up with the tracks on the bottom of the slot. Slowly, I slid in the card and closed the handles on the top and bottom to lock it in. The standby light came on and the card started booting up. It would take a couple minutes for the card to load and update, giving me time to execute the rest of my plan.

I closed the panel and moved to the main terminal. This would be the tricky part, finding the security camera program without raising suspicion. To start the ruse, I typed *Mask System Search* then *Security Cameras* then *Execute*. The search window was blank, in case anyone was monitoring the network.

I pounded away at the keyboard, eyes darting to the screen and back to my fingers as I acted like I was pinging the CC to the system. I knew the *Mask* command hid what was really going on:

*Searching... Searching... Searching...*

I could have been a hacker for the CIA, breaking into the KGB's network and saving the world.

Servers hummed. Lights blinked. Fans whirred. I was waiting for a beep to signify the search was completed.

Seconds passed, but nothing happened. I rubbed my

temples.

*Come on.*

I didn't have all night. There was no way I could tell if Massey or his security people had been alerted to my incursion into their system. A knot tightened in my stomach. I was so close to getting the cell phone. I thought to grab it and run, but I wanted to peek under that blue tarp before I left. It was imperative to shut down those cameras.

I had to stall for time, got up from the main terminal, and returned to the Cisco. Just in case I was being watched, I opened the panel and futzed with the CC, poked it, inspected it, and hoped my actions looked legit.

The computer chirped. I rushed the few steps back to the main terminal and saw Server 4B had popped up on the screen. A message flashed in a red window.

DISABLE CAMERAS? Y/N?

My heart raced. It was game time. Two minutes max. One second's delay would bring Massey and his thugs down on me like a plague over Egypt.

I punched the Y key.

\*\*\*

Detective Mullen gripped the wheel of his Ford Taurus as he followed two NYPD patrol cars through heavy traffic, their overhead lights flashing and sirens wailing. They weaved right and left, hit the shoulder, and squeezed into spaces not fit for a scooter. Sean Calhoun had done a foolish stunt, going in without backup. Mullen could only hope they'd arrive before he got himself killed.

Sergeant Ray McNulty trailed him in an unmarked SUV. All of CAT had been dispatched to Massey, Inc.

Sirens trilled across Manhattan in a desperate race to serve and protect.

The blue and white strobes across the top of Mullen's windshield reflected off the civilian vehicles around him, some giving way, others reluctant to move over into already cram-packed lanes. McNulty's emergency lights flashed in Mullen's rearview mirror, the SUV hard on the Ford's bumper. "Some goddamned birthday party."

A sea of cars and trucks snailed southward on the Major Deegan Expressway. The posse charged along the break-down lane, throwing dust and dirt into a whirling maelstrom. Mullen's Ford Taurus whined like a well-oiled machine and sped past the standstill of regular folks just trying to cope with the ills of life in New York City.

"Coming up on 95," the lead patrolman radioed. "Stay to the right."

Mullen tore up the shoulder and accelerated with the boys in blue leading the charge. His heart raced with excitement and dread. He'd spent his years in homicide solving murders. This was a rare time when duty called him to prevent a murder. "Fucking Sean."

A compact car veered onto the shoulder, the driver obviously panicked by all the lights and sirens. Mullen swerved to avoid a collision, but McNulty wasn't so kind. The SUV bulldozed the idiot into the crash wall and continued the frantic pace toward the George Washington Bridge.

Mullen dialed Sean's cell phone. The call went right to voicemail. Several redials came with the same results. Tendons tangled to knots in Mullen's shoulders. Why would Sean risk his life by inserting himself into the

O'Malley investigation? *Is he trying to one-up me for not solving his father's murder?* He'd better have solid proof against Frank Coletti, or this fiasco could end in disaster.

Mullen's chest tightened as he hugged the patrol car's rear bumper while his escorts pressed and weaved through traffic. He released a breath when they edged onto the Henry Hudson off-ramp, where the flow of cars thinned out.

*This should save us some time.*

He could only hope that Sean hadn't already found a way to get himself killed.

## Chapter Twenty-Seven

In the sub-basement lab of Massey's building, the clock was ticking. Two minutes and counting. I'd disabled the video security system then glanced up at the camera watching me. The blinking green light went out, telling me the cameras had no backup program. Easy-peasy. I snatched the cell phone from the countertop. My heartbeat quickened. The prospect of speaking with my dad again was now in my grasp. I'd just have to get out of here alive.

Pocketing the phone, I had a good idea what Massey and his security goons were doing. Freaking out. Somewhere within the building, in a control room with floor-to-ceiling monitors, I imagined, panic erupted as those monitors went black. Someone had surely sounded the alarm, and security was no doubt troubleshooting the problem, which would soon lead them to my hacking down here at the main terminal. I had no time to lose and sprinted to the blue-tarped gizmo. There was a broken section of the four-foot wood-slat fence around it, so I stepped through the gap, fully prepared to be amazed at some state-of-the-art supercomputer, more modern, intelligent, and much faster than IBM's Big Blue. Instead, I found myself stymied at the array of nautical knots in the tie-down ropes.

"Shit." If only I had a pocketknife. This was going to set me back precious seconds I couldn't afford to lose. I should have abandoned the idea, right then and there, but no. I had to quench my curiosity, so I tackled the knots on the front corner ropes.

Got one loose. *Tick-tick.* Got two. *Tick-tick.* Got three loose then lifted the tarp's corner enough to get a good look under it. Instead of unveiling a new and historic discovery that could connect a cell phone across time and space, I found a giant rock. I raised my eyebrows in wide-eyed shock.

All this trouble for a fucking rock? This had to be some kind of sick practical joke.

*Tick-tick.*

Oh, it was a pretty rock, all right. The granite surface was aglitter with knobby crystals, maybe diamonds, for all I knew, and stranger still, a splay of wires were attached to various places, like the leads of an EKG machine to a fat man's chest. The wires gathered into cables that snaked back to the Cisco I'd repaired, a macabre coupling between eons-old geology and modern-day technology.

*Tick-tick.*

I ran a hand across the crystalline stone and wondered how it could be transferring information to a server, or vice versa. There had to be a computer-to-computer or router-to-router connection, not a stone-to-computer link. Both had to speak the same language and have the same communication protocols. This connection was inconceivable. I'd seen nothing like it during my twenty years in the telecommunications business. I could string together DB9, female-to-male, connectors over a serial cable to hook up a laptop to a router, but this configuration made no sense to me.

## Jim Keane

The Cisco beeped, slamming me back to the here-and-now. A bucket of cold water couldn't have done any better. The CC boot-up and update were completed. My two minutes were up. The main terminal chirped out a RESET, something I hadn't expected, and the video cameras' green lights began to blink again. "Damn." I didn't expect that, either. My heart thrashed against my ribcage. I should have been long gone by now.

I bolted to the elevator, mashed the button, and cursed Carlson for taking it up earlier. Now I had to wait for it to come back down. What a fool I'd been, messing around with a rock when I could have been making good my escape.

*Come on. Come on.*

I swallowed hard and looked back to the lab where O'Malley had faced the same dilemma, back when he too had stolen the cell phone, a decision that had cost him his life. I'd gotten what I'd come for. Mullen would have to sort out his own murder case.

The elevator dinged.

*Finally.*

The doors opened. Frank Coletti lunged out with a gun pointed at my chest. "Where the fuck do you think you're going?"

My breath hitched. Cold fear poured down my spine. Massey and Carlson followed behind him. Neither looked surprised to see me. I'd almost made it out.

*Now I'm a dead man.*

\*\*\*

Sirens blared and misery lights flashed as Detective

Mullen and his posse of police officers screeched to a halt, helter-skelter, in front of Massey's towering headquarters. Thankful he'd arrived in one piece, Mullen shoved the shifter into park and bailed out of the Taurus just as Sergeant McNulty swung his SUV in and slammed on the brakes. The air was foul with the smell of burnt rubber and hot engines. Down the block, fully lit NYPD squad cars had parked catawampus in the intersection, blocking traffic. This was an all-hands-on-deck operation, and Mullen quickly took charge. "Gather 'round, boys."

Uniformed patrolmen and helmeted officers in flack vests and camo emerged from the bright lights and smoke. They were all armed to the teeth. He handed out BOLOs on Frank Coletti. "Here's our person of interest in the murder of Arthur O'Malley. He's armed and dangerous. Nobody tries to be a hero. Understood?"

"He's a punk," McNulty said.

Mullen wanted to dispute that statement. Coletti was a hardened criminal, an ex-Riker's inmate, and he was highly motivated to stay out of prison, with his daughter being sick, and all. As for Frank being a murderer, Mullen was counting on Sean Calhoun to come up with the proof he'd claimed to have. Until then, Coletti was a person of interest and not a suspect. "Don't underestimate him."

Lieutenant Dawson joined the circle. "I've seen his handiwork, boys, so be careful."

"McNulty, Dawson, you're with me." Mullen singled out two other officers. "The rest of you, watch our backs." He led the charge toward the entrance doors to Massey's building. Down the sidewalk and along the curb, gawkers had gathered with their cell phones aimed at the police procession. They were a cop's worst nightmare, all hoping to get video that would go viral on social media: a beating, a shooting, or excessive use of force. His biggest worry was some fool getting caught in the crossfire for five seconds of fame.

"Everybody get back."

Nobody moved as Mullen led his men into the building. He took in the grandiose lobby: the marble walls, floors, and pillars, all shiny and spotless, as he scanned for the black elevator Sean had told him to take to the sub-basement. The aroma of fresh baked bread wafted from *The Real Deal* restaurant and made him wish he was at dinner with his family, celebrating his son's birthday.

"Hey. Hey." The security guard leaped from his desk and ran toward Mullen with his hand out like he was a traffic cop. "What's going on?"

Mullen showed him his badge. "The sub-basement lab. Where's the black elevator?"

"You can't storm in here like Rambo. You'll disturb the restaurant patrons...the residents."

Mullen pressed forward, setting the guard back on his heels. "It's an emergency, god damn it."

"You got a warrant?"

Mullen pulled out his gun. "This is the only warrant I need."

"Okay. Lighten up. This way...and put your guns down, for Christ's sake. Mister Massey isn't going to like this."

"I want to talk to him, too. Get him down here."

"I'll call, but I doubt he'll talk to you."

The black elevator was inset a bit from the lobby. It

would have taken precious minutes to find it on his own. Mullen pushed the *down* button.

McNulty's hand hovered over his holstered gun. "I don't like it, Detective. The confined space of an elevator, no room to spread out in a firefight."

"Calm down, Ray. Let's do this by the book."

McNulty clenched a fist. "We need eyes-on down there first. Who knows what we're walking into?"

"Then I'll go down by myself." He double-punched the button impatiently.

McNulty stepped in front of the elevator, his back to the door, and folded his enormous arms. "No way, Tom. I'm not letting you go down there by yourself."

"Then quit bellyaching." Mullen mashed the button harder. "What's wrong with this damn thing?"

## Chapter Twenty-Eight

**M**eanwhile, in the sub-basement lab, Massey locked the elevator doors open and stepped out behind Frank, who had the Sig Sauer .45 aimed at Calhoun's chest. He had only moments left to live.

Calhoun stepped back with his hands raised and eyes wide. "Whoa. Take it easy, big guy."

Frank clenched his jaw. "I've been looking forward to this." He held the gun out sideways, gangster style, ready to light him up.

"Wait," Massey shouted. He'd seen the untied ropes on the tarp covering the obelisk and needed to know why Calhoun had looked under it. "What's your game, Calhoun? You a spy for Vericom?"

"I just fixed your server and your goon shoves a gun in my face. Is this how you treat your employees?"

Carlson hurried to the main terminal. "He's got the cell phone, boss."

"Give it back, Calhoun."

His bravado faded, shoulders sagged, and his hand trembled as he reached into his coat pocket.

Frank wagged the gun. "Don't try anything stupid. Take it out slowly."

Calhoun retrieved the cell phone and held it up for all to see. "I know why O'Malley stole it."

"You don't know shit," Frank spat. "Let me kill him

now, boss."

"And Frank, I know you killed O'Malley," Calhoun added. "To get that phone back."

"You're not so smart. Bart shot O'Malley. I was busy driving."

Calhoun glanced around. "Where is your sidekick, anyway?"

"In hell, waiting for you."

"So he's dead?"

"You catch on real quick. Just say the word, boss. I got his ticket to ride right here." He jabbed the gun at Calhoun.

"Keep your shirt on, Frank." Massey still had questions, and though his blood pressure pulsed in his ears, he folded his arms in a show of authority and control. "Spill it, Calhoun. What do you think you know?"

"O'Malley talked to his wife on this phone. He told me to protect it with my life...it can connect to dead people."

"Is that what he told you?" Massey scowled. "And you believed him?"

"Not really...not until the cemetery."

Carlson's eyes narrowed. "You made a call from the cemetery?"

"My dad called me."

Carlson looked like he'd been gut-punched. "Boss, I don't get it. A call *from* the afterlife? I don't see how that's possible."

"He's lying," Frank said. "Let me plug him."

Calhoun held the phone out in front of him. "That's why I'm here, to find out how it's possible."

Jim Keane

Massey frowned. "That's unfortunate. You already know too much."

"I was hoping to talk to my dad again."

"That ain't happening. Hand it over."

Calhoun shook his head and gave Massey the phone.

He stared at it, felt a wave of heat roll up his arm. In his hand he held the answer to the age-old question: *What happens to us after death?* What eternity awaited him? Excitement spurred his heartbeat, made his head feel woozy. The image of the Tiki bar on the beach appeared. Warm sand oozed between his toes. The air smelled of brine and tequila. Palm trees swayed in the breeze. His breath shuddered. He took a deep breath, let it out slow. It was time to end this fiasco. "Okay, Frank. Kill him."

"Wait." Calhoun raised his hands again. "Before you unleash your dog on me...answer me one question. What's under that tarp?"

At the mere thought of giving up his secrets, a sharp pain stabbed Massey's chest. "You come into my building and steal my phone then expect me to answer your questions... Are you out of your mind?" He hesitated to take in a painful breath. "Carlson. Check the network...see what else he hacked."

"Just the cameras, sir. Everything booted up perfectly. We're fully functional."

"See?" Calhoun stepped back. "No harm, no foul."

Frank's face flushed. "Can we speed things up here? I want to get back to Chloe before Clarissa divorces me."

"Hold on, Frank." Massey, never being one to miss an opportunity to brag, decided to grant Sean his last request. "Carlson, show him the obelisk."

Calhoun's brow crinkled. "Obelisk?"

"For lack of a better name." Carlson typed in a command. The tarp whipped off the obelisk, slick as a magician's reveal.

Calhoun huffed. "Yeah. It's a rock."

"Not just any rock," Massey said. "It came from the Rwenzori Mountains in Africa. The natives used it to communicate with their ancestors."

"How?"

"Carlson. Tell him."

"Atoms are constantly in motion, so everything vibrates at a range of frequencies depending on mass and temperature. The obelisk vibrates at only one frequency, which perfectly matches the StarTAC."

"But there's no SIM card in the StarTAC. How can it make or receive a call?"

"The crystal chip I put in the SIM slot." Carlson smiled as if he were the smartest guy in the room. "It connects the phone's frequency to the obelisk's frequency, and the obelisk is connected to the afterlife. The Rwenzori's used an Adungu Lute to match the frequency. We use the StarTAC."

"And the Cisco?"

"It monitors the transmission between the obelisk and the phone. Problem is, a call overloads the network. The one you received at the cemetery blew the CC."

"How ironic," Massey put in. "You blew it. You fixed it. And for that, you're going to die."

"You should be thanking me." Calhoun frowned at Frank as if a loaded gun in his face didn't intimidate him one bit. "You got your cell phone back. What are you going to do with it?"

"Talk to dead people."

"Who?"

Massey chuckled. "How about HOFFA? What happened to you? Or HITLER, did you commit suicide or flee to Argentina? Or OSWALD, did you act alone? The biggest mystery in life is what happens after death. Nobody comes back to tell us. With this cell phone, I'm going to find the answer."

"Nothing good can come of that."

Massey handed the cell phone to Carlson. "Reconnect it to the network." He turned to Frank. "Kill him."

The elevator doors suddenly closed, stealing everyone's attention from the murder that was about to take place.

Massey's pulse shot up. "Security must've unlocked the doors. But why? Carlson, put up a video feed from the lobby."

Carlson typed at the keyboard. "It's the cops."

Massey looked at the monitor. He couldn't believe his eyes. Police were boarding the elevator. "What the hell are they doing here?"

Calhoun stood tall. "You guys are going to jail for the murder of Arthur O'Malley."

Massey turned to Calhoun. "You called the cops?"

"Frank almost killed my mom. Damn right I called the cops."

"You son of a bitch." Massey pulled a gun of his own and shoved Frank aside. "Calhoun, you're going to ruin everything I've worked for. I'll kill you myself." He pointed the gun at Calhoun's chest, fully intent on pulling the trigger, but Calhoun made a move Massey hadn't expected, sweeping his left hand into Massey's gun arm, shoving it to the right as his right hand came across and grabbed the gun from the opposite direction. Massey almost lost his grip on the gun, and in the next second, he was in a battle for control of the weapon. As Calhoun tried to twist it from his hand, Massey countered with a twist of his own, but the gun remained firmly in the grasp of four hands.

Massey shoved Calhoun backwards into the main terminal. Calhoun pivoted and slammed Massey against the console.

Carlson got out of the way.

Massey's heart quivered. His breath came in gasps. He gritted his teeth and shifted his weight to throw Calhoun back, but he wouldn't let go of the gun. Staggering back and forth, Massey realized their battle was moving closer to the wooden fence around the obelisk. He saw Frank stepping side to side, his gun waving.

"Boss, get out of the way. I can't get a clean shot."

The elevator doors opened. Footfalls pounded in.

Massey, peering under Calhoun's arm, saw a plainclothes cop leading three uniformed police officers, followed by a huge bearded man wearing a camo Kevlar vest. They had their guns drawn.

"NYPD. Drop your weapons. Let's see your hands."

"Shit." Frank swiveled his gun to the cops and fired as he dove behind a server.

The blast echoed through the lab and rang in Massey's ears. He couldn't let Calhoun get the gun, shoved him against the fence. The wood cracked and splintered.

The police hit the floor and returned a volley of bullets.

Carlson disappeared down the row of servers.

"God damned worthless brainard."

*I could use some help here.*

"Give it up, Massey. Your gig is over."

"Go to hell."

Frank and the cops were fully engaged. Bullets pinged off servers and shattered monitors down the line. Glass shards flew through the air, lethal as any shrapnel.

Massey gritted his teeth, refusing to release the gun. The sounds of gunfire grew distant, echoing away. Blood gushed through his ears, louder and louder. The room spun. He felt suddenly nauseous. The cold fist of death squeezed his heart. Pain gripped his left arm, forcing him to release the gun and fall against the wooden fence.

*This is the big one Doctor Santos warned me about.*

Calhoun stepped back, aimed the gun at him. "Get on the ground."

*Not yet. I can still make it to the obelisk.*

Blood pounded through his veins. His heart slammed against his ribs. He couldn't catch his next breath. Every muscle in his body clenched, but he managed to take two steps to the break in the fence.

"Massey. It's over. Stop."

"Boss." Frank aimed his gun at Calhoun.

The obelisk started to vibrate and hum. The floor trembled, setting Frank back on his ass.

Massey held on to the fence, fighting for his next breath.

Sean jumped back.

"Hold your fire," Massey shouted.

Gunfire ceased.

Servers threw sparks. Cooling fans screamed. Lights flashed.

Carlson raced back to the main terminal. "Power levels are off the charts. The Cisco is feeding juice into the obelisk." He tapped a button on the keypad multiple times. "I can't stop it."

Massey put his hands up to shield his eyes from the bright ceiling lights. His heart thrashed as he watched Frank draw down on Calhoun, but before he could pull the trigger, the big bearded cop jumped up on a server and aimed his assault rifle down on Frank. "Drop it."

"Fuck you." Frank swiveled the gun up at the cop.

*Bang. Bang.*

The cop double-tapped him. The acrid stench of cordite wafted from the barrel.

Frank's face contorted into a mask of agony. A gush of blood spurted from his mouth, and he collapsed to the floor. A pool of blood grew around him.

In that moment, Massey felt no sorrow for Frank. The idiot lived by the gun and died by the gun. Chloe and Clarissa crossed his mind, how they'd have to go on without him, but that was their hard luck.

*Put your money on a loser, you lose.*

The police closed in on Massey. He tottered as footfalls neared and distant voices ordered him to get on the ground. The vibrating rumble of the obelisk became deafening. Cables threw sparks and spewed smoke. Through the haze, ghostly figures approached. If he survived this heart attack, he was sure to spend the rest of his life in a hospital, or worse, prison. He opted for paradise in the obelisk, threw himself against its crystalline shell, and screamed.

The sights and sounds of the lab disappeared in a brilliant flash of light.

## Chapter Twenty-Nine

A burnt-out forest and rocky landscape lay before Massey, a scene of such desolation and despair that he couldn't fathom the depth and breadth of his mistake. Burning embers swirled around him, and every breath singed his nose hairs and boiled the spit in his throat. There was no picture-perfect beach, golden sand, warm sun, and blue ocean swells of the paradise he'd envisioned during his near-death experience in the hospital. He whirled to leave, to go back to the lab and face the cops, but a black wall of stone had closed him in.

Fighting the burn of sheer terror in his chest, he turned to face his new reality. A blood-red sun glowed through a thick blanket of smoke and ash, and a hot wind punched him in the face. "What the hell is this?"

He clutched his chest and realized his heart attack had abated, though this reprieve from certain death had presented him with a new set of maladies. Hot pain shot through him, from his toes up through his torso and exploded inside his head in a blast of whiteness. Dizziness enveloped him. He staggered to stay upright on his feet and discovered his hands were ablaze. The hands and fingers that had made him millions with just a handshake were quickly reduced to blackened bones. His Armani suit spontaneously combusted, along with every stitch of clothing, searing his skin and melting every hair on his body. For the longest time, he was a human torch spewing embers until he was as naked as the day he was born.

The torch flamed out, yet the stench of charbroiled flesh hung in his nostrils, the unmistakable fetor of death. Stooped in misery, he screamed, "What's happening to me?"

*"Welcome to Hell,"* a guttural voice reverberated from the smoke.

"Who are you?"

*"Some call me Satan, others the Devil or Beelzebub, the Serpent of Darkness, but to you, I am your worst nightmare."*

The voice of pure evil sickened Massey's stomach, and he instantly thought of his own death. "Am I dead?"

*"Not yet."*

"I want to go back."

*"That door is closed forever."*

"This is not what I expected."

*"This is what you deserve. Behold your final judgment."*

"Do you know who I am? I'm the richest man in New York City. You can't do this to me."

*"But of course I can."*

"No. I don't belong here."

*"We shall see."*

The smoky haze lifted to reveal a smoldering hill where the obelisk stood at the pinnacle, glistening with internal light. Massey fell to his bare knees on the ashen ground and clasped his hands in prayer. "Please, let it be my way out."

The ground rumbled and embers swirled around him.

The hill was steep, seemingly an impossible climb, but he had to try. He rose to his feet and stepped forward with one foot then the next, each upward step its own agony in the blistering heat, yet he persevered toward his salvation.

The closer he got to the summit, the more doubt set in. Would the obelisk regurgitate him back into the lab to succumb to a fatal heart attack that would land him right back here in Hell? Or would he be greeted by a volley of police bullets and end up in this hellhole anyway? Hopelessness stopped him mid-climb where he buckled over a hot boulder and vomited onto the blackened earth. The spew was wretched and burnt, as if Hell itself was burning inside his soul. Had Bart endured this same misery? What about Frank? Was he somewhere around here, as well? Perhaps the answers were waiting inside the obelisk at the top of the hill.

He pressed onward and upward, on his bare hands and knees, clawing at the fetid ash and dirt, breathing fire and seeing red. At long last, he reached the summit where the obelisk stood. A cleft opened in its center, a welcoming maw of crystal and granite. He recalled when he'd first laid eyes on it, high in the Rwenzori Mountains, surrounded by natives bent in reverence to their ancestors. Oh, they didn't give it up without a fight, no sir, but spears and arrows had no chance against automatic assault weapons and hand grenades. Pride bloomed in his chest, the pride he felt as the netted stone rose from the mountain under the thumping dual rotors of the heavy-lift helicopter. He was home again, and without a thought of regret, he crawled inside to accept his salvation.

Instant relief washed over him, like he'd been through

a baptism by fire and rewarded with cool air that caressed his burnt skin and soothed his tortured lungs. He stood in a cavernous corridor of pillars under a crystal-domed ceiling. Waves of light shined down as if the sky were ablaze. The grinding of stone caused him to turn in time to see the crevice close and seal him inside. Fighting panic, he ran in a circle, looking for an exit, but the corridor shifted and he walked into bright daylight instead.

It took a moment to become aware of his physical self. He was dressed again...but not in his customary Armani suit, red silk tie, and Louis Vuitton shoes...but sporting a second-hand suit coat, black Dockers, and shoes in need of a shine.

"What the hell?" He glanced around and realized he was in Crotonville near the Hudson River. Motorboats skimmed across the water while gulls soared above. His perception of time and place narrowed on a familiar three-bedroom house with glorious river views. "I remember this place."

In front of the house, a real estate sign read: OPEN HOUSE.

A car pulled up behind him. An elderly couple, Mr. and Mrs. Haggerty, got out and plodded toward the house, holding hands like young lovers.

He remembered them, too, and as déjà vu made his head spin, he immediately went into salesman mode. "Welcome," he said with open arms.

The woman released her husband's hand. "We got here as fast as we could." She reached into her purse. "Here's the check."

Massey wrinkled his nose at the measly amount. The

housing market was a boom with low-interest loans but few high-end properties for sale. Cash buyers were at a disadvantage, and Massey preyed on those with means but no solid understanding of the real estate business.

"I know you like this house, but I have another buyer coming who's ready to pay more." Of course, it was a lie, but they didn't know that. "I'm afraid you're out of luck."

Her shoulders drooped. "But we love this house. Our kids love this house. It'll be their house one day, when we're dead and gone."

The old man grumped. "You can't do this to us."

"Homes are selling fast these days. Buyers are lining up. You'll need another hundred grand to stay ahead of the bidding."

"We won't have any savings left."

Massey frowned. "Do you want the house or not?"

Mr. Haggerty shook his head. "That would kill us."

*Time to set the hook, just as he'd done more times than he could recall, but like a first lover, he'd never forget his first marks.*

"How about I carry the balance for you?"

"Thank you so much, Mister Massey. You're a saint."

The obelisk shifted and the sunny sky turned to gray. Under a straight-down drizzle, Massey, sporting an umbrella, strode from his favorite coffee shop toward his waiting limousine. There at the curb huddled Mr. and Mrs. Haggerty, shivering and soaked. He sidestepped them like so much trash in the gutter.

The missus spoke up. "You should be ashamed of yourself, Mr. Massey."

"I don't control the market." *Yes, I do.*

"We lost everything."

"You shouldn't have missed a payment."

Sure. The housing market had crashed, *not my fault*, and he'd sold their mortgage to an investment banker. The couple couldn't make the new lender's payments and got evicted. *Not my fault, either.* The house went into foreclosure and he'd bought it back for a song, jacked up the price, and sold it again. Some said he was a real estate vulture. He thought he was a shrewd businessman, built his empire on the backs of the unfortunate and unwary. As he stooped to get into the limo, a bright flash of light sent him back to the domed corridor in the obelisk, naked again.

"What the hell was that all about?"

The voice boomed. *"Seems your treachery was only outmatched by your greed. And you have no remorse for swindling that old couple, nor for anyone else you scammed to climb your financial ladder of success."*

He shrugged. "It was just business."

*"You've learned nothing."* The voice reverberated and the domed ceiling shook. *"Avarice has blinded you. Your lust for power is insatiable."*

The obelisk shifted and spun in a dizzying swirl that dumped him into an open-air Jeep bouncing along a rutted road through the jungle. He now wore camo fatigues, combat boots, and carried an assault rifle. Behind him, a convoy of trucks lumbered along, occupied by Ugandan mercenaries armed to the teeth. Rotor blades hammered the air as three Sikorsky helicopters flew in a wedge formation above him: a heavy-lift King Stallion and two S-92 transports carrying a crew of excavators and engineers. As the convoy of death wormed its way up into the Rwenzori

Mountains, his heart pumped adrenaline-laced blood. The attack on the village was brutal and heartless. Arrows and spears flew through the air as did bullets and grenades in the opposite direction. Massey screamed with excitement as he popped off rounds at the villagers. Men, women, children, young and old, lay in the dirt as their huts burned to the ground. The bloodletting led to the prize, the obelisk, now uprooted from its mountainside temple and flown over the treetops to a landing strip in a clearing where a plane awaited its cargo. He jumped from the Jeep and ran aboard just as the ramp was closing. Turboprop engines blew down the dusty runway and lifted the plane into the African sky, now scarred by black smoke rising from the decimated village. Massey smiled, as he'd smiled back then. It was a glorious day.

The plane's interior shifted and spun, landing him back on the floor in the obelisk, naked again. He screamed. "Stop jerking me around."

*"It's time to face your final judgment. There's a special place in Hell for you, Ronald Massey."*

"Wait. What about Chloe Coletti? I helped that poor girl. I'm not all bad."

*"Silence, you dolt."* The floor rocked as if the obelisk sat at the epicenter of an earthquake. *"Your act of charity was done for all the wrong reasons. Glory for yourself. Press for your sick ego and narcissism. Not a true act of mercy from the heart. I've seen enough."*

The floor dropped open and Massey plummeted down, down, down, his arms flailing and his feet kicking. He screamed in the blackness, a scream that echoed back from every direction. Finally, he hit dead bottom with a thud that knocked the breath from his lungs. His body writhed with agony. Glowing-hot rock walls revealed that he had landed in a tunnel.

*Is this the culmination of my life, no more than a gopher in a hole? If this is Hell, where is everybody? Is there any way out?*

Cold fear prickled down his spine. He struggled to his feet and surveyed his new surroundings. From far down the tunnel, firelight flickered, so he walked in that direction, carefully, and came to a ledge. The tunnel had opened into a cavern. Its width exceeded his field of vision, but the flickering light below seemed to be a beacon showing him the way down. It looked like a fool's errand, dangerous with all those jagged rocks, and to what end? More torture? He should just sit here and rot, yet some unknown force prodded him over the ledge.

He descended the rock-rubble cliff. Loose stones clattered down into the abyss. Sharp rocks stabbed the tender skin of his feet. At one point, rocks broke loose under his weight, and he'd damned near plummeted to his death, but he righted himself and scrabbled to the cavern floor.

The air smelled of salt, sulfur, and the odor of rotting flesh, which made a knot tighten in his stomach. Water dripped. Mold strangled the rocky terrain. Spiders crawled, and ominous shadows lurked in every crevice. Above him, stalactites hung low like the fangs of a beast. He shivered though the air was hotter than an inferno down here.

The flickering light emanated from another tunnel.

*Something is leading me toward that light.*

There was just enough room to fit his body inside the

tunnel. He crawled on his hands and knees. Ceiling rocks loosened and pelted him as he plodded forward. Hell-heated granite burned his palms and knees, so he had to move quickly. A suffocating current of hot air whipped through the tunnel and howled, as if spawned from the throat of Beelzebub himself.

Working his way through the tunnel, he concluded the floor was slanted downward, and Hell was getting hotter the lower he descended.

The flickering light was close now, just past a bend in the tunnel ahead. Hot air blasted him in the face. As he neared the brightness, the tunnel opened into a cavern where flames shot out from the ground and the walls. Wisps of lung-choking smoke clouded the air. The odor of charred flesh wafted from this giant oven, it seemed, forcing bile to race up to his throat. He swallowed hard, not wanting to see the burnt contents of his soul again.

Amid the crackle of flames, moans bellowed throughout the chamber, and blood-curdling screams caused gooseflesh to break out on his blistered skin.

A motion to his right caught his attention, where a line of stooped and burnt figures ascended a craggy pathway up the wall, their legs bound in chains that clinked and clanked with each staggering step upward. They carried buckets of flaming lava, an endless march of souls feeding the fires of Hell, he knew, and though he didn't know how he knew it, he was sure he wasn't about to do physical labor for eternity and turned back to get as far from this hellhole as possible.

He ducked to the tunnel, but a hot gust of wind blew him back into the cavern. Hissing tongues of fire licked up from the ground and burned his feet, causing him to hop and skip about like some fool in a mosh pit.

The guttural voice echoed. *"Dance, Massey, dance."*

"Stop. Please. I beg you."

*"The fun is just beginning."*

"Give me a chance to make amends for my life of sin."

*"That horse has left the barn. Dance, I said."*

Massey's worst fear hit him like a punch in the gut. *Paradise was a lie. I'm never leaving this place.*

His legs were like noodles as he scampered to the far side of the chamber. When, finally, he made it, he slumped to his knees. "Was that torture entirely necessary?"

"You ain't seen nothing yet, boss."

That voice...it sounded familiar. He scanned the rock face in front of him, and suddenly realized the bumps and cracks weren't rocks at all, but human figures, stretched and distorted beyond belief.

One of the figures shifted. "I warned you, Mr. Massey."

Terror gripped his throat. "Bart?"

His ashen face was wrenched in unbearable agony. He looked like a flaccid corpse, contorted, maltreated, and utterly discarded.

"What the hell happened to you?"

"I'm paying for my life of crime."

All around Bart hung other humans, but calling them human was far too generous. They had vestiges of human traits: heads, grotesquely smushed, bug-eyed and oval mouthed; arms and legs, impossibly stretched and bent in odd directions, and their torsos were ribbed and sunken, each pierced through by a rod that pinned them fast to the rock wall. The sight of such inhuman suffering...such gross and unrelenting torture, ignited Massey's flight instinct. Though he scrambled backward, he couldn't rip his wide-eyed stare from those tormented souls.

Bart's head rose shakily, and his round white eyeballs met Massey's gaze. Agony etched jagged fissures into his forehead, and his swollen lips were wickedly cracked as if every drop of moisture had been sucked from his body. "Now it's your turn, Mr. Massey." Bart's voice sounded like gravel grating on a washboard. "This is all your fault. I killed O'Malley for you, on your orders to retrieve the cell phone."

"You and Frank were criminals long before I hired you." Massey's body shook as he struggled to get to his feet. "He's around here somewhere, I'm sure. Cops shot him dead."

Bart laughed.

The wall of bodies shifted, and a sinewy and blood-smeared figure rose from the mire. Pieces of gristle and splinters of bone protruded from its limbs as if all the skin had been peeled off its body until only muscle and guts remained. It crawled over Bart and the others like a snake immune to gravity. Worse, its serpentine eyes were fixed on Massey.

An icy hand of fear reached through his ribcage and clutched his heart. He turned to flee, ran back through the hissing flames to the tunnel, and dove into it like a cockroach fleeing a kitchen light. As he crawled on his belly, scattering dust and ash, a fiery hand grabbed his leg and pulled him back into the chamber.

*"There is no escaping your fate,"* the snakish demon hissed, its crooked fangs snapping.

Massey held up his hands as he lay on the ground. "Don't kill me."

*"Before long you will beg for death."* The demon grinned a hellish, slobbering grin.

"Who are you?"

*"I am Malkobach, the Collector."* With his free hand, he swept it across the wall of horrors. *"This is my collection of condemned souls. You will join them and suffer here for all eternity."*

"Look, Mr. Malkobach. I'm Ronald Massey. I'm rich enough to buy my way out of here. In New York City, I'm a powerful man. Surely there is some way we can strike a bargain."

The demon lowered his brows to hood his reptilian eyes. *"All your money cannot buy you a single drop of water. Here you are powerless."* The demon dragged him back toward the wall of condemned souls.

Massey raked his fingernails against the rocks, dug into the dirt and ash, but nothing would give him leverage against the force pulling him backwards. He screamed in terror. "No. No. No."

The demon stopped at the wall and stood above him, emotionless. No empathy. No pity. *"Your soul is mine."* Malkobach snatched him up and stuck him on the wall where an oozing, bloody goo held him firmly in place next to Bart. *"You should be quite uncomfortable here,"* the demon hissed.

Massey couldn't move, couldn't swing his arms, couldn't kick his feet. The goo was stickier than a spider's

web, and he was no more powerful than a fly. "Let me go."
Malkobach stood before him and laughed.

Massey screamed bloody murder as he struggled to
get free. The moans of the other tortured souls joined in,
and their voices reverberated into a cacophony of anguish
and misery.

*"Music to my ears,"* the demon said.

"You can't do this to me."

Bart's head shook as he stared at Massey. "Save your
strength, boss. This prick is playing for keeps."

"I'm supposed to be in paradise...with the cleaning
lady."

"Ha. She's a far better person than you ever were,
boss. I can see her now, sitting at a Tiki bar, sipping on a
Bahama Bay Breeze, and watching the surf roll in."

"That was *my* eternity in paradise."

Malkobach grinned. *"I do believe you were
mistaken."*

A warm sensation entered Massey's back. Then a
sharp stabbing pain pierced his body. A rod suddenly burst
from his chest, stretching muscle and tendons until they
snapped back to reveal his skewered heart throbbing and
squirting blood. "Just kill me, you bastard."

*"I already have."*

Massey howled in agony.

# Chapter Thirty

**M**y brain fought to process what my eyes had just seen, the bright flash of light and Massey's disappearance, like some kind of cheap magician's trick. *Where did he go?* I dropped Massey's gun and stepped back. The giant rock vibrated and emitted an eerie drone. Acrid wisps of smoke coiled up from its connected cables as they sparked and crackled. The Cisco server shook and rattled, threatening to break loose from its bolts on the floor. I couldn't fathom how an inert stone created such havoc and exerted such raw power. My heart juddered. I hoped the damn thing wasn't about to explode.

Carlson's cursing brought me out of my mental stupor. Two cops grabbed him and put him on the floor. Though his hands were now cuffed behind him, he kicked and wriggled against the restraints. "Let me go. Let me go. I didn't do anything wrong."

"Where is Massey?" Mullen demanded.

"You fools don't understand. The obelisk has won." Carlson chortled in manic glee.

The obelisk droned louder and vibrated with more intensity.

"What is that thing?"

"The end of the world."

"Bullshit. How did Massey use it to escape?"

Veins jutted from Carlson's forehead. "You

simpletons won't understand. Massey is in Hell, burning to a crisp, for all I know."

"I don't have time for this. Tell me the truth."

"I want a lawyer," Carlson demanded.

"You're not under arrest." Mullen holstered his gun. "So stop with the crazy talk and tell me where he is."

I knew better. Although Carlson appeared to be talking like a loon, I knew the impossible was possible. A phone call from my dad was proof enough for me.

I stepped to Frank Coletti's body. Judging from the size of the blood pool beneath my would-be murderer, I had no doubt he was dead. It didn't have to end this way for him, but when he chose to shoot at the police, he chose the manner of his own death. I was lucky Mullen arrived before Frank shot me full of holes. Problem was, my proof of Arthur O'Malley's murderer had died, as well.

*Damn.*

Mullen knelt to Frank and placed two fingers on the side of his neck. "McNulty, why'd you have to kill him?"

"He should have dropped his gun."

Back on his feet, Mullen stalked to Carlson and yanked him off the floor. "Where did your boss go?" He shook him by the lapels of his lab coat.

Carlson laughed that crazy-man laugh. "I already told you." He pointed to the obelisk.

Mullen shoved Carlson backwards and glared at the big rock. "What the hell is the matter with that thing?"

"It's pissed off." Carlson laughed like he'd lost all his marbles.

"Impossible," Mullen grumped. "It's a rock."

That was obvious, I knew, but I wanted Carlson to

explain all the computer leads attached to it.

Mullen bulled toward the rock. "It's an escape route of—"

I grabbed his arm and pulled him back. "Don't touch it."

He scowled in my face then looked down at my hand that was crumpling the sleeve of his suit coat. "Let...me...go."

I figured I'd better comply before I got arrested. "It's hooked up to the Cisco over there." I pointed in the direction of the bank of servers, knowing he wouldn't know one from the other.

"All right, Calhoun. What do you know about this...this rock?"

"Nothing, but until we figure it out, we best stay clear."

"Okay. Lock it down, boys. This place is a crime scene." Like any good detective, he surveyed the lab, spotted the video cameras set about, and then narrowed his focus on the camera overlooking the rock. "Calhoun. Can you get me the video? I want to see how Massey escaped."

I stepped to the main terminal where Massey had set the cell phone, and with one eye on it and the other on the keyboard, I tapped the *ALT* button several times to shuffle through programs.

"You're wasting your time," Carlson said.

I got the video feed working, clicked on the folder for today's date, then located the time when Massey disappeared. "I found it."

Mullen stood next to me. "Let me see."

We watched Massey fall against the rock. There was a

flash of light, and the next second he was gone.

Mullen's mouth dropped open. "That's impossible."

"Do you want to see it again?"

Mullen pointed a stiff finger at Carlson. "You've got a lot of explaining to do."

"You won't believe me anyway."

"Then tell me something I will believe."

The elevator opened, delivering backup officers led by Lieutenant Dawson. "What do you got?" he asked Mullen.

"Have patrol take this clown to headquarters."

"No. I can't leave," Carlson screamed. "I have to shut down the obelisk."

Mullen grumped. "Sean. Unplug the damn computers."

"Yes, sir." I moved my hand closer to the cell phone, hoping to grab it while everyone was focused on Carlson.

"It's not that easy," Carlson shouted over the drone. "The obelisk is alive, I tell you. It speaks to me. It knows me. I have to be here to calm it down...no telling what it will do without me...it could destroy the city."

Dawson said, "It's a rock."

"Don't mind him," Mullen said. "He's crazy."

While Carlson had Mullen's attention, I picked up the cell phone. Finally, I had it in my hand again. It felt warm and comforting, like my dad's handshake—

"Put that down," Mullen ordered me. "It's evidence in a murder investigation."

"But, detective—

"It may contain vital information. The forensic techs need to take a look at it."

*Damn.*

I set down the phone...felt like I'd cut off my own hand...gouged out my beating heart. So near yet so far.

Two cops loaded Carlson into the elevator. His face contorted into a mask of rage. "You don't understand the obelisk's power. Only I do." His nostrils flared. "You need me here. Don't underestimate its power. You'll be sorry." The doors closed, cutting off his rant.

Mullen stabbed a finger at me. "You said you know who killed O'Malley. You said you have proof. Let's see it."

I glanced down at my proof. Frank Coletti lay on the lab floor, dead. The pungent, metallic smell of blood made my stomach turn. I swallowed hard, thinking it could have been me on the floor instead of Frank. I was lucky to be alive.

However, with Coletti dead and Massey AWOL, my proof went to hell with them. I needed to give Mullen something. He needed proof. I needed proof. The cell phone was Frank and Massey's motive for murder, but the techs wouldn't find anything in it. A chip of crystal in the SIM slot would mean nothing to them, but still, the phone would be buried in the department's evidence room forever. I'd never learn how it was possible to talk to someone in the afterlife.

"Come on, Sean. Tell me what you know."

"I know Bart Marconi killed O'Malley."

"Proof, Sean. Where's your proof?"

I pointed to dead Frank. "He told me, but Bart's dead too."

"Are you giving me the runaround? I can lock you up for obstruction of justice in a murder investigation."

I decided to put Carlson in the hot seat. He had to know everything that went on. "Ask Carlson. Give him immunity. Let him fill in the blanks."

Mullen's brow crinkled. "He's a nut job...has no credibility." He waved Dawson over. "Take Mr. Calhoun back to headquarters. I want to get a formal statement from him."

"Whoa. Wait a minute," I said. "Detective, let me stay. Somebody's got to troubleshoot the Cisco before it blows."

"We'll just unplug it."

"You heard Carlson. He said it's not that easy. It's probably got a fail-safe program running in the background. I've worked on this type of equipment before. I'll find a way to shut it down safely."

Mullen shook his head. "I'll get IT forensics down here to work on the problem. Meanwhile, I need to know everything you know, on the record."

I needed to stay here and find a way to get the cell phone. "But I can help."

"Let us do our jobs. You're going downtown."

A lump formed in my throat as I looked at the cell phone for the last time.

Mullen turned to McNulty. "Lock this place down...and nobody goes near that rock."

"On it, sir."

"Dawson, get him outta here." Mullen pointed at me.

"Sure thing." The Lieutenant stepped behind me and gave me a nudge. "Come on, Calhoun. You heard the man."

I followed Dawson into the elevator, and as the doors

closed, he folded his arms and leaned against the wall. "Why is it every time we meet, you're up to your neck in trouble?"

I punched the *UP* button. "Somebody's got to do your job."

"You could end up dead."

He was right. Playing cops and robbers was a dangerous gig. Ask my mom.

The elevator glided to a stop. As Dawson and I stepped out, I saw a horde police officers in the lobby. Some wore jackets with *NYPD* and *POLICE* embroidered on their backs, others *CSI*, and two read: *CORONER*. They took our place in the elevator, and the doors closed. Before long, Frank Coletti would be in a body bag.

Flashing emergency lights pierced through the glass doors and drew colorful swaths on the walls. I felt a faint tremor in the floor but couldn't hear the droning hum of the rock below. Carlson had warned of a catastrophe in the making. I could only hope he was wrong.

Outside, we weaved through emergency vehicles parked helter-skelter to Dawson's squad car parked across the plaza. I got into the front passenger seat. Dawson slid in behind the wheel, fired up the engine, and flipped switches to activate his overheads and grill-mounted hazards. "Buckle up."

Seat belted in, I noticed all the cop-stuff between us: the dash-mounted brackets for a laptop, canted toward the driver, a racked shotgun, its muzzle pointed upward, a hand-held radar gun in a Velcro fast-draw holster, and a mic for the radio, which crackled with police chatter. The lingering odor of burnt rubber told me he had driven like a maniac to get here. A dash cam hung on the windshield, and when I looked back to see the receding emergency lights, I noticed the 'cage' of wire and plexiglass that cordoned off the rear seat for bad guys. I was glad Dawson didn't make me ride back there.

As Dawson drove toward headquarters, I couldn't believe I was actually sitting in a police car with the Lieutenant, the last place I imagined I'd ever be. Riding upfront like this, I felt kind of important, not at all like a criminal, though I was about to be interrogated like one. I had to wonder if Mullen would have better luck with this investigation, or would he squander it like he'd done with my dad's case. That time he had no suspects; this time he had three: Bart, Frank, and Ronald Massey, all MIA.

***

A cold wind howled off the East River, and with the Brooklyn Bridge lights in the background, Dawson led me into Lower Manhattan Police Headquarters. From the outside, the thirteen story building looked like a giant cube with rows of inset square windows. Inside, a white-faced clock on the wall read 10:30pm. The cavernous cubist lobby was dimly lit, and only a few ceiling lights illuminated the hallways. My heart rattled in my chest. I'd been run through the mill all day, and I wanted to check on my mom, but I was sure Mullen wouldn't let me leave until I gave him everything I knew about O'Malley's murder. The trick would be keeping the cell phone out of the story.

Dawson waved at the Desk Sergeant then pointed down a hallway. "The elevator is this way."

We took it up to the homicide department. Hints of

stale coffee permeated the air in the hallway as we passed the Real Time Crime Center, which looked like a military war room. Flat-panel monitors lined the walls, and terminals with access to state-of-the-art data search engines aided detectives and officers in their investigations.

Dawson pushed through the doors to the Major Crimes department and stopped in front of a door marked *Interrogation.* He opened it, and with his arm extended: "Wait in here for Mullen."

"You got any coffee?"

"How strong is your stomach?"

"Strong enough. It's going to be a long night."

Dawson smirked. "We'll see. I'll be back." He closed the door.

The room was small; I'd seen bigger closets; and a two-way mirror was embedded in the wall. The air was cold enough to make me think they'd pumped it in from Alaska. Furnishings consisted of a marred wooden table, two chairs on one side, and one chair on the other where I sat to await a barrage of questions I couldn't possibly answer. I noticed a steel eyelet anchored in the tabletop and imagined a parade of suspects and bad guys who had been handcuffed to it. I was glad I wouldn't be one of them.

I checked my phone for updates on my mom. Nothing. I shook my head and slumped my shoulders.

Dawson stepped in and gave me a Styrofoam cup of coffee. "Need anything else, let me know."

"Thanks."

He left.

I took a sip and winced. I'd tasted better coffee...and hotter.

I rubbed my temples. I had to prepare for all the questions Mullen would ask me about what went down in Massey's basement lab. My stomach tightened. How would I explain my involvement with Massey, Inc., O'Malley's murder, and all the events that followed? I didn't fully believe it all myself.

It wasn't long before Mullen strode in and closed the door. "Sorry to keep you waiting. I hope you've got something good for me."

"Should I have a lawyer?"

"Why? Did you do something illegal?"

"No."

"Then you've got nothing to worry about. I just need some answers." He leaned forward with his hands on the table. "You told me you had proof. I show up and you've got nothing. I'm a busy man, Sean." His eyes narrowed. "Make my time worthwhile."

I put my hands up. "Okay. Take it easy."

"Tell me what you know about O'Malley."

*Here goes nothing.*

"I was there when he died...just coming out of the bar when I found him slumped on the ground in the alley behind McGee's. He was bleeding...bleeding bad."

Mullen's eyebrows rose. He sat across from me. "Did he say who shot him?"

"No..." My breath hitched. "But it didn't take long for me to figure it out. Two goons rounded McGee's and ran toward me. Bart had a gun in his hand."

"So you figured Bart had shot him?"

"Wouldn't you?"

"I suppose."

"Frank Coletti was with him. Makes him just as guilty. Right?"

Mullen nodded. "What did you do?"

"I got the hell out of there." I skipped the part about the cell phone. "But they chased me."

"Why do you suppose they did that?"

"Maybe they wanted to get rid of me because I was a witness to O'Malley's murder."

"Maybe, but I think there's more to it than that. What aren't you telling me?"

"That's it." I showed him my best poker face.

"Most thugs turn away and run so the witness can't get a good look at them."

"I assure you, detective. I got a good look at them."

"Okay. Describe Bart."

"He was smaller than Frank. Frank gave the orders, made Bart check O'Malley. When I backed up, Bart said O'Malley was dead. That's when Frank pulled a gun and they went after me. But it's all a moot point. They're dead now."

"Yeah. Frank is at the county morgue, but Bart is officially missing, as is Massey."

I shuddered. "Presumed dead, I would think."

"God damnit, Sean." Mullen smacked the table. "That's not good enough."

Someone knocked on the door.

"What is it?" Mullen shouted.

Dawson stepped in. "Carlson's ready for you. He's mad enough to chew nails."

"I'll be right there."

Dawson left the room.

Mullen inhaled, held his breath, then: "Sean, I'm going to need your help with Carlson."

"Now you need my help?" I sounded brash, but I didn't care. "Back at Massey's I was chopped liver. If I'm free to go, I want to visit my mom at the hospital."

"All that computer jargon Carlson knows is way over my pay grade. In case the wacko starts spouting off tech stuff, I need you to observe the interrogation and decipher his lingo."

"Then can I go see my mom?"

"Absolutely. I'll arrange a ride for you."

I really didn't want to listen to Carlson go on and on about his superior intelligence, but he might say something useful to help me understand how I was able to get a call from my dad. "Let's get this done so I can get back to my life."

"Hey. I missed my son's birthday party on account of your bullshit phone call. I want to go home as bad as you do, preferably before my wife throws me out of the house."

"Yeah. I'm sorry about that, but Rambo shouldn't have shot Frank."

"That was unfortunate." He opened the door.

I followed him out, and he led me to a narrow observation room lit by a window in the wall that looked into a bright interrogation room, a clone of the one I'd just left. Carlson sat at the table, handcuffed to the eyelet with his fists clenched. His face was flushed as he muttered, "The chicken or the egg. The chicken or the egg." Video cameras were positioned in the room's upper corners, so I was confident his statements would be well-recorded.

Mullen patted my shoulder. "Remember, he can't see

you."

"Okay, sure." Just to be safe, I stood back from the glass.

Dawson strode in and stood next to me. "Who's got the popcorn?"

"I hope we get some information from this loony-bird before he lawyers up." Mullen left and soon entered the bright room where he sat across from Carlson as nonchalantly as if they were meeting for coffee. "Mr. Carlson. Seems you're having a rough night."

He pulled at his handcuffs. "Take these things off."

"Do I look that stupid?"

Carlson grimaced. "I know my rights. I don't have to talk to you."

"Depends on how you want to play this, Carl. I can call you Carl, right?"

"Knock your socks off."

"Question is, do you want to be a witness in the murder of Arthur O'Malley or a suspect?"

"I didn't kill anybody, but the obelisk will. I have to get back to the lab before all hell breaks loose." His eyes darted around the room, and he cowered as if the walls were closing in on him. "You have to let me go."

I looked at Dawson.

Dawson shrugged.

"Slow down there, cowboy," Mullen said. "I need your cooperation here. I'm on your side. Just tell me, where did Massey go?"

"I already told you."

"Yeah, yeah. He's in Hell, but I'm serious. How does that rock-escape trick work? Is there a trap door, a staircase, a tunnel?"

"You don't know what you're dealing with. The sheer magnitude of the obelisk's power is way beyond your measly intelligence."

I had to agree. Even I couldn't program a computer to control a rock.

Mullen shook his head. "I'll do my best to follow along. Tell me how Massey got out of the basement."

Carlson looked at the door. "I really need to leave."

"Answer my questions."

"You're not listening to me." That came out with a hiss.

Mullen looked at the two-way mirror and then back to Carlson. "Maybe a night in the slammer will convince you to cooperate."

"We don't have that much time. I gotta go now."

Dawson crossed his arms and chuckled. "That bozo's not going anywhere."

I wondered just how much time we had until...until what?

Carlson pulled on the handcuffs as if he could rip the steel eyelet from the table.

"He's nuts, all right," Dawson said.

"Sit down and tell me about Arthur O'Malley," Mullen pressed. "He worked for Massey, right?"

"He was a traitor. A thief. Lower than pond scum. I'm sorry he got himself killed, but that's what happens when you steal the prize."

"The prize? What prize?"

My heart shuddered. *Damn. He's going to blab.*

Carlson slumped. "The cell phone."

Jim Keane

"Cell phone? What cell phone?"

"Ask your boy Calhoun. He knows." Carlson shifted his eyes to the mirror. "Tell him, Calhoun," he shouted. "Tell him how you talked to your dad on that cell phone."

I choked. "He can see me."

"Relax," Dawson said. "He's guessing."

Mullen frowned. "Sean's dad is dead."

"Damn right he is," Carlson growled out. "But my cell phone connects to the afterlife. I can talk to dead people."

Mullen coughed. "That's impossible."

"His dad called him. Ask him. Go ahead."

"You're crazy to think I'd believe that."

I knew it. If I'd told Mullen about the cell phone, he'd think I was crazy too. Good call to omit the phone from my rendition of events over O'Malley's death.

Mullen leaned back in his chair. "You're not doing yourself any favors here, Carl. Let's get back to Massey. Where is he?"

Carlson's eyes got big-around. "The obelisk sucked him inside."

"He's inside the rock?" Mullen huffed.

"It's not a rock. It's a gateway to the afterlife. I guarantee you he's in Hell with Bart...right now...while we're wasting time. The obelisk is going to get its revenge for being ripped from its temple in the Rwenzori Mountains, oh, yeah, and it's not going to be pretty."

Mullen leaned forward. "You gotta do better than that. Where is he?"

Carlson went nose-to-nose with Mullen. "I called Bart on the cell phone. I talked to him. He told me he was in hell. How's that for doing better?"

"You better start telling me the truth."

"You won't believe the truth."

Mullen kept his cool. "Try me."

Carlson rocked back and forth in his chair. "It all started with the chicken and the egg. You know, which came first? Then I thought which came first, the obelisk or the frequency. You need the phone to make the call, but if you don't have the obelisk then you don't need the phone. It's a conundrum."

Mullen's eyes widened.

"You see, Bart disappeared into the obelisk, just like Massey did. Now you see him...now you don't. Poof. Just like that." He snapped his fingers.

"And you called him on a cell phone?"

"Yes."

"You know how crazy that sounds?"

"The crazy thing is I figured out how to do it. I spelled his name on the keypad. B-A-R-T. The next thing I know, I'm talking to him, and I hear screaming in the background... Bart told me he was in Hell. I can call Massey the same way. Just let me get back to the lab. I'll prove it."

"By dialing his name on a cell phone?" Mullen laughed. "You can't expect me to believe that shit."

"See? I was right. You don't believe the truth."

"I believe you're going straight to jail."

"Get me out of here," Carlson raged on. "The obelisk is alive. It knows about everything everything..." He slammed his fists on the table, rattling the handcuff chain. "Except what came first, the chicken or the egg? You can't reason with it. You can't barter with it. It showed me the future, detective, and it's nasty." Drool dribbled from his lips.

Mullen stood. "I can see this is getting us nowhere."

I disagreed with Detective Mullen. Carlson had been very helpful. Now, I knew how to call my dad. The pounding of my heart accelerated. I just had to get back to the lab and get that phone, but fat chance Mullen would let me anywhere near it.

As Mullen stepped to the door, Carlson started screaming. "Let me go, you fools. You don't know the power of the obelisk. Only I can control it. You have to take me back to the lab before it's too late."

Mullen opened the door and spoke to the uniformed officer in the hall. "Watch him."

The cop stepped in and shut the door.

Carlson screamed at the top of his lungs, "You're all dead, you hear. The obelisk will win."

I felt sorry for the guy. His boss was gone. He was now unemployed. Maybe I could get him a job at Vericom, though in his mental state now, everyone would think he'd do well to qualify for mopping duties in an asylum.

Mullen entered the observation room. "That was rough."

I thought for sure he'd ask me what I knew about the cell phone, if I'd seen it, if I'd taken it from O'Malley, if I'd received a call from my dad, but he didn't go there, so I ventured to say, "You really think he's crazy?"

"It's obvious he doesn't know what's real or what's bullshit. We all saw Massey disappear. His escape was made to look like the rock had swallowed him up. We all know that's impossible. Classic lights and mirrors and sleight of hand, but he believes it was something supernatural. He's a textbook case for the criminally insane."

Dawson chuckled. "A real-life mad scientist, huh?" I knew full well Carlson was as sane as a judge.

"The guy needs professional help." Mullen pressed the intercom button on the wall and spoke to the cop guarding Carlson. "Put him in lockup. Maybe a taste of his future will loosen his tongue enough to tell us where we can find Ronald Massey."

I had my doubts, but if I hurried, I could get to the hospital before midnight.

## Chapter Thirty-One

**W**hile Mullen finished the paperwork to put Carlson behind bars, Dawson drove me back to Montefiore Medical Center. He seemed preoccupied with his thoughts and not very talkative as he navigated across the city. Traffic was light during the midnight hour. I dared to venture into a conversation. "Is Mullen pissed off about something?"

"Yeah. You could say that." He spoke without looking at me in the passenger seat beside him. "He's working on another cold case with the O'Malley murder."

"I told him who done it."

Now he glanced at me. "You didn't say anything about a cell phone. Do you know what Carlson was talking about? He says you do."

"He's crazy, remember. You don't really believe my dad called me from the grave, do you?"

"No." He stopped for a red light. "But you seemed especially interested in the phone back at the lab."

"It's an old one, a classic, is all. I'm in the cell phone business, you know...work for Vericom...well...when I'm not on unpaid suspension. It's a lot easier than police work."

"It's a grind." Dawson nodded as we neared the hospital. "Cases don't get wrapped up as fast as they do on television."

I sighed. "I get it now. It's one thing to know who committed a murder, but to prove it—"

"Yeah, that's the trick." He pulled up to the curb in front of the entrance doors of Montefiore. "Before taking a case to the DA, we have to be sure we've done our homework. It takes rock-solid proof to win in court. If we get it wrong, or a defense attorney finds a hole in our case, the perp gets acquitted and we can't prosecute him again. He walks and we look like idiots."

"I owe Mullen an apology."

"How so?"

"I've been giving him a hard time about not solving my dad's murder."

"With you, it's personal. We know justice takes time. Sometimes we get lucky, catch a break. Sometimes not...as in your dad's case. Be patient. If anyone can figure it out, it's Mullen. He may be gruff, but he's got a lot of experience. At the end of the day, he wants to go home to his family."

"Don't we all?" I levered open the passenger door. "Thanks for the ride."

"I hope your mom is better."

"She's fighting the good fight." I closed the door, turned up my coat collar to the cold night air, and watched him peel off down the street. Dedicated. That's what I thought of Dawson as his taillights melted into the darkness. He too wasn't home with his family.

Sure. I should have come straight about the cell phone. Maybe one day I would, but not today. Not until I got one more chance to call my dad.

I hurried into the hospital. The halls were vacant, all

sound was muted, and the air still held the lingering scent of antiseptics and floor wax. Fighting fatigue and enduring that constant worry over my mom's condition, I caught the elevator up to the ICU.

\*\*\*

In the early hours before dawn, the ICU halls and rooms were as brightly lit as if it were mid-afternoon, and just as busy. The sounds emitting from the array of machines down the line were omnipresent and ominous in their precise electronic languages. Nurses scurried about, immersed in their duties, their steadfastness and dedication to helping others a mere undercurrent in their stormy battle against the grim reaper. In one room, in the bed surrounded by a gray curtain, Sheila Calhoun had not an inkling of this activity as she languished deep in the depths of her unconscious mind.

Here, there was nothing to see, nothing to hear, nothing to feel, nothing to think. This was a place where nothingness reigned supreme. An hour could pass, a year, eternity and beyond without so much as a hint of her previous or present existence.

As an intercom in the hallway called out, "Doctor Webber, ER, stat," a nurse strode to Sheila Calhoun's room and pulled back the gray curtain to check her vitals, I-V, catheter, ventilator, and EEG. The nurse inhaled the scent of bleach from the bedding, benzoin lotion, and the aroma of roses from the vase set on the table next to the bed.

To her surprise, the electroencephalogram screen displayed ripples of activity. The nurse raised her eyebrows and her heart accelerated. She ran out to the hallway to summon the doctor on duty. "You've got to see this."

He hurried in and examined the electroencephalogram. "This is very promising. Get her to imaging for an MRI. I believe her brain swelling has gone down enough to bring her out of this coma, but I want to see it for myself."

"Right away, doctor."

***

I rushed past the nurses' desk in the hallway of the ICU and walked directly to my mom's room. To my horror, I found the curtain pulled back and the bed empty. A sudden image of her going into cardiac arrest ravaged my brain.

*Did she die?*

My heart thrashed about. I stared with wide eyes to make sure I had the right room. Her name was still on the door. I bolted to the nurses' station. "My mother...where is she?" My breath came out in spurts.

The duty nurse looked grim. "Slow down. Take it easy."

"Sheila Calhoun. What happened to her?"

"She's in imaging for an MRI."

"Why?"

Her expression brightened. "Relax. It could be good news."

"An MRI sounds like bad news to me."

"The doctor can explain. You can wait in her room."

I paced my mom's room, back and forth, while hope and terror beleaguered my mind. Could she recover from her injuries and be good as new? That would be a miracle.

Or would the MRI reveal permanent brain damage and leave her a vegetable? That would be a disaster.

Minutes later, an orderly wheeled my mom in on a gurney. A nurse followed, and the two of them transferred her to the bed. As the orderly left, I stepped close to my mom and noticed she was still in the same catatonic state as before. However, her head wasn't as thickly bandaged, and the ventilator tube had been removed from her mouth. The nurse secured the I-V bottle stand and adjusted the drip.

"Mr. Calhoun," a voice said behind me.

I turned to see the doctor walk in. "Doc. The nurse said you might have good news."

He stood next to me. "Your mother's brain activity has increased dramatically."

"Thank God, right?"

"It's the first sign we look for to indicate the edema or swelling in her brain has decreased. The MRI confirmed it."

"What does that mean?"

"We can safely bring her out of her coma. I've already started the procedure. It'll take a few hours for the anesthetics to wear off."

"Will she remember what happened to her?"

"Most head trauma patients don't remember what put them in the hospital. She'll be surprised to find herself in this room."

"What can I do?"

"Just be here when she wakes up."

I felt a huge weight lift from my shoulders. The nightmare was about to end. "Thanks, doc."

"You're welcome."

I pulled a chair to the bed and took hold of my mom's hand. It felt warmer than before. I watched her chest rise and fall ever so slightly. As tears blurred my vision, I wondered what I'd say to her, what I'd tell her about what had happened, the cell phone, the call from dad. How much would she believe?

Her body suddenly shook and scared the hell out of me. Just a tremor...or a muscle spasm, or maybe there was a struggle going on inside her head. I thought to call the nurse in, but when I noticed my mom's eye movement under her eyelids, I decided she was dreaming. Maybe she was fighting to come back, or giving in to despair, knowing she'd wake up to a world without Dad. She had to have the will to survive without him, I knew, or she might not ever find happiness again.

***

In her unconscious mind, a faraway dot of light, hazy around the perimeter, drifted toward Sheila. The world she experienced was ethereal, and she seemed to float in the abyss. The dot got closer and enlarged, warm and inviting like a hug from a loved one.

Dermot appeared within the glow. "Sheila. Sheila. Is that you?"

Sunshine flooded her soul. Hope bloomed in her heart. "Dermot. Where are you?" Her voice sounded like a distant echo.

"I don't know. I hear your voice all around me."

"I've missed you every second."

"I'm sorry I left you so soon."

"We never got the chance to say goodbye."

"Don't be sad. We will be together again, someday. Until then, live your life to its fullest. Find happiness. I'll be waiting..."

"Dermot? Where are you?"

"I'll be waiting."

"Dermot." She swam up through the depths of her sub-consciousness toward a new awakening.

\*\*\*

A flurry of activity awoke me. A doctor and two nurses had rushed into the room and were attending to my mom. I bolted upright in the chair and threw off the blanket a nurse had covered me with during the night. "What's going on? Is she okay?"

"She's awake," the nurse said.

Warm sunshine poured into the room.

"All right." I rushed to her bedside, squeezed between the two nurses. Mom's eyes were wide open but had a vacant, faraway look. They had lost their sparkle. Angry bruises expanded from her eye sockets and the corners of her mouth. She just stared at the ceiling.

Tears streamed down my cheeks. "Mom. Mom. Can you hear me?"

A nurse pushed against me. "Give us some space, Sean."

I stepped back. "What's wrong with her?"

"Give her a little time," the nurse said. "She has to process, figure out where she is, and that'll come as a shock."

I could only hope she had no memory of Frank and what he'd done to her.

The doctor adjusted the I-V drip and checked her chest with a stethoscope.

"Blood pressure's normal," a nurse reported.

The doctor nodded. "She's come out of the coma nicely. Looks like she'll be all right."

"Stay close to her," a nurse told me, and they left the room, all smiles.

I stood at my mom's bedside and leaned over her while holding her warm hand. "Mom?" I thought my heart would burst with excitement.

She blinked.

"Mom. It's me, Sean."

She turned her head to me. Her eyebrows arched. She licked her lips and whispered, "Sean?"

"I'm right here." I pulled up a chair and sat, never letting go of her hand. My grin went from ear-to-ear.

"I'm thirsty."

I found a sippy-cup of water on the tray table. "Here you are." I had to let go of her hand to hold the cup and guide the straw to her lips.

She took a swallow, then another.

"Not too much, now." I set the cup aside, and when I looked back, her eyes sparkled with tears. "I spoke to him, Sean."

"Don't talk, Mom. Just rest."

"Your dad called out to me."

My heart gave me a jolt. Did she remember the cell phone? Frank? The beating? How would I explain it? Though I was fighting panic, I had to keep the angst out of my voice. "From where?"

"I don't know. It was so dark...I think..."

I knew it wasn't dark in my bedroom, and besides, she'd never go in there on her own accord. The cell phone must've drawn her into the room, and she didn't remember it.

"In the darkness, I heard his voice."

"You must've dreamed it, Mom. You were in a coma."

"He doesn't know where he is, but I'm sure he's okay." Her battered eyes locked on mine. "He said I'll see him again, someday."

"I believe you will." I couldn't tell her why I believed it, that I too had talked to dad on a cell phone. She needed her own moment with him. "Did he say anything else?"

"He wants me to go on with my life. Be happy."

My angst dwindled. "Smart man. I've been telling you that all along."

She reached up and cupped my cheek with the palm of her hand. "You're a smart man, as well, my son. What would I do without you?"

I grasped her hand and kissed her knuckles. "I'll never be far away."

"What happened to me?"

"We'll talk about that later. You're going to be okay. That's what's important."

"But—"

The nurse walked in and spread open the gray curtain. "You have a visitor."

I turned, thinking it was Mullen who probably needed more information in the murder investigation, but it wasn't. I squinted in the sunlight flowing through the window behind Bridget, an angelic sight to behold. My stomach fluttered. I stood and moved to her. "You came."

"Hey, Sean." She glanced at my mom. "How is she?" Her fingers clenched her purse strap.

"Come in. Come in." I gave her a hug and a kiss on the cheek. The scent of her jasmine perfume didn't escape my notice. "See for yourself."

She stepped past me to Mom's bedside. "Hello, Mrs. Calhoun."

"Bridget. So good to see you, but you didn't have to come."

"It's okay. I want to be here, for you and for Sean."

"Then I'm glad you came."

I could only imagine what Bridget was thinking. The enormity of the situation. Her dedication and affection for me. Her empathy for my mom. This was as real as it got.

Bridget turned back to me. "I'm sorry for calling you a momma's boy."

"I'm sorry for blowing you off."

"You had good reason." She looked into my eyes and gripped my shoulders. "Whatever you need. I'm here for you."

"That means a lot."

She gave me a little shake then turned back to my mom. "They tell me you're going to be okay."

"I don't know why I'm here."

"You're still here. That's what counts."

"I talked to Dermot."

"You did?"

"He's waiting for me. Sean thinks I was dreaming."

"Well...I believe you."

"Sean, you have a keeper here. Make an honest

woman out of this girl. Why don't ya?"

I felt my cheeks heat up. "I'm working on it, Mom."

Bridget smiled up at me. "Me too."

With Mom on the mend and Bridget fully entrenched in my life and the problem with my job resolved, I knew our lives were on the right path. Massey was gone and Frank was dead. Carlson was in jail. The cell phone was in police custody. My dad was in a good place, and though his murderer might never be caught, I could live with that, knowing how hard Mullen had tried to solve the case. That was all I should have asked for. Yeah. I felt things could get back to normal now.

My phone buzzed. It was Mullen. I walked away from Bridget and my mom to take the call. "Yeah, detective."

"Sean, I need your help. All hell broke loose in the lab."

## Chapter Thirty-Two

**A**t my mom's bedside in the ICU ward of Montefiore Medical Center, I tried to make sense of what Detective Mullen had just spouted on the phone.

*"Sean, I need your help. All hell broke loose in the lab."*

"What's the problem now?"

"It's that damn rock. It's going haywire. That crazy bastard Carlson may have been right. It's shaking Massey's building loose from its footings. I'll pick you up in five minutes."

As I glanced back at Bridget and my mom, I felt their eyes boring into me. It was like they were thinking out loud: *What's so important that you have to be on the phone? You're not leaving. We're finally all together again.*

"My mom just got out of a coma—"

"That's great. I'm happy for you. Now listen up. I'm sorry about dragging you back into this, but I'm working on two hours of sleep. My wife is going to kill me, and the Chief is breathing down my neck. I need your expertise."

"You told me your IT forensic guys could handle it."

"I know what I said, but McNulty told me it's scary down there, and he's not afraid of anything. My IT guys won't go near the place."

A chill skittered down my spine. I imagined Carlson laughing maniacally at the ensuing chaos. The thought of his prediction coming true, the city being destroyed, called for urgency in the nth degree...but why me? My mom needed me here. If I left, she might feel abandoned, affecting her fragile condition. I couldn't risk taking that chance. "Get someone else, detective. I'm not going anywhere."

"Don't leave me hanging like this. I need you. The city needs you. Step up and do the right thing."

"Look, detective—"

"Sean, who's that?" Bridget asked from behind me.

I turned and put my hand over the phone. Her face was etched with fear. "It's nothing."

"Then why are you yelling?"

*Oh.* I didn't realize I'd raised my voice. "It's Detective Mullen. He can be really frustrating. Ask my mom."

"Sean," Mom said. "Tell him I'm not angry anymore. I know he tried to find Dermot's killer."

That was quite the switch. "Okay." I put the phone back to my ear.

"Sean," Mullen shouted. "You still there?"

"Yeah. Mom says hi."

"I'm three minutes away."

I clenched a fist. "You're wasting your time."

"If that stupid rock destroys the city, your mom will die. We're all going to die. You can't let that happen."

That gave me a jolt. I looked at Mom and Bridget and imagined them screaming in terror as the room collapsed and their bodies were crushed to dust under tons of concrete and steel. He was right. I'd better at least try to keep that from happening. "I'll meet you at the front entrance."

"You've got two minutes."

I hung up. Heat burned up the back of my neck.

Bridget grabbed me by the shoulders. "What's going on, Sean? You look a little pale."

"I have to leave."

Bridget arched her brows. "Why?"

"It's a long story."

"Sean, you know I love you. You can tell me anything."

"I love you, too...both of you, but this is bigger than all of us." I hugged her and kissed her cheek, wishing I didn't have to let go of her. "I'll tell you all about it when I get back. There's no time now. Take care of my mom."

"We'll be okay."

My mom's eyes were wide as I stepped to her bedside. The poor woman had been through a lot, and I couldn't imagine what she was thinking.

"You be careful, Sean."

That surprised me. "Get some rest." I squeezed her hand.

Bridget clutched my arm. "We'll be waiting for you right here."

"I'm counting on that." I pushed aside the gray curtain and sprinted to the elevator. I could only hope the building would be left standing by the time this was over.

As I bolted out the main entrance, "Sean," Mullen shouted out the open passenger window of his white Taurus squad car. "Come on. Let's go." He honked the horn as if that would make me run faster.

As soon as I got into the passenger seat, Mullen tore off, siren blaring and overheads blazing. Under the extreme inertia, I struggled to buckle the seatbelt. He swerved through and darted around traffic on Gun Hill Road like a maniac on four wheels. "It's bad, Sean. Really bad."

"What's happening at Massey's lab?"

"McNulty says the floor is cracking, plaster is falling off the walls, ceiling tiles are raining down, and light fixtures are swinging on their wires."

"The obelisk is doing all that damage?"

"What else?"

We careened onto the Major Deegan Expressway, southbound, and Mullen had the Taurus pinned at eighty miles an hour. I noticed the traffic was heavier heading northbound out of the city. "Where the hell is everybody going?"

"The obelisk is going ballistic. We don't know how to stop it. Even the IT forensic team gave up and won't go back in. Safety concerns, they said, and I can't blame them."

"I gather unplugging the Cisco didn't work."

"They cut power to all the servers, which only seemed to agitate the rock further. It's vibrating and droning like some alien from outer space."

"Unbelievable."

"More like impossible, right?"

*I've learned nothing is impossible. I'd talked to my dead dad on a friggin' cell phone.*

I braced myself with both hands on the dash to keep from being jerked around. "Carlson said the obelisk could destroy the city. You believe him now?"

"I don't know what to believe."

"Get him down there. Let him fix the damn thing."

"I tried. He's bat-shit crazy. Chicken or the egg. Chicken or the egg. That's all he says. Whatever went on in that lab, it's pushed him over the edge."

As we neared the interchange with the George Washington Bridge and the 9A, my heart slammed against my ribcage at the horrific sight ahead of us. Lightning cracked across a black and cloudless sky. Windows in Massey's skyscraper had been blown out, and interior lights blinked and flashed from the glassless maws. Angry smoke swirled upward from the top floors. It was as if the building was possessed by a soulless evil.

"We're not going back in there."

"Somebody has to."

"Shit." I was stuck in this nightmare with no way out.

At the George Washington Bridge, five miles from ground zero, the NYPD had blocked access to the Henry Hudson Parkway, southbound. The northbound lanes were jammed with pedestrians and vehicles fleeing the area, a chaotic mass of humanity and dust, surging forward under the glow of streetlights.

I gasped. "Jesus."

"I don't know what we're up against..." Uniformed officers waved us forward. Mullen maneuvered around the barricade of patrol cars and fire trucks. "So I ordered the evacuation of the area within a five-mile radius. Inbound highways are closed, and the Coast Guard is blocking all marine traffic on a ten-mile stretch of the Hudson." He accelerated to 100 miles an hour on the abandoned 9A, southbound. "It's all hands on deck."

At the 79<sup>th</sup> Street jump-off, we hit the surface streets, careened right onto Riverside Drive and found ourselves smack dab in the middle of the hysteria. Pedestrians were running from the buildings, pouring onto the street like living streams of water.

Mullen slowed to muscle the car through the throng. People pounded on the hood, pressed their terror-stricken faces against the window glass, and one guy climbed onto the trunk lid, only to roll off, hit the pavement, and get trampled underfoot. The car lurched and jerked on its suspension.

Another guy knocked off the right-hand rearview mirror with his fist. "Give me the car."

"It's the end of the world," another man shouted.

My mouth went dry.

Mullen gritted his teeth and pressed forward, past another barricade that funneled the flow of terrorized humanity eastward on 72<sup>nd</sup> Street, but he turned right onto Riverside Boulevard.

It was like driving into a scene from the apocalypse. Not a living soul stirred. Tires crunched broken glass and litter swirled down gutters clogged with abandoned cars, doors left open, fenders dented, and some were upturned and on fire. I half-expected zombies to lumber from the shadows.

Mullen skidded the car to a stop in front of Massey's building. "I'm not believing any of this shit." He threw open his door and bailed out of the car.

I joined him at the front bumper. It was then that I felt the ground trembling beneath my feet, and a growling drone disturbed the air. We glanced at each other as if exchanging mental goodbyes, as this could be the end of our lives.

We hurried toward the building's broken front doors. I followed him inside; busted glass crunched under my footsteps. The drone was louder, and chandeliers swayed in the lobby. I could barely keep my balance on the bucking marble floor. My legs turned to noodles as we stagger-stepped toward the black elevator.

On the way, I darted my gaze around the lobby. A bomb couldn't have done more damage to Ronald Massey's display of opulence. Planters were knocked over, chairs overturned, and wall-mounted monitors dangled from their twisted brackets. Passing *The Real Deal* restaurant, I saw tipped tables and chairs and busted dishes scattered across the floor. Disaster was on tomorrow's menu...if the building was still standing. I imagined girders snapping like twigs and the whole structure collapsing on top of us, burying us alive. My chest tightened and my breath came out in spurts.

We made it to the elevator, and I was surprised when the doors opened. I was standing there dumbfounded when Mullen grabbed my arm and pulled me inside. "Quit gawking."

Descending, the elevator shook. My stomach dropped, and I groaned, fighting a terror I'd never known.

*Holy shit. We're going to die.*

I pictured the faces of my mom and Bridget as I held on to the handrail for dear life. However, the elevator descended into the bowels of the building, shakily but intact.

"You should try to get Carlson again. He would know how to fix this."

"He wanted full immunity in exchange for saving the city. The DA wasn't buying what he was selling, so he went off his rocker about the chicken or the egg. We're on our own."

The elevator rattled to a stop and the doors squealed open. The drone was deafening. When we stepped into the lab, our hair stood on end, there was that much static in the air. Lights flickered and popped. Electrical cables sparked and spewed smoke. White hot tendrils of ionized atoms shot from the obelisk and struck the ceiling and walls, leaving black carbonized tracks in their wakes. I smelled the acrid odor of burnt computer components. A quick glance at the Cisco told me it was offline, as the indicator lights were out, as well as all the other servers on down the line.

The obelisk rumbled. The room shook. A tremor created a fracture in the floor, one of many, I noted. Goosebumps burst out all over my arms. I assessed the situation as hopeless until I spotted the StarTAC still resting on the main terminal counter. "I have an idea."

"Whatever you're going to do, you better do it fast.

As I ran to the main terminal, I remembered what Carlson had said about where the obelisk had come from, the Rwenzori Mountains in Uganda. It was just a rock until he paired it with the StarTAC cell phone...something about a frequency match, a stable frequency that had caused this much devastation. I remembered taking the cell phone apart the night of O'Malley's death and how stupefied I was when I saw the SIM card had been replaced with a chip of crystal. And now that I looked at the obelisk closer, I recognized where the chip had come from.

The drone of the obelisk grew louder. My mind put two and two together.

*The cell phone is the culprit.*

My pulse raced as I snatched up the phone and stared at its folded case and little antenna. It was a connection to my dad. All I had to do was dial D-A-D and I could speak with him again. So simple, yet so dangerous. I sensed Mullen looking over my right shoulder. "That's the cell phone Carlson was talking about?"

"Yes."

"You knew about it all along."

"O'Malley stole it from the lab. He was killed when Bart and Frank tried to get it back, but he gave it to me and I ran like hell."

"Let me get this straight. Carlson wasn't crazy when he insisted you used this cell phone to talk to your dad?"

"He called me."

"You know how crazy that sounds. He's been dead—
"

"I had a hard time believing it too, but I've learned that we don't know anything about the universe, eternity, Heaven and Hell, but I do know there's something out there bigger than all of us combined. So sometimes crazy shit is solid gold."

"What are you going to do with it? This building can't hold up much longer."

To save the city, I had to cut this link to my dad. I'd have to wait to talk to him again. In Heaven. It was the only way... I snapped off the back cover before I could change my mind. The sliver of obelisk crystal in the SIM slot glinted under the sway of ceiling lamps. My heart pounded.

*I love you, Dad.*

I pulled out the crystal and crushed it on the floor with the heel of my shoe.

The obelisk fell silent; the room stopped shaking; and the lights stopped flashing. Static bled from the air, and our hair returned to normal. The building emitted an audible groan of relief. I glanced at the obelisk, which now looked like a harmless singed boulder.

Mullen gave me a slap on the back. "You did it, Sean. You saved the city. You're a hero."

I didn't feel like a hero. My dad had just died all over again. "Let's get out of here."

"How about McGee's. I've got the first round."

"It's a little early to start drinking, don't you think?"

Mullen grumped. "My wife's going to kill me, anyway."

"Rain check. I want to get back to my mom."

We rode the elevator up and paced across the lobby. Streaks of sunlight streamed in through the glassless entrance doors, and birds fluttered in through broken windows, chirping with glee at the dawn of a new day. A cool winter breeze filled my lungs, and my racing pulse settled down.

As we walked outside, we encountered pedestrians shuffling by with dirt and soot on their faces.

"Is it over?" one man asked.

"It's safe to go home now," Mullen said.

A raucous cacophony of cheers echoed down the streets and across the city. They had NYPD to thank for their salvation.

"You should have told me about the cell phone, Sean. I could have wrapped up this case sooner."

"Nah. You've got no proof for none of it."

"I've got Carlson."

"He didn't kill anybody, and it's not illegal to go crazy."

"You've got a point there. I'll see to it he gets the help he needs. Want a ride to the hospital?"

"I thought you'd never ask."

## Chapter Thirty-Three

**A**t MSK Kids, in a room adorned with posters of childhood heroes: Mickey Mouse, Buzz Lightyear, and Captain America, and balloons with smiley faces floating above the bed, Chloe awoke on the seventh day after her first stem cell treatment. She gripped Snowball under her arm and hugged the stuffed dog tightly.

"Good morning," Nurse Debbie said. "How are you feeling?"

"My legs feel funny." *Tingly.* That was the word. "My legs feel tingly, like little needles are trying to get out. Where's my mommy?"

"She's downstairs with Dr. Bradshaw. She'll be back soon. I bet you're excited about walking today."

"What if I can't?"

"Think positive, little one."

"I'm scared."

"Of what?"

"That I'll need a wheelchair for the rest of my life."

Nurse Debbie put her hand on Chloe's. "Don't think like that. Besides, you know what that tingly feeling means?"

"No."

"It's your legs saying they want to wake up again."

"Does that mean I can walk?"

"You'll never know unless you try."

"What if I fall?"

"What if you don't?"

A tear trickled from her eye. "I don't know what to do."

#

Meanwhile, in Dr. Bradshaw's office, Clarissa's emotions were off the charts. Juggling grief for the loss of her husband and hope for Chloe's future, she sat in front of a poker-faced doctor and felt like a withering bundle of nerves.

"Today's a big day for Chloe." He showed her an MRI image of the tumor. "The good news is, the tumor is shrinking."

To Clarissa, the mass in Chloe's spine looked like a monster, and she wished they could cut it out and burn it. "It still looks horrible."

"What we can't see is how well the spinal cord has fared. Though the pain has eased, the big question is, can she walk."

"And if she can't?"

"Spinal cord damage is irreversible. Any further treatments would be a waste of time."

"What then?"

"Rehab. Physical therapy. Prayer, if you believe in that sort of thing. Most likely, she'll never walk again."

That brought tears to Clarissa's eyes.

*Please, God. Help Chloe walk today.*

She did believe in that sort of thing.

Bradshaw stood. "Let's get upstairs and find out which way this will go."

#

Jim Keane

Finally, Chloe's mother walked in, followed by Dr. Bradshaw. She tried to sit up in bed, but as usual, Nurse Debbie had to help her. She set Snowball aside and opened her arms to her mother. "Mommy. Where were you?"

"Talking to the doctor, sweetie." She gave her daughter a big hug.

"Where's Daddy? He still hasn't come to see me."

Clarissa glanced at the doctor, and he gave her a nod. This was the first time she'd asked about her dad.

The downcast looks on their faces scared Chloe. "Mommy? What's wrong?"

"Honey..." She held Chloe's hand. "Daddy can't make it."

"Why?"

"He's in Heaven now, sweetie."

Chloe's lips trembled. She blinked away tears that came out all by themselves. "Daddy...died?"

"It was an accident."

Her mother's forehead wrinkled. She always did that when thinking of something to say but didn't know what.

She squeezed Chloe's hand. "I'm sorry, but we have to get on without him."

"I don't want my daddy to be dead."

Clarissa smoothed Chloe's hair. "He's watching over us, baby, and today he's going to see you walk."

"I don't want to walk. I want my daddy."

"The doctor needs to see if you can walk. It's important. Please give it a try." Her eyes were wet and she sniffled. "Just a couple of steps for me. You can do it, right?"

"No." She threw herself back down on the bed. "Why

did Daddy have to die?" She cried big tears and her chest heaved with big sobs and her heart hurt so bad.

Nurse Debbie leaned in close to Chloe's ear. "You want to go home, don't you? Play with your friends? Go back to school?"

"I want my daddy."

She patted Chloe's shoulder. "I know. I know. It hurts, and it'll always hurt, but for now, let me put you on your feet so you can show your daddy that you can walk."

"Honey," Clarissa said. "That's all he ever wanted, to see you walk again. Do it for your dad."

Chloe blinked. "For Daddy?" She rolled over and, with bleary eyes, looked up to the ceiling, past the floating balloons with the smiley faces tied to her bed. "Is he really watching me from Heaven?"

"I believe he is."

"Me too," Nurse Debbie added.

Chloe looked at Dr. Bradshaw.

He nodded. "What do you believe, Chloe?"

"I want him to be proud of me."

"Then let's make your dad happy. Show him you can walk."

Chloe held her arms out to Nurse Debbie. "I'm ready."

Her mom smiled. "That's my girl."

Nurse Debbie lifted her from the bed and set her feet on the floor while steadying her upright with both hands under her arms. "Just take your time."

Across the room, Clarissa got down on her knees and held her arms out to Chloe. "Come to me, baby. Walk to Mommy."

The needles in her legs got out. Now she could wiggle her toes. She found a wobbly sense of balance and felt Nurse Debbie let go.

Her mother's smile brightened. "That's it. One step at a time. For Daddy."

Her legs felt like spaghetti. "I can't, mommy."

"Sure you can."

Nurse Debbie said, "I'm right behind you. You won't fall. I promise."

"For Daddy." Chloe managed one shuffling step.

"That's right. You've got this."

Another step, then another, each one stronger than the last until she fell into her mother's arms. "I did it, Mommy. I did it."

"I'm so proud of you." Her eyes were all wet again, and tears streamed down her cheeks. "You did great."

Nurse Debbie clapped her hands.

Dr. Bradshaw strode to the door. "She's going to be fine."

"Thank you, doctor." Clarissa hugged her daughter. "Daddy is so proud of you."

"I love you, Mommy."

"I love you too."

*I miss you, Daddy.*

***

On a crisp, sunny afternoon in Van Cortland Park, not far from my mom's house, we sat on a bench near Indian Field where I'd once played little league baseball with the Boys Club. My mom sat on my right and Bridget sat on my left. Sitting between them like this, holding their hands, warmed my heart. I wondered if Dad was looking down at us from the heavens. He had to be watching; he'd seen Frank enter the cemetery; he'd told me to run. I felt his eyes shining down on me, embedded in the brilliant rays of sunshine that dappled in the treetops.

"It's nice to be outside, don't you think, Mom?"

She winced when she smiled, not fully recovered from the injuries Frank Coletti had gifted her, but she looked a hell of a lot better. "I thought I could never leave that house, that safe place that turned out to be an illusion anyway."

Bridget squeezed my hand. "It's a dangerous world."

Mom surveyed the baseball field. "Not long ago, your father and I rooted for you to hit a home run."

"Seems like an eternity ago."

"You grew up so fast."

She had no idea how close I came to dying. I returned Bridget's hand-squeeze. "Thanks for being here for us, Bridget."

"Where else would I be?"

My mom leaned into me. "Bridget kept me company while you were saving the city. When are you going to make an honest woman out of her?" She coughed. "Hint, hint."

Bridget laughed. "He's always playing hard to get."

My heart jumped. "All in good time, Mom."

"I'm not getting any younger, son. I want some grandbabies."

I peered up to the heavens again. "You hear that, Dad? Grandbabies, she says. What do you think?" A warm breeze wisped by. "Is that a yes?"

My mom laughed. "It better be, Dermot, if you know what's good for you."

Yeah. She was feeling better about her life, looking forward to the future, grandbabies and who knew what else. "Do you think you'll ever remarry?"

My mom wiped a lone tear from her eye. "Dermot told me to make the best of my life, so maybe I might." She looked up to the sky. "I know I'll see him again. He's waiting for me." She raised her hand, a finger pointed up. "But I'm not ready yet, Dermot. Got some living to do. Ya hear?"

I laughed. "It's good to have you back, Mom."

"I see you and Detective Mullen are all buddy-buddy now. What's up with that?"

I thought about the punk who got away with murdering my dad. It would be a victory to see his killer behind bars, and someday he might be apprehended. After collaborating with Detective Mullen, I found him to be a tenacious hunter for justice. "He's a good man...once you get to know him."

"I knew he was trying, but his lack of progress pissed me off. I'm over it now."

"Who knows, Mom. Someday, he might get lucky and solve the case."

"Maybe." Mom stood. "Let's start back toward the house. Along the way, you can buy me some flowers at the Rose Nursery."

"Me too," Bridget said. "You've never bought me flowers, Sean."

"We don't have much history together, yet, but we'll start with the flowers."

She hooked her arm in mine. "You're so romantic."

I'd seen the apocalypse. A serious romance was exactly what I needed.

Arm-in-arm, we strode beneath the trees, down the park path, and into a promising future together.

# Epilogue

**D**awn broke over the Ugandan jungle, and a thick mist blanketed the treetops. Before long, the day would turn hot and muggy. In a clearing below the Rwenzori Mountains, a flurry of activity disturbed the quiet morning air. Inbound to the dirt landing strip, *Grey Bird,* a massive US Air Force C-130 transport, descended through the mist, settled to earth, and blew up a trail of dust in its wake. Four turboprop engines screamed in retro, slowing the aircraft to a stop at the end of the runway. Something big was going down.

The mist swirled above as a US Army Chinook thundered from the sky and disappeared in a cloud of dust as it found purchase on the ground. Before the dust cleared, while the dual rotors continued to swoop around at idle, soldiers were already rigging cables and chains for the heavy lift operation ahead.

Whining hydraulics announced the lowering of the ramp on the C-130, which immediately revealed the crystal-studded rock netted to a pallet. It rose and moved down the ramp under the power of a Red Horse reciprocating forklift, its knobby tires as tall as the aircrew running alongside it. Within seconds, the forklift rolled up to the soldiers and set down the pallet just beyond the reach of the circling rotor blades. Ladders leaned against the rock. Soldiers, carrying chains and a giant steel hook, climbed up and clipped the rigging to an eyelet on top of the net. Seconds later, they were down, ladders were removed, and the forklift backed away. The twin T55 Turboshaft engines wound up to a deafening roar and lifted the Chinook and the netted rock up into the mist, leaving only the sound of thumping rotors to recede in the distance. Under the guidance of the aircrew, the forklift rumbled up the ramp and lumbered into the fuselage where it was chained to the floor. The ramp whined up and latched with a thud.

Moments later, the four Turboprop engines wound up to a roar and blasted *Gray Bird* down the dusty runway, and with a nose-up pitch, it clambered back into the mist from which it came. Once again, all was quiet in the Ugandan jungle clearing.

That was not the case upslope as the Chinook beat its way higher and higher, flying over the treetops, its precious cargo swaying beneath the heavy-lifter. It was a ten-minute pull to the crag where the natives had chipped out a temple for the stone of their ancestors. Even as the Chinook lowered the rock to the precipice from which it was stolen, the faithful natives rushed forward to witness the return of their heirloom. When it settled into the cupped bosom of the mountain, the net locks released and the Chinook rose and banked to the west while the rigging was winched into the fuselage.

Everyone below cheered and danced as if today was the best day of their lives.

Jim Keane

# About the Author

Born in the Bronx, **Jim Keane** holds a Bachelor of Arts in English from Mount Saint Mary College and has completed many creative writing courses. He's written several short stories and three novels and has more in the works. Jim resides in Westchester, New York, with his family.

**Enjoy more short stories and novels by many talented authors at**

Made in the USA
Middletown, DE
19 September 2022

73417961R00176